wait for me

Mallory Family
Forever Mine

Book 1

Deborah Garland

ALL RIGHTS RESERVED

Wait for Me Copyright © Deborah Garland 2020

WARNING: The unauthorized reproduction or distribution of this copyrighted work is illegal. No part of this book may be used or reproduced electronically or in print without written permission, except in the case of brief quotations embodied in reviews.

This is a work of fiction. All names, characters, and places are fictitious. Any resemblance to actual events, locales, organizations, or persons, living or dead, is entirely coincidental.

Originally published in 2017 as Must Love Fashion
Library Congress Registration Number: TX 8-467-292
Copyright Registration under Wait For Me # 1-11926147951

Proofreader:
Julie K. Cohen
Cover Artist: Bookin It Design

Published by Deborah A. Garland
www.deborahgarlandauthor.com

DEDICATION

For Mom

Because all debut novels should be dedicated to Mom.
Full stop.

DEBORAH GARLAND

FOREVER MINE SERIES

Millionaires and Small Town Heroes.

The new Forever Mine Series featuring the Mallorys is the Mashup Series you need in your life.

Book 1: Wait for Me: A Hot Office Romance

Book 2: All for Me: A Hot Second Chance Romance

Book 3: Live for Me: A Hot Single Dad Romance (Winner of the 2019 Carolyn Readers' Choice Award)

Book 4: His Christmas Surprise: A Sweet Holiday Romance

ALL BOOKS BY DEBORAH GARLAND

Wild Texas Hearts (Cowboy Series)

The Cowboy's Forbidden Crush ~ The Cowboy's Last Song
The Cowboy's Accidental Wife ~ The Cowboy's Rebel Heart
The Cowboy's Christmas Bride ~ The Cowboy's Wedding Planner

The Billionaire Harts (Billionaire Standalones)

The Good Billionaire ~ Daring the Billionaire ~ Bossy Billionaire ~ Rebel Billionaire

Undeniably Yours (Billionaire Standalones)

Accidental ~ Unexpected ~ Convenient

Houston After Dark (Romantic Suspense)

Off-Limits Lover (Prequel) ~ Rough Lover
~ Hard Lover ~ Untamed Lover

Astoria Royals (Mafia Romance)

Sinful Vows (Prequel) ~Savage King
~ Sleeping with the Enemy ~ Deal with the Devil

ACKNOWLEDGMENTS

Updated for 2020

It was a hard decision to dramatically re-work my debut novel, Must Love Fashion. I learned so much in the three years since its release by a small publisher. Gwen and Andrew's love affair was a story I was determined to tell. Even if I had to change all the scenery and details around them. They are still the same couple and deserved their love story to invade readers' hearts.

All the help I received from the original versions of this love story were building blocks to make the Gwen and Andrew 2.0 stronger than ever.

Thank you, Julie K. Cohen, for your excellent proofread and putting up with me as I stripped this story apart for what we both hope is the final time.

I'd like to take this opportunity to give additional thank you to a wonderful friend, Sal Puglia who gave me spirited input and more accurate Italian translations. Sal passed away from Covid-19 the summer of 2020 and my heart broke when I found out. My condolence to his family and other friends.

CHAPTER ONE

Gwen

I tapped the toe of my left shoe during my interview at Prada. Discreetly, since those red sling backs weren't Prada.

Enrico Petrillo, Director of Operations for the US Corporate Offices in New York City, with his wavy salt and pepper hair, scanned my resume. I bragged for several minutes about my degree from the *Fashion Institute of Technology* and *embellished* my years of industry experience since graduating from FIT eight years ago.

The director removed his tortoise-shell glasses and studied me with warm, brown eyes. "So, Gwendolyn Foley, what could you do for Prada that we have not already thought of?"

I sat up in the guest chair and smiled, pushing past the frustration of being called a name I didn't want anymore. "I want to make sure *every* girl has at least one Prada label in her arsenal. I see a campaign saying something like, '*Think about the one thing in your closet you love the most. That* one *thing should be Prada.*'" I flashed my hand like a banner in the air. "And considering many Manhattan closets are no bigger than pantries, valuable real estate shouldn't be wasted on rayon and polyester, am I right?"

"We always hope to sell more than *one* thing to our customers," Enrico said with good humor and handed my resume to Salvatore Corella, New York's head designer. His cologne made me dizzy and not in the good way.

Salvatore barely glanced at my resume before he tossed it on Enrico's polished desk. "What is in *your* closet?" His thick accent would take some getting used to.

I tugged the skirt of the *Simply Vera* coat dress I'd bought at Kohl's. "Is my *current* wardrobe part of the interview? The average person cannot afford Prada, gentlemen." I wanted to change that.

Waving off the misunderstanding, Enrico said, "No. No, of course not."

"The *one* thing in my closet right now is a Michael Kors dress." I wisely didn't wear *that* to the interview.

Enrico gave a soft chuckle.

I hoped my hand-me-down little black dress, or my vintage colorful wrap number, or even one of my many pencil skirts from Target wouldn't get me laughed out of the building. I couldn't afford much else at the moment.

Six months ago, I quit my job at Starlight Elegance—a small fashion house specializing in scandalous lingerie. Despite being the promotions manager, a title I walked through fire for, the owner had forced me to wear thongs and push-up bras at fashion shows. It wasn't my job to show off the clothes. In fact, I held models in silent contempt.

Enrico stood. "*Scusa*, please. Salvatore and I need a moment to…discuss. Can I get you anything while you wait? An espresso?"

I unfolded myself from a burgundy suede wing chair I could fall asleep in. "No, thank you."

The door clicked shut behind the men. I'd met Enrico last year during Fashion Week when Starlight had a brief time slot to feature its spring line. When a head-hunter friend emailed me with Enrico's cute, retro

Must Love Fashion job post last week, I emailed him directly, explaining my dire out-of-work situation. Let's just say he remembered me thanks to the black see-through bra and scrap of lace attempting to cover my ass. But he'd been eager to meet with me to discuss the Publicity and Marketing Executive position at Prada because he needed someone fast.

It often took months to complete the hiring process with such high-profile companies. Enrico had fast-tracked me through H.R. and explained he had an L.A. fashion show coming up in less than a month.

Wringing my fingers, I focused on the magnificent view of the New York City skyline. I passed the time by checking my phone, praying my last active credit card wasn't being canceled.

I kept my money troubles to myself. I didn't want that interview to be about hiring a colleague who desperately needed a job. I'd been swimming in a small, murky pond with big-fish ideas that wouldn't have translated in the lingerie world. A prestigious fashion house like Prada was the next logical step for my career, anyway.

Five minutes later, Enrico returned. Alone. "Well, Gwendolyn, I hope you have a big enough closet for your new *Prada* clothing allowance." He put his hand out to me and I almost wept in it. "The job is yours if you want it."

The earth moved beneath my cheap shoes. Containing my emotions, I shook Enrico's hand. "Thank you. I... I *won't* let you down."

"I am sure our brand manager, Andrew, who you'll be working closely with, will love your ideas," Enrico said. "He is in Milan right now."

Andrew? I wondered why *Andrew* had not been

brought up until now. And how close would I have to work with him?

Musing about the mysterious Andrew, I gathered my portfolio and turned to leave.

Enrico, however, leaned in and said, "I will be sure to tell Michael I hired a woman who spent hard-earned money on one of his dresses."

I just smiled and kept my mouth shut that it was a *Michael*, by Michael Kors and sold at Macy's. *A girl's gotta do, what a girl's gotta do.*

I signed a thirty-page contract and agreed to start the following Monday. A whole new life was waiting for me on the other side of the weekend.

On the subway, it hit me.

"*I work at Prada!*" I pushed back in my seat and laughed.

"Congratulations," a homeless guy said, stopping in front of me. "Can I have a dollar?"

Frowning, I handed over the last of my cash.

Yes, a single dollar bill was all I'd had left in my Coach wallet bought at the East End outlets last year.

My roommate, Kelsey, and generous best friend from FIT kept *me* from being homeless. The two-bedroom sweeping pre-war apartment most people would commit murder to rent was paid for by her wealthy father. When I'd quit my job at Starlight, I'd offered Kelsey everything from IOU's to vacuuming to back rubs to make up for my share. She refused them all. Her dad also paid for a cleaning lady once a week, and her boyfriend rubbed her in places I'm sure she didn't need me to address.

I bounced up Second Avenue to my free apartment on the corner of 78th Street, proud and prepared to force money down Kelsey's throat. I hated taking handouts.

Outside my building, a man in a suit, with wide shoulders and dreamy cologne caught my breath. Then he turned around.

"Greg?" I shook my head at my brother. "What in the world are you doing here?"

I jumped into his arms, missing his yummy hugs.

He rarely left the North Fork. "I had a meeting downtown," he answered, and I could hear the ocean in his voice, making me miss my hometown.

"A meeting with who?" I worried he stormed the news studio where his childhood sweetheart, Faith, worked as an executive producer.

"Just met with a guy I went to the academy with who's now with the FBI."

"FBI?" My jaw slacked open, and I keyed into my building. "You're going to work for the FBI?"

He shrugged, his rumpled chestnut brown hair brushing against his suit collar. "I'm getting a little restless doing patrol. Just checking out my options."

"What did Dad say?" I folded my arms in the elevator. I knew our mom, who passed away from breast cancer when I was in high school, would have been thrilled.

"I didn't tell him yet." Greg fiddled with his phone following me to my apartment, but his head popped up seeing Kelsey in my kitchen. He lowered an eyebrow to her.

My brother was a bit of a hound on the outside. On the inside, he was a heartbroken jilted groom. Love was a taboo subject for him since Faith had bolted out of town a few days before their wedding five years ago.

"Kelsey, this is my brother, Greg," I said, tamping down my excitement because I was proud of the big lug.

My roommate opened her eyes wide enough to take

him and his green eyes in. "Um." She wiped her hands on her yoga pants. "Hello."

"Hello," he responded and quirked a smile.

No. Just *no*.

"We'll be in the living room," I said and pushed him out of the kitchen before it combusted.

"Wait," Kelsey called out and slinked up to me, her eyes on Greg. "This was delivered a little while ago."

"Thanks." I kept pushing Greg, but brimming with curiosity, I tore into the sealed envelope.

"Something good?" my brother asked after I'd gone silent.

"Depends." I shoved the stapled set of legal papers with a blue cover back into the envelope. "I'm sure you'll think Dan divorcing me is a good thing."

"No comment," he grumbled.

"Let's get a drink."

I'm getting my Mallory name back after all.

♥ ♥ ♥ ♥
Andrew

I left my office carrying a purse. Discreetly, since it wasn't Prada. And it was *a purse*.

"Take this." I pushed the white alligator bucket bag with braided saddle straps into Marcello's chest. "Now let me do the talking with the creative director."

"*Si*," Marcello answered, clutching the Mui Mui prototype.

In Italian, I asked the director's assistant for a moment with her. Full and glossy lips puckered at me. The assistant rose, smoothed her skirt, flipped her hair, and strut to her boss's office.

Marcello smirked and rocked on his heels.

The woman could have used the damn phone. As an ex-model, I recognized a practiced turn. I wasn't interested in any of the models, assistants, interns, or cleaning ladies who gazed longingly at me with lust in their eyes.

Blessedly, Stefania didn't flirt. The creative director pawed at the bag, tugged at the tassels, and yanked on the straps. After a nod to me, she jotted notes on a scrap of paper, then slid it and the purse across her desk without making eye contact.

Even though Prada was one big happy *famiglia*, the competing accessory lines in Milan operated like Interpol spies.

"*Grazie*," I said and handed the purse back to Marcello.

Ten steps from the production floor, a flurry of bodies hopped and skipped toward the lobby.

Checking his phone, Marcello said in his exaggerated accent, "Eet's five o'clock." He always spoke English when he wanted something.

I'd not only brought years of valuable fashion experience from both on and off the runway to those months training Marcello in Milan, I also brought my arrogant American work ethic.

Sighing, I took the purse back and said, "Have a good weekend."

"*Ciao!*" Marcello bounced away already on his phone making plans for a night of partying.

I brought the sample with the creative director's notes and suggested alterations to the production manager myself.

The portly man read the requested changes and cursed in Italian for several minutes. Then he looked at me with a sheepish grin. "*Scusa.*"

"*Non ci pensare*," I replied, nodding.

Facing an empty wing of offices, where all I heard

were the echoes of my own footsteps, I exhaled and shuffled to my office. Calling it a day as well, I slipped my work bag across my shoulder. After three months of training Marcello to be the new Milan-based brand manager in Italy, I was dying to get home to New York. My job as brand manager there needed attention.

I left the building and hurried past a crowd of cute young girls. No matter how many times I refused, they always asked me to join them for after-work *cocktails* which amusingly translated the same in English.

Hey, bello! The girls called out to me, even though I'd kept my head down. At six-foot-four, not being noticed had always been a challenge.

Seeing the old stone church a few blocks from my flat stirred me with mixed emotions. I'd stopped there often and lit dozens of candles to pray for my wife Cate's recovery. It seemed hypocritical to blow past the church now that she'd passed away.

Swallowing, I climbed the cracked steps and pushed through a worn wooden door, ripe with splinters. Inside, the smell of perfumed smoke and varnished pews always made me think about the priest who'd given Cate her last rites at the hospital back home in New York.

I never expected to be a widower at thirty-eight. That only happened to older men. Those who sat on a park bench looking sullen and said, *one day at a time,* when asked how they were.

Soon, Catherine will be with her king, Father Reilly had said that day almost two years ago, closing warm palms around my cold, clammy hands. The priest's words were meant to comfort me, but I would have preferred my Cate there with *me*, rather than with some king in the sky.

What was grief supposed to look like? Working sixty hours a week? Saying little, if anything, to avoid choking on words, knowing something would remind me of Cate? Grief wasn't the one-night stand I had a year after she died, when I'd given in to the burning loneliness and took a stranger to bed.

The memory smacked me in the heart like a loud slap of thunder. Thinking of that woman who wore her exotic lingerie at a fashion show set me off balance even now, so I trained my brain to *not go there*.

Wiping my brow, I dragged in one more hazy fragrant breath of candle smoke and left.

For October, the sun felt stronger than usual against my face and by the time I reached my moderately sized flat, drops of sweat had beaded up on my forehead. From the top floor and across the city, the River Ticino sparkled in the distance. Like most nights after work, I dragged a chair to the window and sat with a glass of wine to enjoy the serene view.

The neighbor's black cat snuck in through my open window again. The friendly feline, purring like a gentle humming engine, rubbed his head beneath my chin, breaking me out of a trance.

I tugged on soft ears. "I'm going home next week." Giving the cat a full-body stroke, I asked, "Are you going to miss me?" With only a week left in Milan, I had to speak English more often.

The cat sat back on his haunches and narrowed yellow eyes at me as if he understood perfectly. That was impossible. Even if someone had taught the handsome furball to understand simple sentences, the cat must have been trained in Italian. Still, he looked put-off by my pending departure.

An hour later, the sun set and my furry companion

slipped back onto the ledge and disappeared. The cool breeze from the open window felt good in my lungs, but my heart ached.

The time had come to move on. Everyone had told me so. My mother had been the most vocal on the subject. She was such a force in my life that her opinions always resonated the loudest.

That fashion show in Los Angeles would give me plenty to do, and I looked forward to long hours that would keep my body busy and my mind occupied. Enrico had sent me resumes to review for a PR manager, but I'd dragged my feet, preferring to work alone.

My boss would never hire someone behind my back.

CHAPTER TWO

Gwen

For my first day at Prada, I chose the Michael Kors red shift dress with a shiny brass exposed zipper and sleeve adornments.

The dress gave off the perfect smart-girl vibe so business executives would take me seriously. I draped a coordinating scarf around my neck to hide the MK monikers, just in case my new co-workers didn't have a sense of humor.

The elevator shuddered to a stop, and I teemed with excitement. I gave the short skirt a tug and when the doors opened, all I saw were empty desks.

I stepped into the open floor plan and murmured under my breath, "Where the heck is everyone?"

Tiptoeing to where I'd signed my contract, I checked my phone and sat on a soft tufted bench.

Ninety minutes later, the HR receptionist arrived. The young woman took her time getting situated and pulled my new-hire file while slurping at a Venti cup.

"I was beginning to worry today was an Italian holiday no one told me about," I said with a smile.

"Yeah, we don't come in exactly at nine a.m.," the woman remarked back.

After being processed as an official Prada employee, I ambled to Enrico's corner suite carrying several company policy binders. He had strolled by earlier and told me to meet him in his office when *you're finished with all of that administration stuff.*

Thalia, Enrico's assistant, greeted me with a pleasant smile. Long crystal-blonde waves framed her pretty Northern Italian features. She brought me into

Enrico's office and announced me as if I were a foreign dignitary.

"Come in, Gwendolyn." My new boss stood behind an old-world walnut executive desk. Its intricately carved legs and patterned veneers suited someone of his European sophistication. "I am so glad you are here. Andrew is still in Milan. He will be back next week."

"You said in your email he signed the endorsement contracts. Has Salvatore started interviewing models for the L.A. fashion show?"

"*Sì.* And now I need you to work on the publicity." Enrico led me out of his office. Several doors down, he stopped and fumbled with a set of keys.

"I'm getting my own office?" I asked with a shiver of disbelief.

"Eh... In a way."

The door opened and a hint of musky cologne floated past me. Such an odd smell for an empty office. Except, there were binders, file folders, and books piled up on what looked like a desk.

I turned to Enrico. "*This* is my office?"

"*Sì.* You will have to share with Andrew until we find a better place for you."

"Um, Enrico, there's no place for me to sit." I pointed to the *one* messy desk. Was I supposed to sit on the guy's lap?

"I have a sleek writing desk on order for you. That should get you through until an office opens up."

Nodding, I eyed the large file cabinets I had a feeling weren't empty. The bookcases were filled with more binders, stacks of papers, and shoeboxes I bet didn't have any shoes in them.

"IT has a ticket to bring you a laptop computer," Enrico said. "They will give you all of your log-ins."

"Well, all right." I put my work bag down on the desk, careful not to send any of the piles spilling over the side.

This isn't the best way for me to start a job.

Enrico had hinted my position was sensitive and that the Andrew Morgan guy didn't even know I'd been hired to take over the brand's PR responsibilities. Now he'd come back to New York to find his job had changed *and* he had an office mate.

Not good.

Preparing to voice my concern, I spun to face Enrico, but he was on his phone, half lingering out the door. I exhaled and gingerly lifted a paper or two on the desk to see how many layers deep the pile went until I reached an actual wood surface. I stopped, however, when my scarf caught on my charm bracelets.

Needing more light to untangle myself, I stepped to the window. Wide as the office, it drenched the space with natural light. Past a few smaller buildings and structures in Riverside Park, I stared longingly at the Hudson River. The sun shimmered off the calm current, filling me with the first sense of ease in several months.

"Not a bad view we have here, Mr. Morgan," I mumbled over a growling stomach, reminding me I'd missed breakfast. I hoped my Yelp app would find a cheap food cart close to the office.

Thalia breezed in with a stack of thick glossy magazines and placed them on the desk. I figured out where much of the mess came from. The hard shove Thalia had given to find a secure spot knocked over a picture frame I hadn't noticed earlier.

Before I leaned across the desk to set it back on its easel, Enrico was there lifting it up himself. "I wouldn't want Andrew to find this picture of him and his wife toppled like this." Enrico placed the frame back in its original spot, his thumb brushing across the glass. "Poor Cate had been sick for many, many months. God rest her soul."

"How did his wife die?" I asked, the realization I'd be working with a widower waking up something very visceral in me. "Was it recent?"

"Cancer. Two years ago. *Terribile*."

The C-word hit me like a physical blow and I felt lightheaded. *Cancer*. Just like my mom.

"That's so sad. I'm sorry to hear that," I said.

"Andrew has not been the same. I'm ever hopeful something or," Enrico set his gaze on me, "someone will bring him back to us. The way he used to be."

My cheeks flushed, though, surely Enrico didn't mean to suggest me. Still, I couldn't help but feel moved by how much Enrico cared about Andrew. Prada already felt like a family environment. Warm and caring. Those Italians and their *amore*.

I glanced at the picture, noticing the woman first. The frail blonde clutched her husband. Poor thing. Tucked under his arm, she almost disappeared against his body. My eyes wandered further to take in the mysterious and conveniently absent Andrew Morgan. Tall. Built. Obsidian colored hair and expressive bushy brows to match. Gray hypnotic eyes. *Uh-oh*.

I froze.

My mind tumbled back to last year's Fashion Week. The most stunning man I'd ever seen, the man who bought me a drink one very late night, in a very dark hotel lobby bar, the very last night after a weeklong grind of shows, parties, and kissing media ass.

My one and only one-night stand with a stranger. So, his name was Andrew. I never got his name that night. Now I worked with the guy! My heart pounded and my throat dried up.

"Gwendolyn, are you all right?" Enrico asked, looking concerned.

The man in the framed image *was* him. I hadn't forgotten that strong chin and those dark carbon eyes that warmed me from the inside out.

That wild night had also been the last time I'd had sex. My husband, Dan, and I had separated a few months before that.

I swallowed past a tight throat and nodded, wondering if my new boss would have a heart attack when he read the resignation letter I was writing in my head.

I blinked for a few seconds and regained my composure. "Yes. *Si*."

"*Eccellente*. I will let you get started." Enrico smiled and closed the door, oblivious to my meltdown.

Started. My career at Prada might have just come to an end.

*

On the advice of counsel — my sister, Skye — I kept my job. By Friday, I'd put the impending showdown with Andrew out of my mind, determined to create a kick-ass PR package proposal for the L.A. fashion show as a distraction. Or a peace offering.

I know this is awkward as hell, but look, I'm actually good at what I do.

I'd found publicity contacts and previous press releases buried in Andrew's confusing filing system. He was due back in the office on Monday, and now I needed to put all those folders away. Looking at the stack, I panicked. I forgot which cabinet drawer I'd plucked each one from.

"Okay, okay, calm down. I'm not done with them, Andrew," I said, practicing my excuse.

He might already be pissed at Enrico for not only hiring me without his input, but hiring a woman he'd slept with while in the throes of grief and heartache. A trashed office would only make Andrew go postal.

"Andrew, forget we had a night of naked passion. I'm in charge of publicity now." The more I practiced, the easier it sounded. "I will put everything away in *my* file cabinet." I glanced around, dreading the task of emptying one out.

There was no point in leaving the office messier than I found it, however. I leaned across Andrew's desk to organize the folders. Pulling one out from under a tower of binders caused them all to slide down and crash into the framed photo of him and his wife. In horror, I watched it shoot off the desk. The sound of shattering glass made my legs wobble.

I crouched down to retrieve the frame. Thank goodness Andrew wasn't back in the country until next week. I tucked the mess under some papers on his desk. "Now I have to buy a frame."

Annoyed, I draped my scarf around my neck and put on my coat. Those frayed edges once again caught on one of my charm bracelets, but dragged the scarf through the armhole.

"Son of a bitch." My free hand reached up to loosen the scarf from my neck before it strangled me. When it snagged on the clasp of my necklace and twisted, trapping me as if I were in a straitjacket, I growled, "Are you *kidding* me?"

Cursing under my breath, I shrugged out of the coat, sending it flying across the office.

"Excuse me." A familiar deep gravelly voice drifted

in from the doorway.

I swung around and locked eyes with the most devastatingly handsome man I'd ever seen. *Andrew!*

Oh shit.

"Oh, hi!" I held up my hand not meaning to reveal the tangled mess I'd made of myself.

"That's an interesting way to wear a scarf." Andrew put his bag down and moved toward me with powerful long legs covered in what I knew had to be a pair of Prada dress slacks. In an instant, he was touching my hand and…my neck. "Can I help you with something?"

He hadn't…recognized me. Was that possible?

Just go with it!

"I need a pair of scissors." I backed away, startled to be so close to him again.

My memory did *not* do that man justice. He was even more stunning under a harsh bath of fluorescent lights versus the flickering candle separating us in the bar that night. The rest of the sepia tinged space around us had blurred the background. And the world, apparently, for him.

Andrew shook his head. "I have scissors in my desk." He opened the top drawer, but paused. "Or, at least I had scissors."

"Try that other drawer. I moved some things around." I pointed to the left pedestal.

"*You* moved them?" he bristled.

Men and their stuff.

"Yes. When I was looking for—"

"Wait. Who *are* you, anyway?" His gaze swept over his desk then back to me. "And why are you even in my—" The horror-filled look on his face twisted my stomach. "You?" he said, taking a step back.

"Yes. It's me. My name is Gwendolyn. Gwen. Gwen

Foley." I held out my hand. "I work here now."

"Is that so?" He crossed his arms instead of touching me.

Huh, boy. Enrico had a week and *still* hadn't broken the news.

I gulped down the embarrassment. "I know this is awkward, but—"

"Are you one of my new interns?" he asked, wiping sweat from his forehead.

A thirty-year-old intern? "No. I'm your new PR Executive."

Andrew jerked back. "I don't need a PR person."

"Enrico hired me last week. We have a fashion show coming up." I yanked down hard on the scarf to free myself. If I couldn't tie a scarf around my neck, how would I convince Andrew I could market a high-end fashion event?

"I *know* we have a show coming up," he snapped.

"But there's been very little marketing. The media events haven't been set up for that week, and the programs need... Where are you going?"

He rushed past me, only stopping to notice the broken frame sticking out from under a pile of papers. He slid it out. The photo of him and his wife was now under a spiderweb of cracks. Without looking at me, he stalked away, and barreled toward Enrico's office.

"I was on my way out to replace that," I yelled and chased after him.

CHAPTER THREE

Andrew

"Andrew!" Enrico's eyes lit up with surprise and he stood up behind his desk. "We were not expecting you until Monday."

"I took an earlier flight back." I glanced at the woman trailing behind me as she tried to unravel herself. It was *her*, the woman I'd slept with last year to give me a few hours of pleasure instead of the relentless heartache.

"Gwendolyn, what have you done to yourself?" Enrico pointed at her.

"I just got my scarf caught in my bracelets. That's not important now," she answered. "Enrico, can you please explain to Andrew—"

"Here." I grabbed the scissors from Enrico's desk caddy and thrust them at her.

"Who taught you how to hand someone a pair of scissors?" she snapped with a disapproving frown.

I looked down to see the tip and blade side facing her. Taking a breath, I turned them around. A rush of heat raced through my chest when she grabbed them and brushed our hands together.

Dangling the scissors in her free hand, she attempted to slide her fingers through the handle.

"Oh, for goodness sake. Who taught you how to *use* scissors?" I took them from her and held her wrist, her pulse thundering beneath the surface.

My thumb brushed against skin I'd forgotten felt so soft, igniting a spark deep in my bones. With palms beginning to moisten, I picked through the row of charm bracelets and found the one that had snagged the scarf. The silver rings jingled softly, tickling a nerve inside me. I tucked the scissors under my arm and ripped the scarf free. The impact smacked her arm right into my chest. Long manicured fingers lingered against my shirt. I swallowed, watching her slide her hand away.

My gaze locked on her face, unable to let go, like that night she'd captivated me. So quickly, so easily, so fiercely. I'd not looked at another woman since losing Cate. Only her. Gwendolyn? I hadn't bothered getting her name that night. Not that she'd asked me for mine.

The woman cleared her throat. "Thank you. I'll get it out of the necklace."

"Turn around," I said with the voice I used when I wanted a woman. The same one I'd used that night.

Her blue eyes sparkled at the familiar command and she turned in a fluid and sexy swirl. Yeah, I remembered all that hair, the sable waterfall I got lost in. Her hands reached back, lifting the wild mane from her shoulders. Moving her hair out of the way released a scent that knocked me off balance.

Feeling bold, I took the strands from her, grasping the bundle of silk and draped it across her right shoulder. With the back of her blouse exposed and the scissors in my hand, a wild desire to just slice the center seam and expose that aberrant creature coursed through me. Only something unnatural could drive me to such a state in a short amount of time. Again.

"Do you have it?" she whispered, twisting her neck.

I only saw her pink lips, shiny from that damn gloss that I remembered tasted like peaches.

"I see it." With the scissors back in my hand, I snipped a section of the scarf, and with my fingers, picked the left-over frays out of the necklace's clasp.

Her neck blazed hot. The skin was so fair, like she'd hidden that part of her body from a man's view.

Had she been alone all that time as well?

She slid the scarf away and turned around. She looked lost in confusion, and I suspected I wore the same stunned gaze.

"Thank you," she said, staring at the scarf clenched tight in her fist like the moment had struck her the same way, and she also couldn't bear to maintain eye contact.

One thing resonated, I didn't like the thoughts going through my head. I'd stuffed away the shame of feeling so much pleasure and joy from another woman's touch. Now I had to face that shame every day.

Forcing away how she made me feel—or I'd go insane—I turned back to my boss. "So, Enrico..." My voice shook. "What exactly is going on here?"

Enrico tilted his head, as if to say, *you tell me*. Instead, he spoke to the woman. "Gwendolyn, it's almost six. You should go home. Enjoy your weekend."

"Are you sure? I can stay," she said, her voice soft, but also a little shaky.

"No, we got it, *Gwendolyn*," I interjected with a *let the men handle this* tone. I regretted it immediately when her smile faded and blue eyes narrowed at me.

"Thank you, *Enrico*," she said, looking at my boss. "*You* have a good weekend as well."

She spun around and stalked off. The way she moved and the sway of her hips held my attention. I was glad she left, though. Her hair smelled like a field of wild roses, and the scent made my head fuzzy.

Clearing my thoughts, I turned back to Enrico, the man I'd worked with for years. The man who had said, *anything you need*, in my time of despair. Enrico had heart and soul, and treated me like a son.

"Andrew, sit down." Enrico pointed to a guest chair in front of his desk.

"I was sitting on a plane for nine hours," I said, folding my arms.

"You have been gone for three months—"

"I've been in Milan." I pointed to the two luggage cases sitting outside my office. "On an assignment you gave me."

"And while distributing your workload, it occurred to me I had been overworking you." Enrico removed his glasses. "You can imagine how that made me feel, knowing those last few months before Cate…"

I shook my head. I expected Enrico to assign my day to day tasks to others. Working with the Milan brands re-energized me about my work.

"*Sì*, yes, the position had gotten a little overwhelming. But being with Marcello forced me to hone a few of my processes that could help get our marketing campaigns out sooner." I opened a production binder sitting on Enrico's desk. "For example, even before the designers—"

Enrico reached across the desk and cupped my shoulder. "I cannot wait to see what you have come up with. But it's late, you have been traveling." He straightened his spine, suggesting he was about to be the boss. "Andrew, I hired Gwendolyn to run the PR side of your brands' strategies."

Press releases and dealing with the media gave me a stomach ache, but I'd still rejected every candidate's resume Enrico had emailed me. The last thing I wanted was some PR know-it-all telling *me* how to run a fashion show. Heck, I wanted to bury myself in my work and have everyone leave me the hell alone.

I sighed, though. It was done. Gwendolyn was

there and a small sense of relief settled into my aching back from the long flight.

"I'm sure someone else could do a better job at PR than me. But you should have at least told me you went ahead and hired someone. I came here and found that...that woman in my office. What else—" I stopped and looked around.

Startled, I realized Enrico had jammed every cubicle on the marketing floor with people and every office was occupied. *Oh God*, she'd have to work *in my office*. A woman I'd slept with. A woman who'd stung my pleasure sensors like a hornet. A woman I'd also just insulted.

"You are right." Enrico ran a hand through his hair. "I'm sorry I did not tell you beforehand."

I nodded to avoid belaboring my intense displeasure with the situation. I knew Enrico had meant well. To help me. At least Prada didn't hire just anyone. *Gwendolyn* must have come from another prestigious design house.

"I know you and Gwendolyn will work well together. She is very smart and had a stellar CV." Enrico pushed a few papers around on his desk. "Here. Salvatore approved of her as well."

I bet he did. I looked over the resume. "Starlight Elegance?"

"Everyone has to start somewhere." Enrico smirked. "You have had quite the journey yourself. Remember where you started in this business."

Hmph. I was surprised Enrico brought up my unorthodox *foot in the door* as a runway model after so much time. I handed the resume back to my boss. "Have a good weekend, Enrico."

"Get some rest, Andrew. You and Gwendolyn have

a lot of work to do."

I walked back to my office, frustrated. *Starlight Elegance*. Last year at Fashion Week, I'd blushed at the skimpy thongs and lace bras all over the place. So, *she'd* treated me and everyone else to that visual display of skin. Got my attention all right.

Gwendolyn's soft perfumed skin had shot fire through my veins, bringing me back to life for one night.

My heart raced wondering if under her skirt just now…was she wearing that lace thong I'd slid down her thighs with my teeth?

I shook my head, annoyed. Those were not the thoughts to have about a co-worker. Especially in today's office climate. Had I run into her at another show, I may have had enough drive and desire to ask her out on a proper date.

Not now. Damn, a stab of gloom zipped through me.

Two porters lumbered by carrying a writing desk through the corridors and headed for my office. While they set it up, I rearranged my desk to the way I'd had it before I left for Italy. Moving the mouse back to the right side of the monitor gave me pause.

She's a lefty.

That's why she couldn't manage the scissors when I handed them to her. And I mocked her for it.

Asshole!

Frustrated, angry, and shoving away misplaced sexual tension, I fired off a harsh email to Gwendolyn to set the parameters of our working relationship.

Despite the added bonus of her being a one-night fling, I'd not delegated my PR responsibilities before. These unchartered waters were going to be choppy.

Strap in, Gwendolyn.

Gwendolyn. She even sounded like a goddess. With curves, ample cleavage, beautiful eyes, and an infectious laugh, that night turned my world upside down.

When I closed my eyes to clear my head, those piercing blue eyes blinked at me in the back of my dirty mind. Sapphire blue...yes, that was the color. Like the ocean, wide and deep.

Now I'd have to look at her every day. Dodge her stares, only she hadn't ogled me earlier. Hadn't flirted with me. And she hadn't let me snap at her. She fought back. Stood up for herself.

The slit in her short kick-pleat wool skirt had sparked the memory of her toned muscular thighs when she marched out of Enrico's office.

Thighs I remembered wrapped around my hips and...

Stop! How was I going to work in the same office with that woman if I already couldn't stop thinking about her?

♥ ♥ ♥ ♥
Gwen

I went straight to the train station after work aching for the solace of a weekend at home on the North Fork. As the train slogged its way to Darling Cove, the view changed from cityscapes and tall apartment buildings, to small-town suburbia, quaint shops, and vast acres of farmland.

At the station that time forgot, I hopped off the train. I breathed in and sighed happily. Late harvesting grapes ready to burst off the branches in nearby vineyards perfumed the October air. I adored the North Fork, a thin stretch of coast made up of unique glacial soil surrounded by the Long Island Sound and Atlantic

Ocean.

The whoosh of the departing train propelled a gust of chilly air against my bare legs. I bounded down a set of metal stairs and hoofed it the mile to my childhood home.

Greg's schedule always changed, my sister Skye would never remember to pick me up since she was so buried in her legal work, and my dad... I sucked in a breath.

My dad was still on medical leave from the police department after being attacked. I couldn't help but wonder if that's why Greg wanted to get off patrol and go sit behind a desk under the emblem of *Fidelity, Bravery, and Integrity*.

I caught a faint hint of my mother's perfume when I stepped into the living room. "Hey," I called out.

Using a cane, my dad limped from the kitchen. "Hey, pumpkin."

We had the same dark blue eyes, and even though Martin Mallory had two other children, I noticed an extra sparkle when he looked at me. "Did Greg pick you up?" he asked.

"Nope. I walked. I need the exercise." I'd never been a size two, but being around runway models messed with my head.

"Says who?" Dad snapped as if I could name a playground bully for him to rough up.

"I work for a fashion giant. I want to look good in their clothes."

"How's the new job?" Dad asked, settling into a lounge chair in front of the fireplace.

I moved the screen to get a fire going, knowing the warmth would make him feel better. "Good, so far," I answered, thinking it'd been going well. Then Andrew had showed up. Now I wasn't so sure.

That intense moment Andrew and I shared threatened to linger between us for some time, not letting either of us forget that amazing night. No, I wouldn't let him, his gorgeous face, *or* the way his body made me feel get in the way of excelling at my dream job.

"I'm happy I'm finally in a *professional* fashion environment. Prada is the reason I went to design school." I felt it wise to remind him my expensive education was paying off.

"Does everyone speak Italian?" he asked.

"Some do, not everyone." I'd heard the velvety, romantic language here and there.

"Twist the papers first before you lay them on the logs," Dad said, referring to last Sunday's New York Times to get the fire going.

"Got it." I lit the ends and sat on the hearth.

"And have you made friends at work?"

You'd think I was still in kindergarten. The hassle of being the youngest. "It's only been a week, Dad, but so far everyone has been nice."

Except Andrew. *Nice* didn't really cover how he'd acted around me. He was the person I needed to work the closest with and he made me sizzle and sweat. It had *super complicated* written all over it.

"Nice is a good start," Dad said, drumming fingers on the chair's arm, showing how restless he was.

Dad had pulled over the town drunk and found out the hard way Derrick Hannigan bought a gun. Derrick drove off, running my father over, breaking his leg. Then, the drunk got out of the car and made the fatal mistake of pointing a loaded pistol in a cop's face. Dad had no choice but to shoot the poor guy.

The investigations continued and Skye had been working on the case. In between her real estate closings. Dad needed a better attorney, but I didn't know if my voicing that would scare the hell out of Dad or insult Skye. In the meantime Dad's doctors hadn't signed off for him to go back on patrol.

Feeling the warmth of the fire against my back and the love from my Dad's proud smile, I let go of the tense moment at the office with Andrew.

"Pizza!" Skye breezed in with two boxes, and her golden retriever, Casey.

"Who else is coming?" I asked, lifting my butt to help her get paper plates and hot pepper. "Does Casey eat pizza?"

"Greg said he'd stop by. Have you just met our brother? He can eat an entire pie himself," Skye said, helping Dad into one of the dining room chairs.

"Midnights aren't so quiet anymore," Dad said and settled into his seat.

"I also got some red." Skye took out two bottles of cabernet from her work bag.

I assumed she got them at the liquor store while waiting for the pizza and didn't drink in her law office.

We ate and chatted. Dad went to bed and Skye left to walk Casey, musing how she loved the sweet smell of fire smoke in the crisp fall air.

They left me alone in the kitchen with my third pizza slice and a splash of wine.

Not making size two anytime soon.

I pushed away any sad feelings to focus on the positive. A small shock of pleasure slipped under my skin knowing I'd finally steered myself on the road to a better life.

And I have a paycheck to prove it.

"Paycheck!" I perked up and moved through the living room to dig my laptop from my work bag. "Let's see what my take-home pay will be."

Clicking through various screens to find the ADP app and see my stub, I noticed a Prada icon on the bottom toolbar.

I opened my work email and saw the message on top was from Andrew Morgan. There was nothing in the subject line.

Oh great, no way am I reading this sober.

I stomped to the kitchen to open that second bottle of wine.

CHAPTER FOUR

Gwen

By Monday morning, I still hadn't responded to Andrew's message. Email made it too easy to fire off a response in anger, knowing the person on the other end could walk away and think *I'll deal with that bullshit later.* Instead, I printed it out and made notes. The practical side that often overshadowed my creative nature would deal with Andrew Morgan. In person.

Any face-to-face conversations, however, would be a challenge. The man dripped with raw masculine intensity. I'd have trouble completing a sentence around him.

Over the weekend, I'd read and re-read the message. In addition to saying he would go through his files and decide what to hand over, he stressed he'd do it in his own time. He must have found the mess I'd left behind.

He notified me that the porters had delivered and set up my writing desk, but reminded me it was *his* office. As *Brand Manager*, he had a staff. Employees came to him with personal issues and to maintain their privacy, he would need to close and lock his door for those sensitive meetings.

I understood this office situation inconvenienced *him*. His complete lack of empathy toward how his hogging the office would affect *me*, a fellow exec who also had responsibilities, was just downright rude.

With each word I read, I expected him to address the obvious source of tension between us. Nothing. How would Andrew avoid discussing our one wild night together, though?

My locked office door answered my question and sent me over the edge. Fuming, I hunkered down in a nearby conference room with my laptop resting on my thighs. The room currently doubled as an audition studio to conduct the last round of model auditions for the L.A. fashion show.

I spent all morning tucked into the corner trying to write a press release while listening to Salvatore's thick accent.

"Walk, turn, come back. Now do it again with feeling. Is that all your hair? Extensions, she will need extensions."

To the next model with wild tresses, "That is way too much hair for the delicate frock she will be wearing."

Salvatore had not only softened since my interview and turned gracious, he became a relentless flirt. Smoothing his Northern Italian blond hair, he had offered me the pastries and paninis laid out on the other side of the room. The photographers, assistants, and stage director munched on the sandwiches and sweets. Yet the models eyed the table like it festered with poison.

In a fresh email, I addressed the locked door situation:

Good Morning, Andrew. I'm in the west conference room if you need me. Please let me know when I can get into the office. I'm starting the press releases and will need to access the files from the last show.

Thank you.

On a small plate, I packed half of a mozzarella and pesto panini, an assortment of olives, and a tasty looking scone. Balancing everything on my lap, I unwrapped the sandwich and dragged the napkin across my legs. I hadn't realized how starved I'd been until I opened my mouth to take a scrumptious bite.

"Gwendolyn?" Andrew drawled my name low and controlled.

I looked up and my heart pounded from him standing over me. I put the panini back on the plate. Wiping my hands on the napkin, I answered, "That's me."

"Why don't you come in and we can go over the press releases." Something told me Andrew wasn't the type to embrace a working lunch. When I left the untouched plate on the metal chair, he pointed and said, "You can finish that in my office."

Fearing intense hunger and low blood sugar may make me dizzy, I picked up the plate. "*Our* office," I mumbled under my breath.

"What?" Andrew turned back sharply.

I exhaled. "I'm sorry. It is *my* office, too, right?"

He pursed his lips together then took a breath. His perfect white teeth bit into a plump lower lip. "Yes, it is."

"I, um, read your message and I'll give you space, if you give *me* the consideration I deserve. I'm an executive here, too."

He grumbled, but nodded. He turned away and his long legs carried him down the central corridor while I scurried to keep up.

At the office door, he pointed to one of the guest chairs on the opposite side of his desk and I made myself as comfortable as I could. I balanced my plate of food on my thighs while resting my laptop and notes on the second chair. The meeting table tucked into the corner, hiding under a mound of crap, would be a better place to work, but I kept my mouth shut about that.

I considered it a small blessing when his phone rang as soon as I sat down, giving me an opportunity to take a few discreet mouthfuls of my panini.

When he began speaking perfect fluent Italian, my jaw dropped, food nearly spilling out of my mouth.

I turned away to hide the potential mess. *Get it together, woman.* After a fortifying swallow, I looked back. Andrew had stood and searched for something on his desk.

He lifted folders open and slid loose papers in and out. I gave a soft sigh. Damn, that man made *filing* look hot and steamy.

All his movements were slow and measured like a panther stalking his prey. My eyes wandered to his beautiful hands and long fingers. I gasped, noticing a braided gold band on his ring finger. *He's wearing his wedding ring.*

Had he worn it that night? I wouldn't claim to have been drunk, except high on Andrew's kisses and touches. I may have missed it because I couldn't take my eyes off his face.

"*Ciao.*" He hung up and met my eyes. "Sorry about that."

The moment grabbed me, but swooning over a man still in love with his deceased wife was ridiculous. "Before we get started, Andrew, I wanted to say I was very sorry when I heard about your wife."

My own loss had taught me to respect the suffering of others. A kind word of acknowledgement had significant meaning to people who had lost a loved one. Having lost my mother, I could relate.

Andrew's body froze, though, and his lips curled

into a shape that suggested he tasted something bad. "Excuse me?"

Uh-oh. "Enrico told me what happened. I'm just letting you know that I'm very sorry. Cancer is—"

"Okay. That's kind of my personal business." His fists were tight, and a vein in his neck looked ready to pop.

"I didn't mean to upset you." I released a sharp breath. "I just thought it would be rude to sit here, look you in the eyes…" as gorgeous as they were, "and not say something. That's all." I folded my arms across my chest.

He stared for a long moment. "She'd been gone just over a year when…" He coughed. "You and I…"

My hand shot up to stop him. *Dear God, don't say it. We know it's best if we don't talk about it.* "I…get it. I'm still very sorry."

"Thank you." He pursed his lips like saying those simple words were difficult. "She was everything to me," came out just above a whisper, but he'd meant for me to hear it.

"Everything," I repeated softly, watching him.

Andrew looked back with dark questioning eyes, but said nothing. He filled a room with his presence. To say a woman was everything to *him*, was deep to say the least.

I cleared the emotion from my throat. "Back to the show, I've written some preliminary press releases. Can I see the event planning that went on at other shows to make sure I'm not missing anything?"

"Yeah." Andrew spun gracefully and sauntered to the row of file cabinets.

God, he was tall. In a flourish, he yanked out folders, binders, accordion files, and large brown envelopes. One by one, he piled them all in front of me. Some almost toppled to the ground before I caught them.

"Here," he said. "This is everything you need to create the media kits, write the press releases, and set up the interviews."

"That's a lot of paper." I organized the pile. "Ever hear of this thing called the computer?"

He flattened his smile. "Your computer skills went to good use at Starlight Elegance?"

My eyelashes fluttered. "Excuse me?"

"I'm sorry. I just don't understand how a promotions person at a *lingerie* company—"

"I was the promotions *manager*. And I don't remember you having a problem with Starlight's lingerie when you peeled them off my body."

Yep, we're going there.

The blood drained away from Andrew's face, leaving a startled ghostly expression. *Damn it!*

I pushed the pile aside. "Listen, I'm sorry. I know it's best if we never speak of that night, but I will defend my experience."

The color in his face hadn't returned. I'd pushed him too far. And on our first day working together. Stupid. He'd done that job by himself all those years and never had to open up or let anyone in.

The messy office was a symbol of what Andrew had become. *Lost.* Just as Enrico had said.

He rubbed one thick eyebrow, suggesting I'd given him a headache, and said, "Please have everything completed before we go to L.A."

It was best to let him cool off. I slipped a brief look in his direction, hoping for another chance to apologize. Then his cell phone rang.

Looking at the screen, he said, "I need to take this, and I need to be alone."

I nodded. "Right. Sure."

He gave me a great view of his back and answered his phone. "Mira, what is it?"

With the bundle in my arms, I stood, and stepped toward the door. Once I passed the threshold, it slammed behind me, sending a burst of air across my shoulders. My long hair flew forward and around my face. I spit out a curl that lodged inside my mouth.

And who might Mira be?

"Oh, my gosh." Thalia had been walking by and must have heard the commotion. "Let me help you with these."

I gently released the pile. I assumed Andrew didn't label or date his documentation. "Thank you, Thalia."

"Come on." She shook her head in Andrew's direction. "Enrico is at Flagship for the rest of the day. You can sit in his office."

Walking by desks of people, I brushed off the mixed reactions of smirks and smug chin lifting. I suspected many of those women salivated over Andrew and were probably jealous as hell of how close I got to work with him.

Heh. I just make it look fun.

♥ ♥ ♥ ♥

Andrew

On Tuesday morning, I sat at my desk across from a model crying hysterically when Gwendolyn whirled in like a tornado.

"Sorry. Subway delays." She plopped a slate blue trench coat and a creamy white leather tote on her desk. "Let me get my laptop, and I'll get out of your way."

Before she could fly out of the office, I stood.

"Gwendolyn, wait."

She stopped and slowly turned around, a look of mild panic on her face. "Yeah?"

I'd been too harsh with her yesterday. Dragging Starlight Elegance into the conversation was a low blow. I'd planned to apologize as soon as she came in, but then the weepy model showed up.

"This is Mira, she's a model in the L.A. show," I offered.

"Oh! Hello." Gwendolyn sounded like I'd shown her a puppy.

I huffed. Mira's depressed mood swings were triggered by reactions such as that. Models felt like objects. The scrutiny got to them more than the starvation sometimes.

Mira attempted to compose herself with a weak smile. "Hello."

"Mira, look at Gwendolyn." I spun her chair in that direction. "She's what? A size four?"

"Four?" Gwendolyn smoothed her black pencil skirt.

I shrugged, figuring I guessed wrong. It didn't matter what size she actually was. Her figure was phenomenal. Perfectly proportioned. Her cheeks glowed with fresh skin and she looked so incredibly healthy. Full of life. Full of fire. Her mouth, the way she kissed…

"So?" Mira whined, interrupting my thoughts.

"*So*, if she looks so good as a size four—"

Gwendolyn blinked feverishly at the *so good* comment.

I shook my head and continued, "Anyway Mira, *you* are not fat."

"You think you're fat?" Gwendolyn asked, sinking

into the chair next to the model, her face full of questions.

Mira threw up her hands. "I've put on a few ounces."

"Ounces?" Gwendolyn dropped her chin.

"Mira, it's fine. I promise you." I placed my hand across my heart. Beating. Rapidly.

"Tell that to the *master*." Mira pushed herself off the chair with an impressive amount of force for someone who weighed less than one hundred pounds.

Gwendolyn's eyes trailed upward taking in Mira's impressive six-foot height. "Who's the master?"

"Salvatore," I answered, spite slipping into my tone. I looked at Mira and said, "If he gives you an issue at all for the show, you come to me. Okay? I'm in charge here. Not him."

Mira ran long thin fingers down her neck. "Okay, Andrew." Her eyes narrowed at Gwendolyn. "Can I speak to him in private for a moment, please?"

"Oh, yeah. I was leaving," Gwendolyn said and marched back to the door.

I blocked her path. "Actually, Gwendolyn and I have a lot of work to do."

Winking, I sent her a message that I didn't want to be alone with Mira any longer. After a nod, Gwendolyn inched back toward her desk. She made a good wing girl. *This could work out.*

"Right." Gwendolyn nodded. "For the show. I'm in charge of publicity now. You want people at your show, don't you?"

The way Mira sized Gwendolyn up bothered me. Her hawkish look of disapproval said, *I know what you like, Drew, and she's not it.*

Ha! Think again. Someone like Gwendolyn may not

have turned my head in the past, but after a taste of that woman's luscious curves, skin and bones wouldn't satisfy me ever again.

Mira grabbed her Fendi wristlet and draped her fur-trimmed vest over a long forearm. "I'll see you in L.A. then, Andrew." She held out her hand to me.

I clasped her cold fingers out of politeness, gave her hand a quick squeeze, and dropped it even quicker. "Sure thing."

Mira spun a perfect practiced turn and sashayed out of the office. Her movements were precise and robotic...and she had about as much appeal to me as one of Salvatore's hollow dress forms.

Gwendolyn watched her leave, smoothing her hands across her pencil skirt again. My eyes tracked the motion until she picked up on my stare.

She raised an eyebrow at me and said, "Does that happen often?"

I wasn't sure how to answer the question. Sure, models fled to my office for either comfort or a job. And in the past, for a date or a meaningless hook-up.

Then I married Cate. The aggressive ones didn't respect my marriage, though. The idea of *that* starting up again made me queasy. A generic answer for Gwendolyn right now was best since I loathed for her to see me as some kind of man-whore.

I jammed my hands in my pockets. "Sometimes."

"Let's make sure to link our calendars so I'll know when to avoid the office. I find them...creepy."

"Find what creepy?" I asked.

"Models. *Runway* models," she clarified.

A rush of heat slammed against my neck. "Uh, what...what about *male* models?"

Her body turned in my direction, her eyes

regarding me. "I don't know. I don't have experience working with any, yet. Starlight didn't make thongs for men."

My chest tightened, my eyes grazing across her body. *Is she wearing* that *lace thong right now?* I pulled on my tie. "That would be something to see."

"It's like anything else, there's always a double standard. The male models I see in ads are usually tall and really good looking." She stopped, her eyes sweeping up the entire length of my frame. "The whole androgynous thing done to women on the runway doesn't do it for me."

"*Do* it for you," I said quietly, listening and thinking.

At that moment, I wanted to tell her *I* had modeled at one time. She would never figure it out. I'd used the name Drew Michaels. Michael being my middle name. No one at Prada knew…except Enrico.

Gwendolyn leaned against her writing desk and began emptying contents of the tote bag, starting with a laptop. "If there were aliens watching us, I'm sure they would look at all the models and say, *never mind boys, some other extra-terrestrials have already landed on that planet. Let's see what's happening on Mars.*"

I released a soft laugh, grateful for the break in my self-inflicted tension. A girl with a sense of humor. No, not a girl. She was a woman. Mature. Smart. Confident. Sexy and…silly. Sexy, I caught last year. Silly, no. Then again, it had been a bitch of a week.

I didn't think I would find funny endearing. Pouty and annoyed had turned me on for years. I took a breath and said, "It's a battle I've been fighting since I got here. Trying to work with models who represent the average woman."

"Except, the average human being can't afford our clothes. Try making them less expensive, first." Her unexpected response, perked me up further.

I enjoyed the witty banter. I liked the way she talked, expressive, full of emotion. Eager to see how far I could take that game, I said, "I have a better shot at sending down a model with two percent body fat than lowering our prices."

"You both have zero shot," Salvatore said from the doorway. He walked in, all swagger and ego. "Hello, Gwendolyn, how are you today?"

"Good. You?" She leaned on her desk, smiling. Her right leg bent like she enjoyed the attention.

"I am much better now," Salvatore responded, grinning stupidly at her.

Really? I stepped back, aghast to see Salvatore make such a blatant play for someone at the office.

I took a sip of my coffee, wondering why the designer wanted Gwendolyn, when it hit me. Hard. The same reason *I* did apparently. I choked, realizing how much I still wanted her.

"Are you okay, Andrew?" She rushed to me and laid a hand on my arm.

"Yeah." My skin tingled from the touch of her fingers. So warm and comforting. Yet, confusing.

After years as a husband, and now a widower, I didn't know who I was anymore.

Gwendolyn's large blue eyes searched my face to make sure I was all right, Salvatore forgotten.

It rang so fucking clear in my head, yeah, I wanted her. Her charms had pulled me in once. If I didn't watch out, I'd get completely lost in her.

Lost was *not* the destination I had in mind, returning to New York.

CHAPTER FIVE

Gwen

Andrew had been too quiet for my taste the last two days. The lively interaction after Mira left our office was the last time he'd spoken more than two words to me. Things had looked hopeful between us. He'd been on the verge of warm and friendly. What had cooled his heels?

I tapped the end of my pen against a folder on my desk, almost hoping he'd look up and tell me to stop. *Tap tap tap.* Nothing.

A dinging noise made me glance at my laptop. Another email from Salvatore gave me a faint smile. Since I'd sought refuge in that conference room a few days ago, he'd acted as if I'd gone there to send a message. I couldn't tell if any of the charm he'd poured on was real. Did he think he needed to seduce a good PR strategy out of me? For the time being, I acted polite, even while turning down invitations for coffee or a drink after work. He was handsome enough, but I wasn't interested. Not even a little.

Andrew continued to work at his desk in silence, typing away at his laptop. Oh, how those fingers felt on my bare skin. *Stop it.*

He sat hunched, completely unaware of the mountain of mess around him. What the hell did his apartment look like? His hotel room had been neat enough.

He'd said something about being between apartments. Thinking about where he lived now, my mind's eye wandered through what I thought his place looked like. Simple kitchen with maybe a few dishes in the sink. A plain living room, maybe a pop of color. Andrew *did* work in fashion. I swallowed, thinking about his bedroom. Was he a man who left an unmade bed? Did his scent linger on the sheets?

I slapped my hand over my mouth. Remembering how he pushed me down on that hotel bed, sent a hard thump between my legs. I tugged at my skirt. A man that good looking and great in bed must have had his share of women between the sheets. Maybe he'd had more than one at a time to prevent a line from forming at his door.

My eyes wandered to the picture frame on his desk, the one I replaced earlier in the week. Had I been the first woman Andrew slept with since his wife's death? The last? Somewhere in the middle?

I looked down and sighed. Those crazy thoughts were getting me nowhere. Except frustrated as hell. I shook out my damp palms and twisted my fingers. Now my entire body ached from being turned on thinking about Andrew. Not good because he would never touch me again. We had to work closely together. Office romances were problematic. Now more than ever. I had to keep things professional. I couldn't afford to lose that job and as far as fashion gigs went, it didn't get much better than Prada.

Andrew still sat there, typing away. I'd emailed him ideas for the press releases two days ago, but he had yet to respond. It left me in a holding pattern. There was no point in going to the art department if Andrew hadn't approved the copy.

Bored and restless, I stood and stepped to the window. Through its reflection, I saw Andrew still in his own little world. My movements hadn't made him budge. Next to his desk, someone had stacked a tall column of boxes up against the wall with folders wedged in between. It looked very unsteady, like I shouldn't go near it.

I skulked toward the boxes anyway. Being closer, I got a better look and saw labels with other shows' dates and cities.

Way up high, I spotted a box labeled with the last fashion show Prada did in L.A. *Bingo!* That box probably was chock-full of info I could use. I considered asking for help. Some men jumped through hoops to help women. Andrew's body language at the moment suggested I shouldn't disturb him.

I removed a chair from the messy meeting table we still hadn't used and carried it to the stack. I slipped off my shoes and stood on the vinyl seat.

"What are you doing?" Andrew asked in a booming deep voice, cracking a hole in the deafening silence.

I spun in his direction, flailing for something to keep me steady. Andrew jumped from his seat to catch me, his strong hands gripping my waist. The hold made me feel like falling even more. His fingers sent shock waves through me, shooting to my breasts and tightening my nipples, then south to soak my panties. Like my brain remembered his touch.

That. Want that!

I gazed down, hoping his gray eyes would tell me he felt the same. Just so I didn't think I was crazy or alone in my attraction. But Andrew looked...mad.

Flushed and shaking.

"Thank you." I spoke to fill the silence, and smiled, still wanting a reaction. Nothing. The release of his grip gave me back my sanity.

"What do you want?" he asked.

For a moment I thought he'd read my mind.

"Want?" I whispered.

"Why are you on this chair?"

I exhaled. "Oh, um, I see that box up there has an L.A. label on it. I wanted to look inside."

"There's nothing in there for you." When I crinkled an eyebrow at him, he backpedaled. "I mean, there's nothing in there, publicity-wise."

"Okay, but this is my first really big show. I would still like to see what you've felt was so important that you kept it in a box for six years."

He huffed, still red in the face. "Fine, let me get it."

"I'm right here. I can reach it," I said and leaned forward.

I hooked my fingers under the box and slid it from the stack, only my charm bracelets caught on the box below. The entire heap began to wobble, and with my hands full, the only thing I could use to stop it from crashing to the floor was my body.

The quick movement made me lose my footing again and my stomach did a little flip as I started to fall. Andrew lunged to catch me, lifting me away from the spectacular splat on the carpet. Next, I was against the empty wall where the boxes were, Andrew pressing his body into mine to keep me upright. Binders, fabric, brochures, wristbands, access cards—Andrew's entire career at Prada was dumped on the floor and scattered around our feet.

He stayed utterly still. He clutched my waist keeping me in place. His commanding hold made me feel like Lois Lane when Superman soared through the sky, caught her, and said, *I've got you.*

The solid heat of Andrew's body thrilled me.

I took that moment to watch him. I expected him to

be brooding over the mess I'd made or gawking at the office door, where anyone could walk in.

No. His eyes stayed locked on my face, my eyes really, once I had the courage to meet them.

My breath hitched at the fire in his gaze. I could feel his stare like hot strokes against my skin. Flirting and coy conversation got me into his bed the first time.

That look he just laid on me was different, he let me see the quiet power of his seduction. My heart pounded in my chest. Despite the distance he attempted to keep between us, it wasn't working.

That man wanted me. Again.

Andrew was no longer a stranger. We worked together at a job I needed in order to pay my bills and give me the career I always wanted.

Kissing him, or doing anything with him, would threaten that.

No.

Using my own superhero strength, I looked away because, holy moly, I could gaze at that face all day. I gently pressed down on the hands still wrapped around my waist.

He released me instantly and stepped back, his head tipped forward still staring at me. I pushed a mess of hair out of my face with shaking hands and looked down at the clutter of papers.

I'm in so much trouble.

Trembling, I said, "Andrew, I am so, so sorry. I'll clean all this up. Just go back to…doing whatever you were doing. You won't even hear me."

His face remained expressionless and he said nothing. *It's when they don't yell that you have to worry.* He picked up the box that had fallen the furthest—the one marked L.A. He shook it and the sound of broken glass from inside meant I may have destroyed something important. *Oh crap!*

"Here." He shoved the box at me. "Can you work in the conference room for the rest of the day, please?" The lack of emotion in his voice sent a chill through me.

"Please, let me clean the rest up." I reached for him out of some wild instinct. Just a touch to calm him down.

He wrenched away. "Stop! No more."

I staggered back, feeling like he'd slapped me. "You know I didn't want this to happen."

"Just go." His stinging words and rejection stabbed my heart.

I slinked away with my head down. Again. That became our narrative. I'd gotten somewhere with the man. Then crash. Either I'd say something he didn't like, or touch something he didn't want me to. *Or* make him touch me. The tangled scarf, the unsteady chair... Each time, he sprang to my rescue then vaulted away even further.

It didn't even matter what was in that damn box anymore. I was too afraid to go through it now. Seeing a precious shattered trinket he'd kept for so many years would break my heart.

Prada was my dream job, but from day one nothing had gone as planned. Enrico hired me behind Andrew's back and shoved me in his office. Andrew was a proud man who preferred to do his job, his way. Alone. He was also recovering from a terrible loss. I'd gotten too close to him and now he acted like touching me made his skin crawl.

♥ ♥ ♥ ♥
Andrew
Full of regret, I lined the fallen boxes in front of the

window. Enrico trekked in holding the box marked L.A. When my boss closed the door, I grew even more concerned.

I'd acted abominably toward Gwendolyn. It would have been dumb of her *not* to go to the boss, so I struck first. "Look, I know Gwendolyn must have said something to you. I'm just out of sorts."

"I know." Enrico's calm voice made me more nervous. "Do you need some time off?"

"No!" shot from my lips. The last thing I wanted was time to myself to think and wander the streets where every corner held some memory of Cate. "I'll apologize. I was wrong."

"There is an open office on the designer floor. Gwendolyn asked me if she can have it. I will have her desk moved out of here tonight." Enrico set the box down, clearly annoyed.

"The designer floor?" A small twinge of panic swelled in my chest.

Salvatore's fawning had been irritating to watch. The idea of Gwendolyn sitting near that man every day made my teeth grind together.

I'd been trying to make sense of my feelings. Watching her when she didn't realize it. Listening to her talk to others just so I could figure out who she really was. Meanwhile, Salvatore stomped around trying to lure her into having lunch and drinks after work. The invitations were crude and demanding. *Women don't want to be dragged around by the hair anymore, Salvatore.*

"Andrew?" Enrico prodded me out of my thoughts.

"Let me talk to her first. I'll straighten this out. It would be a waste of time to make her move twice when an office opens up on this floor. Plus, I need to visit some of the newer local retail stores. We won't be in each other's way so much."

"You must understand, if she comes to me again…"

"Understood." I made a fist against my heart. "I'll make this right."

While I feared I'd botch my explanation for why she couldn't have an office to herself right now, I also didn't want to spend all weekend thinking about what I would say. After searching the entire marketing floor and stalking the ladies' room, however, I realized Gwendolyn must have left for the weekend. If she were still here, I would have spotted her immediately. Her lush curves and long silky hair stood out against the sea of bland assistants and interns. My fists curled in frustration. An apology would have to wait.

Stepping into the evening air cooled my ears which had been burning all afternoon. I drew a sharp breath, sucking in the crisp hint of pine and sweet seasonal nuts. The holidays were approaching. Last year had been miserable and I didn't want to feel that way anymore.

With no one to rush home to, I crossed Eighth Avenue to walk all the way downtown. A sophisticated bar looked inviting, so I turned back and gave in to the urge for a drink. The amber border around the sidelights and the crackled glass blurred the faces inside. The silhouette of Gwendolyn's body, however, was unmistakable. She'd imprinted on my psyche and I would soon know her anywhere. Even though I still wanted to speak to her, I needed to find someplace else to have a drink. We were off the clock.

I released the handle, letting the door close, but a group of men at a table in the corner leered at her. Pointing. I knew how men looked at women they wanted. My chest pounded at the thought of one of those men having her.

Enrico should have picked up on the frustrated attraction I couldn't seem to shake, disguised as kindergarten hair-pulling. Sitting across from her every day, I'd struggled to tamp down the excitement I got from just looking at her. And remembering what it'd felt like to hold and kiss her. My body needed sex so badly and my darkest fear was that I'd do something very stupid. If she ended up pressed against me again, I wasn't sure I could control myself to not yank up her skirt and screw her right in the office.

A man in a business suit from that corner table strolled across the bar and seated himself next to her. Rage soared through me, forcing my hand back on the wooden handle. I wrenched the door open with unnecessary force. I still hadn't figured out what I would say, I just wanted that man away from her. Now.

Ignoring the usual gawking stares, I strode across the planked floor to rest a hand on Gwendolyn's shoulder. Her sparkling blue eyes widened as our stares collided in the long mirror behind the bar.

She twisted around and small creases formed above her nose. "Andrew?" She looked around like she didn't believe I was real. "What are you doing here?"

"Can I talk to you?" I gave a sour expression to the suit. Cheap, not Prada. "Alone."

After a stare of contempt followed by the once-over I expected because of my height, the man took his drink and slinked away from the bar.

Gwendolyn released a ragged breath. "Okay."

Relieved, I slid into the open stool next to her. "I want to apologize. To start, I want to make sure you know, you've done nothing wrong. I just—"

"Do you want a drink?"

I blinked several times, curious she didn't let me

finish apologizing. Most women would pounce on the opportunity to make a man grovel. It became clear as crystal to me right there...Gwendolyn wasn't like most women.

"Yeah," I answered, relaxing.

I ordered a pint of Blue Moon from a woman behind the bar who attempted to flirt with me. Gwendolyn smirked into her wine glass, watching the whole exchange. With the beer in my grasp, I took a sip.

"You don't put the orange in the beer?" she asked, her voice light and friendly.

Long fingers, absent of any rings, flicked the fruit slice into the golden liquid. The silver charm bracelets lined up along her wrist and clanged softly. Ever since I'd helped her detangle herself from the damn scarf, that jingle-jangle had been making me salivate like Pavlov's dog.

"Now take a sip," she said.

I did and smiled. "Yes, it does taste better this way. What are you drinking?"

"A Malbec." She swirled the dark burgundy wine around in her glass. "It's not the best, but not bad for ten bucks."

"The next one is on me. And that one if you haven't paid."

She clinked my pint glass. "The guy you kicked off that bar stool paid for it."

CHAPTER SIX

Gwen

Andrew's smile tingled my toes. And other places, but that was dangerous. I could *not* fall into his bed again.

He wasn't very attractive when his shoulders were up around his ears. I liked him better relaxed, sitting with his spine softened. The man I'd met a year ago slowly slipped through.

I opened my mouth to keep chatting, but my phone lit up with a call.

Andrew looked at the screen and wrinkled his nose.

Holding up a finger, I said, "Yeah, Greg? Yes, I'm taking Dad to the doctor visit tomorrow. I'll call you when I'm on the train. Tomorrow." *I'm sorry*, I mouthed to Andrew. "I'm out now, Greg. At a bar. No, I'm not alone. No, you can't talk to…I have to go. I'll talk to you tomorrow. Love you. Bye." *How embarrassing.* I tapped the screen and turned back to Andrew. "Sorry."

"If that was a boyfriend, he sounds a little possessive," Andrew said hesitantly.

I dribbled my sip. "That was my brother."

"Oh…" His eyebrows dipped. Damn, he was so hot when he did that. "Older?"

I nodded. "Greg's not married, so he stalks me and my sister, Skye. He was engaged a while ago to his childhood sweetheart. But…"

"But…what happened?" Andrew asked with sincere interest.

Yes, better to discuss someone else's disastrous love life. "A few days before the wedding, she took off."

"Ouch."

"The great Mallory family scandal," I said.

"Why Mallory?" A puzzled look fell upon his face.

"Mallory is my maiden name."

"You're *married?*" The poor man had gone from thinking I had a boyfriend to a husband in ten seconds, no wonder he turned red.

Except, I didn't know how to answer a very simple question. Was. I. Married? "*Technically*, yes. I'm in the middle of a divorce."

"Oh, dear God, please tell me it wasn't because we... Because I..." He grabbed his tie. Did he think our wild night was all his own doing?

I exhaled, time to get it all out there. "To answer you, no. My husband Dan and I split way before I met you."

His lips quirked in the corners. "Met me. That's putting it mildly."

Met him. And let him have his way with me. Again, and again. I swallowed, watching his smoldering eyes take me in. "Should we talk about it? Just once, get it out there, so we can move on?"

His eyes fluttered suggesting he was searching for something to say.

"I mean, there's no way that's going to happen again," I assured him. "We work together. And I *need* this job."

"I, uh. I agree." He exhaled. "Office relationships are dangerous, anyway."

"Right. See, that wasn't so hard." I punched him in the arm to be playful, the memory of those solid biceps lifting me up and down crashing through me.

The fire in his eyes came back strong like my touch ignited that same memory.

"Sorry." I pulled my hand back and grabbed my

wine. "I'm a bit of a touchy-feely person."

"I remember." He fisted his beer. When he finished a nervous sip, he asked, "So, why aren't you divorced?" His face fell. "Do you have…children?"

I shook my head. "No. No. Thank goodness. He recently filed divorce papers. I have to sign them."

"Oh." Andrew looked down, appearing more confused than before.

I took another sip of my wine and made direct eye contact. "If we can also get something else out of the way. I'm very sorry I brought up your wife the other day."

He tried to jump in, but I quickly shushed him placing my fingertips against his lips. They were so pink and full. Remembering how soft and moist they felt on my mouth, sent a shock of pleasure through my body.

I lowered my hand. "We have to get to know each other *professionally* before we should discuss anything more about our personal lives," I said in one breath. "*If* we do that, I mean. I won't do anything to risk my job. I need the paycheck. And I'll do whatever *you* need me to do to make our working relationship successful."

"Gwendolyn, you're doing a great job." He kept his gaze on me, his smile sincere.

"Really? I'm so excited about this fashion show. I want to make someone like you proud."

"Someone like me?" he asked, surprise in his eyes.

"Yeah." I glanced down at my glass. "You were right about Starlight not being very—"

"No, I'm sorry. That was completely out of line."

"I just need you to trust that I can do this," I said.

Andrew stared until he inched closer. "As long as we're talking about former employers, I'll tell you something about me that only Enrico knows."

My mouth hung open the entire time Andrew revealed his secret past as a male model. It wasn't hard to imagine. He was the perfect specimen of a man. Tall, broad shoulders, prominent cheekbones, and full lips.

"Is that why you asked me what I thought about male models?" I regretted my response now and my choice of words. Something about being creepy, aliens, and men in thongs.

Good one!

Although, if Starlight had designed male thongs, I'd have signed up Andrew as one of my models in a heartbeat.

"Self-consciously, yes," he responded, sounding troubled. "It's something I'm proud of, but at times, I'm ashamed of my past."

"Being rewarded because you're tall and beautiful is—" I forced my eyes away. *I just called him beautiful.* Licking my dry lips, I finished, and said, "I mean, having someone think you're good enough to show off their clothes is nothing to be ashamed of."

"Thank you." His head lowered, but his dark eyes stayed glued to me.

"Thank you for confiding in me," I responded, humbled. My head spun and not because of the wine.

"We're a team, right?" Andrew had become a different person. He spoke to me like…a friend. A new version of the man had emerged.

"Absolutely." I clinked his glass again.

Andrew smoothed his tie and sat up straight. "Speaking of being a team, Enrico said you asked for the office on the designer floor."

My cheeks blazed with heat. I'd almost forgotten about the request. So, his making nicey-nice was business. *Not* pleasure. I took a breath. "It's hard to share an office. No matter what the circumstances." Ours was a doozy.

"I'd really rather you not sit on the designer floor," he admitted with a firm gaze locked on me now.

I leaned in, mesmerized. "Why?"

"That floor is chaotic. *I* can't think straight when I'm down there."

I sat back, regretting how I wished he'd given another excuse. "I think it's kind of fun." I shrugged. "Lots of energy. It'll be like watching *Project Runway* every day, all day." I wiggled my shoulders, my passion showing through. "I love the creative process. Seeing the designers take a bolt of fabric and with a few clips of the scissors and stabs of the sewing machine needle, *voila*! A dress. It's really quite fascinating." I paused and stared into my wine to break the eye contact. "Besides, you can't like me being in your office."

"Actually, I do."

I looked up, shocked by the confession.

He pressed his fingers together. "I thought it would be annoying. But you're pleasant enough to be around."

Pleasant enough... *Oh yeah, Mr. Morgan, you can talk dirty to me better than that.* "I have to be honest, the mess and clutter I have to look at every day is kind of getting to me."

"I'll work on that. I promise." He finished his beer and took out his wallet. "You won't like listening to Salvatore yell all day, trust me."

"Yeah, but it's mostly in Italian." My fingernails scraped the bottom of the empty pretzel bowl, but I felt too embarrassed to ask for another refill.

"Thank goodness. I'm sure if it were English, we'd have dozens of lawsuits on our hands." He wanted to keep me away from Salvatore to protect the company from a lawsuit. How very *corporate* of him.

I exhaled. "Okay. At least until the fashion show, deal?"

"Deal." His lips agreed, but his eyes said, *maybe*.

My phone buzzed with a text from Greg.

Are you still at that bar?

I dumped my phone in my purse. I didn't want him or my father to worry about me, but I was an adult and lived on my own for years. I was allowed to go out after work and come home late.

Or…not at all.

"Do you have brothers or sisters?" I asked Andrew with wary eyes as he paid for his beer.

"Nope."

A knot of emotion settled in my throat. How could a man be so handsome? Jet-black lashes tipped his round, deep-set eyes. Thick and expressive eyebrows curved down toward his Roman nose. His fair skin held on to a few shades of a left-over Italian summer tan. When he smiled, his square jaw would make a Hollywood heartthrob jealous. Underneath, the gentle curve of his throat made me gooey. The soft skin I'd bit and nibbled at. He liked that, all right.

Gasp. Stop. Stop. Stop. Hooking up with a stranger had already shoved me way out of my comfort zone. A fling with a co-worker, one I had to sit across from every day for the foreseeable future, was a bad idea.

"Well, this was…fun. But I should get going." I slid off the seat and my head felt lighter than I had expected.

"I didn't realize it was this late." For the first time, Andrew checked his phone. Its glossy screen had stayed dark and silent the entire time we'd been talking. "Are you okay to get home?"

"Sure, sure," I answered, not looking at him and checking the area around me for all my bags.

"Where do you live, Gwendolyn?"

"Upper East Side."

Andrew stared with questioning eyes, his cheek twitching.

"You?"

"Downtown. Or I would have suggested we share a cab." His voice shook with nerves and tension.

"I wanted to walk for a little bit, anyway," I said, pulling my laptop bag over my shoulder. "And please, call me Gwen. We have secrets to laud over each other now."

The way he smiled made me wonder if getting that man to soften up was such a good idea. What if he *did* want me again? Would I have the resolve to say no?

He followed me out the door and bent his body into a bow. "Have a good weekend, *Gwen*."

I'd made so much progress, anything but a smile now might push us back. An uncontrollable urge overpowered my better senses. I leaned in and hugged him. *God*, he still felt so good. His powerful body made me shiver.

While I hugged him, reveling in how good it felt, Andrew's body, however, stiffened like a piece of plywood.

Uh-oh.

I jerked back and glanced down at the sidewalk. "You have a good one, too. Bye."

I sprinted away from Andrew as fast as I could, my high Prada heels wobbling with every repentant step.

♥ ♥ ♥ ♥

Andrew

I didn't move. Couldn't move. The feel of Gwen's body again, strong and healthy against mine, took my breath away. I'd been cold and mean to her for a couple of days, yet it came so easy for her to forgive and embrace me. She wasn't a petty person or a grudge-holder, and those unique qualities elevated her in my mind.

And the desire to have her again seared through me. *Shit!*

A cutting wind woke me out of the trance I'd been in. I trekked a few feet toward my subway station, but stopped, and trudged back to the office instead.

I strode through Prada's quiet marketing floor and reached my locked office. Once inside, I closed the door behind me.

How did this office get so out of control?

I never thought I'd be under a microscope. Shows were the priority, not cleaning out my office.

I dropped my work bag on the messy desk and put my hands on my hips. The unoccupied office on the designer floor made me curious. I turned to check it out, but smacked into a body.

"Sir?" A startled man stood there. "Is everything all right?"

"Sure." I got my breath back. The white patch on a blue shirt caught my interest. *Maintenance.* "Is there a way you can give me a hand with something?"

"Of course, sir."

I brought him down to the designer floor. Ah! Just what I'd hoped, a large office and a small desk. "Okay." I turned to the maintenance man. "What are the chances we can move this desk upstairs and move my desk down here?"

The man nodded and seemed eager to help. I'd bet

he spent every Friday night sitting on a chair with nothing to do. In two hours, a team of porters had my old desk emptied, dissembled, brought down to the designer floor, and reassembled. Another team took the smaller desk and did the reverse.

When I tried to help, the porter cheerfully dismissed me. "No, no sir, we got it."

While the desks were being switched, I rifled through my file cabinets. In the staff lounge, I grabbed a box of extra-large garbage bags. I'd been at Prada long enough to know I could toss fabric samples from a fashion show six seasons back. I emptied several drawers which weren't even full without any stress at all. Two whole cabinets were moved to Gwen's side of the office. *Our* office.

In my bookcases, fancy binders lined the first few shelves, but I'd filled the rest with crap. I tossed the crap, consolidated the binders to one bookcase, and gave the other to Gwen, as well.

By three a.m., there were six black trash bags in the hall, and I'd transformed the office into a comfortable neat space with two desks on opposite corners. The walls were now neatly lined with bookshelves and file cabinets. I wanted it to look perfect and even wiped the furniture down with polish. I also dug out my round conference table from under a blanket of old newspapers. Now Gwen and I could sit together and have meetings.

The new space excited the hell out of me, made me feel I could be more productive. I'd been accumulating junk. Each year in the time-span between lines being released, there'd always been a pipedream I'd have time to clean. That never happened. Enrico used that down time to whisk me all over the world.

Exhaustion took ahold of me. On my final scan of the office, I spotted loose papers peeking out from under Gwen's desk. One of the porters must have knocked over the trash can. I picked up the papers and crumbled them in my fingers. Something didn't bend like the other discarded papers and I opened my hand to have a look.

I unfolded the mini envelope. Loopy handwriting, I didn't recognize read: *Gwendolyn*.

It looked like a card I expected had accompanied a floral arrangement. There were no trace of flowers, dead leaves, or wet muck that accumulated at the bottom of a vase anywhere in the office or the trash.

I guessed it came from the soon-to-be ex-husband. Maybe asking her to take him back. What idiot would let her go in the first place?

Waiting for the elevator, I stared at the sloppy script, my heart pounding with anticipation. I opened the envelope feeling as if I were about to sneak up on the woman who fascinated me to distraction.

My eyes filled with rage taking in the words scrolled across the card. Nope, not the ex.

Think about it, bella- SC.

CHAPTER SEVEN

Gwen

Skye picked me up from the train station. I'd not gotten much sleep the night before, unable to get Andrew off my mind.

Listening to Kelsey and her boyfriend having loud sex hadn't helped. Not to mention kept me frustrated.

My sister's blonde hair sparkled in the fall sunlight shining into her Audi, and her shoulders and legs looked toned as ever. Running agreed with her.

"I bought you your favorite latte," she said, handing me a warm cup.

"Bless you, my beautiful sister." I breathed in the steaming black silk heaven with a hint of mocha. "Are you coming to the doctor with us?"

"Got work to do. I'll be at the house later to help him get settled."

"Greg working?"

Skye gave me a look.

"What?"

"Faith's back in town." Her voice dropped to that dangerous tone of a protective sister.

Skye never forgave Faith Copeland, my childhood best friend, for breaking Greg's heart.

"Is he working all these hours to avoid her?"

"I guess. He won't talk about it."

I exhaled, wondering if any of us would get love right. I was getting a divorce and pining for a widower I worked with. Skye got dumped on Facebook by a rockstar last year. And Greg, try as he might to look like he was over Faith, was stuck on the only woman he ever loved.

"What's up with you?" Skye asked, noticing my frustration.

"Nothing." I couldn't talk about how I'd woken up with hard, sore nipples and a throbbing between my legs.

I'd dreamt Andrew and I were outside the bar again. I'd been standing outside myself, watching it like a movie. Andrew hadn't reacted to my hug last night, but in the dream, he devoured my mouth with those full pink lips and a warm, velvet tongue.

It'd felt so real because seeing him again had awoken the dirty memories of what he'd done to my body. In another flash, we were in his office, *our* office. He'd lifted me up and laid me out on that messy desk, shoving papers and folders aside. His free hand dove under my skirt where he found me slick and waiting. I'd thrashed around, my body sizzling, as his long fingers slid inside me to make me come in my sleep.

"Are you sure it's nothing, Gwen?" Skye asked. "You're all flushed."

I'd not told a soul about that night because I wasn't a one-night-stand with a stranger kind of girl.

"There's a guy I work with who's really hot," I said, hoping to leave it at that.

"How hot?"

"You wouldn't believe it." I leaned my head against the cool passenger window in hopes to lower my body temperature.

"Tall?" When I pressed my eyes closed and let go of a sharp breath, Skye hissed with delight. "You like 'em tall. Which is why I never understood what you saw in Dan. What else?"

Ignoring the dig on Dan's short stature, I swallowed, and figured, what the hell. "Actually, I slept with him last year. But I didn't know who he was."

Skye shot me a look. *"Really?"*

I waved away the pouncing I knew I'd get. My crazed family were full of protective lunatics. "I'm not in a mood to get into it. I met him in a bar, we had a drink, and then I went back to his hotel."

"With a *stranger* who could kill you?" she rasped, sailing through a red light on Center Street.

Talk about getting killed.

"You sound like Greg," I grumbled. "If you tell him, I'll kill *you*. Do you see? I'm fine. Oh, the guy slayed me all right. It was the best sex I ever had, Skye, which is why this is so hard now."

"What is?"

I pushed through the fire burning beneath the surface of my skin and reminded myself out loud while answering Skye, "Andrew is completely off-limits."

"Is there a no-romance policy at Prada?"

"Just the opposite. It's like a meat-market there."

"What's the problem?"

"I'm an executive now. I can't go home with a *co-worker* and then show up the next day in the same clothes." Although I had plenty of opportunities to get more clothes, nice ones if I ever dared to let Andrew have me again one fine day after work.

"Hmph." Skye pouted, annoyed that I'd denied her juicy details about Andrew and that night in his hotel room.

"Anyway, I love the job. Thanks for asking about that."

"Of course, you love the job. It's Prada. I'd haul my ass to the city every day to work there."

"And give up your nice little law practice here in town?" I gulped my hot coffee and burned my lower lip.

"I'll see you later at the house when we get back from rehab?"

"Yep." She swung into the driveway and my dad waved from the front porch.

Dad dealing with that injury where he could have lost his life, kicked me in the stomach because we'd already lost my mother.

I waved and got out of the car, wondering how I would ever tell my family my last mammogram came back abnormal.

♥ ♥ ♥ ♥

Andrew

"Andrew Morgan," I answered my cell phone, all groggy with sleep.

"That's very formal for a Saturday."

"Hi, Ma." I licked my dry lips and glanced around. I was face down on my bed, still fully clothed. I'd been too exhausted to remove anything except my shoes at four a.m. "What time is it?"

"It's almost noon."

"I got in late."

"Were you on a date?" she asked with too much enthusiasm.

Gwen's face rushed into my mind as soon as my mother said the words and it damn near unsettled me. "No, and please stop posting those inspirational greeting cards to my Facebook page."

"Have you found the chance to get out and meet anyone, my handsome boy?" My mother had always boasted about me, introducing me as her polite, good-natured, smart, and considerate son. And handsome, she'd always added. That would be more her accomplishment than mine.

Last I checked, I was a *man*, and not a boy, but I

didn't mind that she wanted me to move on. I'd considered telling her about Gwen a year ago, just to give my mother hope I was on the mend and ready to get out there again. Except, being with Gwen had only set me back.

"Not really," I answered after a moment. "I've only been back a week and I have a fashion show coming up. I'll be even busier." I wandered into my kitchen and cursed at the few scattered grains of coffee laughing at me from the bottom of the Café Bustelo can.

"What about trying to date someone at work?"

The metal container slipped from my hand and clanged against the ceramic tile floor, spilling what could have been at least one small cup of coffee.

Before Gwen, getting involved with a co-worker had always been on my *to-don't* list. I pinched the bridge of my nose. "Ma, Cate passed away—"

"Two years ago."

"Twenty months." I considered counting the months a step in the right direction toward letting go. It started with hours, then it was days, and then weeks. Now I counted the months, and soon it would be…years. "I'm still—"

"You're too good a man to be alone."

I hadn't planned to stay celibate for the rest of my life. Cate had even told me to move on. *'Drew, you're a good man. Promise me you'll find someone when you're ready. I don't want to leave this world worrying that you'll be alone.'*

Those words had cut through me like a knife. Even now, the pain still ate at me.

I sighed in relief when Ma changed the subject to the gossip in her Fifth Avenue building. Half listening, I ambled back to my bedroom to put on workout shorts and a tee-shirt.

Before I got a sock on, Ma interrupted herself and said, "Your father's calling me from the golf course. Bye, love you!"

"Love you, too." It struck me how good it felt to say that out loud.

I sat on the edge of my bed and took a few breaths noticing the large brown envelope I'd just received from Cate's sister. Apparently, my wife had tucked away some racy honeymoon photos in several of the books I'd let Julia take. All the photos from that trip to Paris were postcards from happy ever after. All I had now was...after.

I kept a hat box with other photos from our life as well as my past on the top shelf of my closet. I took the envelope off my nightstand, ready to slip it in the box, but breezed through the junk mail inside the package first.

"What the hell?" I gripped the Victoria Secret catalog, wondering why Julia would give that to me.

Must have been an oversight, but the cover model—a striking brunette, caught my eye. And stopped my heart. Her long wavy sable hair called out to me like a mountain begging to be climbed and conquered. I pawed through the thick glossy catalog. I found the model again and again, but one image made me go rigid. She wore a lace thong and covered her bare breasts with her hands while flashing a sneaky smile.

It reminded me so much of Gwen when I'd had her down to a thong and nothing else. The memory grabbed me by the throat. I stirred from the swelling in my groin. I kept growing hard whenever I dared to think about Gwen or remember what she'd felt like beneath me as I slid my cock deep into her tight wet folds.

I blew out a harsh frustrated breath. I wanted her again. But it could fuck up my career to sleep with a woman who worked for me.

CHAPTER EIGHT

Gwen

An envelope taped to my office door on Monday morning caught my attention. I shifted my work bag, my purse, and a lunch cooler to one arm. Balancing the pile, I tore the envelope down and lifted the flap. A jingling sound intrigued me. Inside, were two sparkling silver keys on a thin, round wire fastener.

All my bags tipped to the side and began to fall. I caught the laptop case by the strap, but the rest went flying. "Son of a—"

"Ciao, *bella*." Salvatore greeted me with a velvet accent and scooped up my spilled belongings.

"Oh, hi." The keys felt cool in my hand as I slid one into the lock.

With a slight turn of the handle, the door swung open. I froze for a moment. "What the heck?"

On Friday, I'd left an office that looked like a tornado had struck. There were still two desks, but now mine didn't look like a dinghy floating behind a crowded yacht. Behind my desk were two bookcases, and to the right, a file cabinet.

"I see you redecorated," Salvatore said, dumping my bags on the desk.

The windowsill looked clean and dust-free. The sloppy depository for fashion programs now showcased Andrew's travel souvenirs, and in the center was the squat violet plant I'd brought with me. On my first day, I'd crammed it into the few inches of available space to catch a hint of sunlight. Now, it sat front and center, soaking up the rays streaming in from the window.

I fingered the plant's velvety leaf when the reflection in the window changed from the city view to Andrew's hunky body in the open doorway.

I spun around to face him. "Did you do this?"

He held a tray with two coffees and his canvas work bag slung across his broad chest. "Yep," he replied and put the coffees down. "Good morning, Salvatore. Can I help you with something?"

"No, no. I was helping Gwendolyn."

"Really? With what?" Andrew asked.

"He just grabbed my bags for me." I moved in Andrew's direction and his posture immediately relaxed. "I got the keys you left me."

"The porters did that actually. They must have made them up this morning."

"Andrew, this is so amazing. Thank you. But you didn't have to do this alone. I would have helped."

He peered down at me, ready to respond, but he glared at Salvatore instead. "Do you need me or Gwen for something? Because she and I still have a lot of work to do for your show."

Salvatore's leather jacket squeaked when he brushed a hand through his thick blond hair. "Gwendolyn, are you free for lunch? I'd like to talk about what I mentioned last week."

"What was that?" Andrew jumped in.

I stepped back to watch two elegant beasts size each other up. Salvatore had been needling to see me outside the office. I considered saying something to Enrico, but so far, the advances had been harmless.

Andrew's acceptance of me, rearranging the office, and now the daggers he threw at Salvatore, *that* shocked me. He'd been working there long enough to witness Salvatore woo and wine many women in that office and must be protecting me.

"Actually, Salvatore..." I wedged myself in the middle of the men. "Andrew and I are planning a kick-off meeting where we can talk about the theme for your show. I've already reached out to the art department to get a few samples of a logo I have in mind."

"That is very proactive of you. Yes, I will look forward to your invite on the Outlook." Salvatore stepped away eyeing the reorganized office and the desks gleaming with fresh polish. His light eyes moved back to Andrew, and he gave a formal nod. "Mr. Morgan."

"Signor Corella."

The designer shuffled out of the office, glancing back at me. I gave a little wave, but Andrew closed the door before he could wave back.

"So, when is this meeting we're having?" he asked.

"I have no idea." I smiled at the cardboard tray he brought in earlier.

"Oh, I didn't know how you take your coffee." He pulled a cup from the tray. "I just got you my favorite, a mocha latté."

My favorite was...his favorite.

"That's perfect." I played it down and enjoyed the warm cup in my chilly hands. "How much do I owe you?"

"Don't be silly. It's a coffee."

So, it didn't mean a thing. Cleaning out the office for me, also nothing. Probably just making amends for his bad behavior on Friday.

After a sip, I scanned his side of the office. "Is this the same desk?" Either I'd grown a few inches wider or the desk was smaller.

"No, I downsized so you'd be more comfortable in

here."

"Andrew!" I put the cup down. "I said I would move."

"*I* needed to declutter. It was a good thing for *me*."

My heart squeezed seeing my map of the world pinned up on the cork board in the corner. On Friday, I'd left it rolled up and lying under my desk, fearing there would never be a place for it. "You hung my map," I said, pointing.

"Yeah." He nodded, acknowledging what he'd done. "It's great. I wouldn't have thought to hang something like that in here. But we *are* a global brand. Manhattan can be so confining and feel so closed off."

"It's easy to forget there's a big world out there." I crossed to Andrew's side of the office where the map hung closer to his desk. My fingers floated over the length of the Italian peninsula, settling on the base. "I've only been to south Italy."

My family had taken what we called *The Elizabeth Mallory Memorial Vacation* a few months after my mother had died. We landed in Naples, drove to Sorrento, and stopped in Pompeii. We took day trips to Capri and drove up the Amalfi coast. It had been my mom's dream holiday. We kept her memory alive by taking the trip in her honor.

Milan, the landlocked city, seemed a world away. "What's *Meelano* like?" I asked Andrew.

"You don't have to pronounce it that way around me." He was close enough now that even from behind, I sensed his intense heat. "*My* impression of Milan is, it's New York, London, and Paris all wrapped up into one."

"Have you been to Paris?" I turned around, eager to talk about the city I loved.

He looked down and flattened his lips. "Uh, yeah."

His head hung a little lower. "On my honeymoon."

Here we go again. One step forward and two steps back. Think, think. Draw him out. He doesn't want to be sad. *Make this about you, Gwen.* "It's a beautiful city. I lived there for a summer."

He perked up. "Really? When?"

My shoulders relaxed. "I took an art class there while in school. It's a great place to vacation. But living there, you feel as if you're a part of the city, you know, walking among people as neighbors. You've stayed in Milan for extended periods of time, right?"

"Yeah." He sounded like the conversation exhausted him, but he smiled and said, "I'm sure you'll get to Milan eventually."

"You think so?" With our bodies inches apart, the trace of coffee on his lips with a hint of mocha was sexy as hell.

"Of course." His height made me feel vulnerable, but excited. He watched my eyes, as his darted from side to side like he was searching for something to say next.

Damn, I liked being close to him. A sizzle shot through my veins, and my body came to life, especially my nipples. *Uh-oh.*

"We have a lot of work to do," he said while my stare lingered.

When he retreated, I looked down. The thrill I got from him put my arousal on display. I crossed my arms and ambled to my desk.

"Shall we?" He pointed to the clean and cleared-off meeting table.

"Sure." I grabbed a spiral notebook and sat.

"Here are some notes." Andrew showed me the printed emails I'd sent with my press release ideas.

The red ink splashed all over the pages made me sink in my chair. I reached out to take the pages back. "Wait, let me have another shot at this."

His hand covered mine. "No, it's fine. I just added some teasers in Italian."

"Teasers?" I asked, thinking about him as a model, sauntering down the runway, his eyes hooded and his lips parted. He may have been showing off the latest suit, but I bet every woman must have been wondering what was underneath.

"Yeah, Enrico likes it. Just plop them in when you write the final draft."

"Okay." I tucked the papers in a folder and took out an image I found for the program. "What did you think of the cover art? I kind of like this visual of L.A."

The slanted image forced our heads to tilt in the same direction. My hair swept across his shoulder making his nostrils flare.

"I think it's great, but I would crop the angle a little." He took the paper from my hand, his fingers brushing against mine. "We have to keep in mind that people may view it on their phone."

"Right. Don't want to cause pile-ups on a California freeway."

He stood to get his laptop.

God, that man has such a great ass. Even covered in pants! That. Want that!

He returned with the file downloaded from my email. With a few swipes of his long fingers, he played with the embedded image to resituate it.

"Wait, that's too far. Now it looks like we just made it crooked." I leaned over and played with it myself.

The warm keys tingled under my touch. My arms stretched out and crisscrossed over his, but he didn't move.

"Yes, that's perfect," he whispered, his eyes no longer on the screen.

"It really is," I agreed in a breathy rush.

Andrew's dark guarded eyes studied me. Long arms tangled with mine, our heads dangerously close. With one puff of his chest, I would feel his lips. One delicate flick of the tongue, I'd taste its lush surface. A feather-light wisp was all I wanted at the moment.

Oh, God. My heart was ready to explode. "Andrew…"

"Gwen?" he whispered, his shoulders tensing.

The ringtone on my phone drew my attention. The annoying clatter came between me and Andrew like an iron wall.

I sucked in a breath and slid my hand away. "Dan?"

"When are you going to sign those papers?" my soon-to-be ex grumbled.

"Hang on," I said into the phone and looked at Andrew, who sat back. "I need to take this." I stepped out of the office. Dan calling me out of the blue alarmed me. His FedEx surprise a few weeks ago had been his only contact in months. "Hello to you, too. So now you're in a rush to get divorced? We split up a while ago."

"I just want this official so we won't have to file joint taxes again."

I rolled my eyes in exasperation. "You're concerned about your *tax bracket?*" The whirlwind of my new job, the fashion show, and figuring out Andrew, made me forget to get back to Dan with the list of concerns Skye had with the divorce papers. "I'm sorry to ruin your plans for the New Year, but I have some issues with that document."

"Your sister is not a divorce attorney. Give it to a professional. Now."

"Don't order me around." I tried to remember Skye's objections. "I didn't have a job for months, I can't afford a lawyer."

"Oh yeah? I hear you're at Prada now. Does it pay well?"

I wanted to smack my forehead. My new job at Prada must be the talk of my hometown. "Glad you're now keeping track of my life. You weren't interested in my career before."

"Get a lawyer, Gwen," he said, ignoring my charge. "And sign the papers."

"Stop telling me what to do!" I looked up and spotted Andrew walking toward me with his coat on. "Hang on, Dan. Andrew, I'm sorry. I'll be back in the office in a few minutes."

"I have a meeting at Flagship, and I forgot, I have a… There's somewhere I need to be after that. I sent that revised image to you. You should finalize the program." He was all business. No hint of the man who had almost kissed me.

"Okay. Andrew, wait." I held the elevator door before it closed. "I have a…thing tomorrow morning. I'll be a little late."

His eyes pinched in irritation looking at the phone in my hand. "Fine."

The doors closed with his gaze laser-focused on me. It became difficult to stand. And made me hate the man on the phone even more. I may very well have been in that elevator with Andrew, kissing him, going to Flagship with him. It would have been my first time, and I wanted it to be with Andrew. To see the store through his perspective.

"Gwen!" Dan shrieked.

"Okay! I'll sign the papers, but there's one thing I have to have, or the deal is off and I'll get some shark to tear you apart."

"What's that?"

"Your lawyer forgot to include one important provision in that decree."

"I don't have all day, Gwen."

"I want my damn name back. It's Mallory, in case you've forgotten." I clicked the phone off.

♥ ♥ ♥ ♥

Andrew

After a visit to Flagship, I slogged across town to Sloan Kettering with dread in my heart. With every step, though, I grew more and more relieved to be there. After today, I'd never have to go back. Ever.

Cate's very wealthy family had given a huge endowment to the hospital after she passed away. The result was a new radiology center and a generous yearly allowance for their research labs. I had expected *The Catherine Reese-Morgan Women's Pavilion* to be unveiled on the anniversary of her death. They finished almost a year late.

Cate had lived very much like me, a starving model, both literally and figuratively, refusing to live off her family's money. I'd loved that about her because while my father was a high-powered and successful lawyer, I lived as my own man and made my own way in the world.

Just when I thought Cate's medical bills would bankrupt me, I was shocked to learn she'd set up a trust for me. I was technically a multi-millionaire.

The outside of the MSK building and the lobby still looked the same. I hoped for some kind of change, so the memories of my previous visits didn't feel like a punch to the gut.

The new radiology center, much to my dismay, was located on the same floor where Cate had died. I had to go back to the scene of the worst day of my life.

After stepping into the elevator, I pressed the button for that level with trembling hands. Mercifully, I was alone. As the doors closed, so too did my eyes.

"Okay, I'm here. I'm back," I whispered. "Come on in. Come to me," I called in the memories I'd locked away in the dark part of my soul, even past the shattered pieces that had been mourning Cate.

The brutal disease's effect on her had scared the hell out of me the most. It'd been like witnessing a gruesome murder. Every day.

Never again.

The elevator door chugged opened and I stepped off. Project leaders had shared details of the new wing with me as the construction progressed. Only now that it was all finished and I skimmed my fingers across the fabric of the lounge chairs in the waiting room, felt the silkiness of the privacy curtains, and ran my hands along the embossed wall covering, did it hit me.

My connection to that place was done.

"Andrew, we're in here," Julia called out to me, standing outside the administrator's office.

Julia was strong, like Cate. Her other sister, Diana, however, was a mess.

"Diana, please get it together." Julia's impatient tone irritated me.

"I'm being forced to remember what my sister went through. I'm allowed to be upset."

"Be upset. Just stop blubbering." Julia put an arm around me. "How are you, Andrew?"

"Fine." I stifled my annoyance at their bickering. Even as my temper rose, my heart squeezed painfully in my chest.

The administrator shook my hand, not meeting my eyes. Yeah, I remembered there'd been a lot of that. On the way to the actual ceremony, I trailed behind everyone. As Cate's husband, I should have been the Grand Marshal of that pity parade.

No. I'd walked many runways as a model. Felt eyes on me. Admiring me. Wanting me. Feeling worshipped under the spotlight. Now, I preferred the quiet anonymity.

The ceremony ended and I acted detached leaving the hospital, even though I felt more devastated than when I'd gone in.

I made a silent vow to show as little emotion as possible from that point forward. I'd feel the pain, but wouldn't burden anyone with my messy feelings.

No, I wasn't ready to move on.

God, I'd almost kissed Gwen again. Right there in the damn office and didn't think I'd stop at just a kiss.

On the street, while waiting for a taxi to go have a strong drink, I spotted Julia and Diana leaving. Diana grabbed her sister's hand. They would be all right, I thought warmly to myself. They still had each other.

I had nothing. No one. Just a job at Prada.

CHAPTER NINE

Gwen

On Tuesday morning, I waited for the radiology doctor at Lenox Hill Hospital.

My mind wandered to Andrew. *Back* to him really. I'd not heard from him the rest of the afternoon yesterday. I'd gone to bed last night wondering what if Dan hadn't called? The jealous look in Andrew's eyes made me tingle, but the way he'd taken off hinted at a battle going on inside his mind.

Would it be easier if he were divorced as well? Sitting in a hospital waiting to discuss my abnormal mammogram thinking about his deceased wife felt surreal.

I typed *Cate Morgan* into Google to pass the time. A few blogs announced the news of her death. *Catherine Reese Morgan, former Lanvin model, died in early December...*one old blog post started. Ah ha! She'd been a model, too. Must have been how she and Andrew had met. My eyes shot to the cold tile floor. It would make sense if Andrew didn't want to get involved with someone else in fashion.

I clicked a few more links. I had a strange desire to see a picture of Andrew in that old world of his, but found it odd there weren't any pictures of him on Cate's blog. "If he were my husband, I'd get tee-shirts made up," I mumbled to myself.

In the photo on his desk, Andrew looked different standing next to Cate. That must have been his brave face. Now, his smile seemed peaceful, especially when he looked at me. Perhaps the man he used to be — the person Enrico hinted at — was indeed returning.

But who was the man I'd slept with?

The door to the waiting room swung open and Dr. Sage, a thin cheery blonde breezed in. "Hey, there."

"Good morning." I let my phone slip into my bag.

"I found a batch of suspicious cells in the upper quadrant of your right breast that I want to get a better look at," she said, pointing to a spot on my X-ray.

A dark reality crept over me, I'd no longer be covered under Dan's health insurance once I finalized my divorce. Prada had a ninety-day probation period. Even then, my coverage may not be as good.

"Let's do a quick biopsy. There won't be much of a scar," Dr. Sage said, leading me to the procedure room.

On my phone, I opened my calendar to account for the additional time. I typed in the words: *Biopsy*. I'd shared my schedule with the entire marketing department, so everyone would know I was out of the office for legitimate purposes.

My throat went dry thinking of Andrew. After a nervous breath, I backspaced and retyped: *Emergency Appointment*.

♥ ♥ ♥ ♥

Andrew

"Andrew, I found this *bellissima donna* in the lobby," Enrico said, smiling at my mother wearing a stylish trench coat.

"Enrico, my mother, Sarah Morgan," I said to my boss. "Ma, what are you doing here?"

"I was in the neighborhood." My mother tucked a lock of her dark mocha bob behind her ear, revealing a firm jawline.

"You were wandering up and down the West Side Highway?" I stood and folded my arms. "Enrico, thank you."

"My pleasure." In his suave Italian style, Enrico took my mother's hand and kissed her knuckles. "Until we meet again, my lady."

My mother's face beamed with excitement and a hint of mischief. I would have to remind my father to get off the damn golf course once in a while.

Ma swung into the room. "What a gentleman."

"Can I get you an espresso?"

"No. Vile stuff. I prefer tea. But not until later." She stepped to the window and gazed at the view. "When did you get this office?"

"About four years ago. I've invited you, but you keep turning me down."

"Your father's job keeps me busy."

"You stopped being his legal secretary decades ago."

"You think those little girls in that office know what they're doing?" She turned and ran her fingers along my desk, still smooth from my cleaning blitz. Her eyes settled on the framed picture of me and Cate. Ma pursed her lips and turned away. Pointing to Gwen's work area, she asked, "What's this?"

"It's a desk, Ma."

She narrowed her eyes—the same color as mine. "I see it's a *desk*. Whose is it? Did you get a new secretary?"

"No. She's not my secretary." I purposely said that loud enough to squash the rumors swirling about Gwen. No one knew her true role at Prada because Enrico had kept hiring her on the down-low. Even from *me*. "She's a new PR exec."

"Public relations. So exciting." Ma lifted a folder from Gwen's desk, but put it down to pick up a bronze frame. "Is this her?"

I hadn't noticed the personal items on Gwen's desk.

In the frame, a younger version of my new co-worker sat cross-legged in the center of a group of people I assumed was her family. On her left, a cute blonde had similar shaped eyes, and to her right, a young man kept his hand on her shoulder. *Must be her brother, Greg.* Why had I remembered the name so easily?

An older man graying at the temples and an older blonde woman smiled with pride in their eyes. I should have noticed *her* first. Gwen's mother looked sick in the picture, frail and thin. Hopefully she was better now.

On a tack board behind Gwen's desk, hung a few more photos. More recent, I could tell. In the close-up someone had taken of Gwen, I could count the freckles on her nose. Her husband? A tinge of anger bubbled up inside me.

In a photo below, she appeared again with the blonde from the other picture. In the backdrop were rows of vineyard vines, a bright blue sky, and a halo of sunshine on the horizon.

All I wanted to look at in that picture was Gwen. "Uh, yes, that's Gwendolyn."

"Gwendolyn?" My mother nodded with approval. "That's fancy. Where is she from?"

I smirked. "No."

"She's from a place called *'No'*?" my mother asked sarcastically, reminding me of how Gwen often joked. *Uh-oh.*

"It doesn't matter where she's from." I took the frame out of my mother's hand and put it back on Gwen's desk. I'd grown up listening to my mother make hypothetical matches for me. I was an only child, and my father had lost a brother in the Korean War. The responsibility for the entire Morgan bloodline rested on my shoulders.

Mom had 'put up with' my dating model after model. Waiting for me to get it out of my system. When I'd married one, she'd gone through the roof. It didn't matter how much Cate had adored me.

I'd been shocked to find out Cate didn't want children. I hadn't faulted her for her decision to remain childless, except she hadn't told me how she felt until *after* I'd married her.

When I'd painfully confessed to Ma that Cate didn't want to have children, my mother refused to see or speak to me. For years.

Cate may have come around to the idea of children, but shortly after our first anniversary she'd been diagnosed with terminal cancer. I'd gone into my marriage thinking I had a beautiful sophisticated wife who'd give me plenty of sons to ensure the Morgan name.

Instead, I ended up a widower. Heartbroken and alone.

"Let me buy you lunch," Ma said, taking my arm and leading me out of my office. "There's a nice lawyer in your father's office I want you to meet."

Grunt.

♥ ♥ ♥ ♥

Gwen

A trace of perfume lingered in the office when I returned. Draping my coat on the task chair, I noticed someone had moved the picture of me and my family. I narrowed my eyes at the girls who'd been slinking by my office, peeking and leering at Andrew—stalkers with astonishingly small waists and thighs.

Everyone in that office wore a size two and below. As a curvy size six, I felt like an elephant tromping through the narrow lanes of desks and cubicles.

I popped a piece of gum in my mouth to cover the spicy taste of the pizza I wolfed down in the cab.

Andrew walked in a few minutes later, frazzled and jittery. "Oh, you're here."

"My appointment took a little longer than I'd hoped, sorry." I twisted so the icepack in my bra to reduce the swelling didn't fall out.

"No problem." He looked at his phone. "Something wrong?"

I wanted to place a hand on top of his and return to the moment we shared yesterday. "I'm sorry about yesterday." I searched for a reaction to know if he tossed and turned about it like I had.

All he tossed was his phone on the desk. "For what?"

For...almost kissing him. Taking Dan's call. What had I been thinking? The moment had clearly passed. Or he was ignoring it. Two can play that game.

"Nothing. Do you want to go over the schedule for tomorrow and the rest of the week?" I still needed to wrap up all the loose ends for the fashion show. It'd crept up so fast and nerves were setting in.

"Sure." He patted his desk looking for something and brought one hand to his hair which had a mussed-up quality about it.

A shock crashed through me. Had he been with a woman?

In response to how *I'd* made him feel?

He had every right to be with someone. A harsh reality set in, making me shiver as if a hairy spider crawled up my arm. If I continued to work there, I had to accept Andrew would date *someone* eventually. Those potential someones were all over the place, lined up and waiting. *Ugh.* I'd have to watch him be all gooey with another woman.

"What is it?" Andrew asked, noticing what must have been a strange look on my face.

"Um, nothing." I wore my best crooked smile. "Are *you* all right? You seem a little...off."

"I just had lunch with my mother."

His mother. Oh, thank goodness. The idea he had a little lunch date with his mom warmed me. "That's so nice."

He shook his head in frustration. "I love the woman, but she makes me crazy."

Having a big family who was always in each other's business, I empathized with him. "My family likes to meddle, too. My dad's protective. At least you're a man." When Andrew abandoned his futzing and watched me with curious flat lips, I clarified, "I'm sure your mom doesn't hover over you, always thinking something bad is going to happen to you."

"Oh, I would expect a father to be like that." He swiped a notepad and dragged his chair across the room to my desk. "And mothers hover. In other ways, you know what that's like, I'm sure."

My stomach clenched and I hated to correct him. "My mom passed away right after I graduated high school."

His eyes were full of regret glancing at the photos on my desk. "Gwen, I'm so sorry. I didn't know."

I shrugged. "How could you know?"

He released a sharp breath. "I still feel terrible. I feel like I bit your head off when you first mentioned Cate."

"Andrew, that's different." I took a seat at my desk. "My mom died a long time ago. Your wife passed away recently. Plus, it was your *wife*. The person you're supposed to be the most...intimate with."

"But I think losing a parent is different. I mean, I'll eventually get another wife." He rolled his eyes, turning red. "Okay, *that* came out wrong. What I mean is—"

"Of course, you'll *eventually* find someone else. You're a young man." I snuck another look at the sea of faces peeking at us above their monitors. "It's not like you won't have any takers."

He caught me looking that way. "I certainly can't date anyone out there."

"Out there?" I jammed my thumb at the entire marketing floor.

He released a slow breath. "They all work for me."

"That would be messy. Right?"

"Yeah, and illegal...right?"

"Are you asking me or agreeing with me?"

He released a low chuckle. "I get that people at work hook up. But if I were to put my job at risk, it would be for a person I just couldn't stay away from. No matter what." Andrew studied me for a moment.

Imagining that man going all in to take a risk on someone choked the breath out of me. More and more I wanted to be that someone. Except I couldn't be with Andrew. We had an awkward brief history and now worked closely together. Surely, he hadn't meant me.

"Anyway..." I opened my laptop, knowing it was best to start speaking about work. "I sent that image to the art department. They worked up a draft program. I'll print it out." I stood to run off to the copy room.

Andrew's hand closed around my wrist, freezing me in place. "Gwen...is everything all right with you?"

"Sure," I squeaked out, shivering at his touch.

"Your husband isn't *bothering* you or anything, is he?" Andrew asked with a tight jaw.

"No. And he won't be my husband for long. He just

called yesterday asking for the signed divorce papers."

"Oh."

"The only reason I haven't signed them is because I've been so caught up with the new job and...and with you." I absorbed the eyes fixed on me. "And the show, of course."

"Right." His gaze shifted to the doorway.

"Is this yours?" Thalia stood there with the program I'd printed.

I took it. "Thanks."

Yesterday had happened so organically, it was futile to force me and Andrew back to that place. I handed the program to him and leaned over his shoulder while he looked at it.

"This looks amazing, Gwen."

"Hold on, Mister. Wait till you see what else I can do." I winked and sauntered out of the office.

CHAPTER TEN

Gwen

I stood in one of the Prada bathroom stalls with my head against the partition. The phone call I'd received about my biopsy left me breathless and confused. Those *suspicious* cells came back *negative*, but I'd need more regular screening under the care of a specialist.

I couldn't tell my family. Considering what happened to my mom, they'd lose it. I needed to get myself together before I got in the airport limo with everyone going to the fashion show in an hour.

My thoughts got rudely interrupted when two women started gabbing by the sinks.

"Don't do it, Charlize," one of the voices warned.

"Why? He's single."

"That's only because his wife died."

My ears perked up. They were talking about Andrew and the gabbing just got interesting.

"She died like, five years ago," Charlize whined.

I shook my head at the wildly inaccurate timeline.

"Besides, I heard even before his wife, he only dated models," the unknown voice said. "I'm sure that's who he'll end up with again. You know, once you go model you don't go back."

"I can pass for a model."

"You're barely five feet tall, Charlize."

Ah ha! I placed Charlize. Ironically, she shared the name with a tall gorgeous actress, only *this* Charlize was a little troll. That troll worked for Andrew, and she had the power to roll in our office and kick me out. I swallowed, worrying Charlize might draw Andrew into some childish, but dangerous game.

"At least we know he won't go after that cow penned up in his office. Who did *she* kill to get that spot?" Charlize asked, seething.

Hey!

"She's not a cow."

Yeah, I'm not a cow! I only wished I knew who that voice of reason was. Someone deserved a nice souvenir from L.A.

"Charlize, I think you need a macchiato or something. You're out of control if you think Gwendolyn is fat."

Hearing my name unsettled my stomach enough, but taking in Andrew's dating habits prior to Cate made me stop and think for a moment. Had he truly *only* dated models? And now, with all the fashion shows coming up...

"Anyway, that *cow* is not a threat." Charlize sounded overly confident.

"I don't know. She's gorgeous, if you ask me."

I sucked in a deep breath and in a bold wave of confidence flushed my bowl. The chatter by the sinks came to a screeching halt. Upon reaching the women, I focused my glare on Charlize, who turned white. The other woman, someone I didn't recognize, cringed—perhaps in solidarity for her friend.

I rinsed my hands, my eyes locked on Charlize through the mirror. I wrung the loose droplets into the sink and stepped to the paper towel dispenser. I winked to the other girl before walking out of restroom, feeling victorious. Little Charlize and her friend might be right about Andrew only wanting to date models.

Before.

The way he'd been looking at *me* lately hinted Andrew Morgan may want something different this time around.

His tone asking about Dan, worrying if the slime ball had been bothering me, and how he'd sneered often at Salvatore, tipped me off on the key ingredient to prod Andrew out of his shell. *Jealousy*.

♥ ♥ ♥ ♥

Andrew

"On behalf of myself and your Atlanta-based Delta crew, welcome to Los Angeles."

Fucking finally! I hadn't felt six hours take so long since I'd been in middle school waiting for the bell to ring on the last day before summer vacation.

Other planes were fuzzy visions in the distance while mine sat on the runway for several more excruciating minutes. Oil sizzled on the tarmac, blurring the departure line into a rainbow of colors. My ire fumed hotter than the ninety-plus degree temperature outside the oval window to my left.

For the entire flight, all I'd heard was Gwen's laughter. From four goddamn rows back. Nothing could get her voice out of my head, not listening to music with my headphones on, not watching the movie I'd been dying to see, not reading the book I'd been so drawn to at home in New York. Nothing.

All I heard was Gwen. Talking and laughing. How Salvatore wrangled a seat next to her infuriated me. Why had the company travel agent randomly paired *them* up? Enrico lounged in first class, while Thalia sat alone in the row behind me. Even her snoring couldn't distract me. Or the little kid next to her who kicked my seat most of the flight.

From the moment Gwen re-entered my life three weeks ago, I hadn't been able to get her out of my head. I'd played it cool. That's where guys got into trouble and good women got away.

Still, I didn't want Gwen to grow attached to Salvatore. The business constantly evolved from one extreme to the next. The most beautiful, praised, and famous dress had a short shelf-life. There was always another beautiful and praise-worthy dress ready to be celebrated.

There would be other shows and other designers. Gwen would be promoting not just clothing, but also the accessory lines. Even shoes were a different animal. Showcases were not the same as fashion shows. They were more business-oriented and less glamorous. Gwen might find herself sorely disappointed when the Miu Miu line released their spring handbags.

Okay, not really. I'd seen the sketches and some of the samples with my own eyes. Gwen would love them. I imagined her face lighting up, handing her that white bucket bag. It brought a small smile to my own mouth. Until I heard that cackling laugh of hers. Again.

The plane finally parked at the jetway. Thank God! I hoped Salvatore enjoyed those six free hours. Designers put in eighteen-hour days before shows. "Soak her up, buddy. You won't have time to take a piss once you get off this plane," I muttered to myself.

Salvatore's phone had not stopped ringing, and messages started dinging as soon as he turned it back on. He and his team of design assistants had to pick up trunks of clothes, shoes, and bags for the show from the cargo area.

"Hey. Where were you all this time?" Gwen asked me in a cheery voice, getting off the plane.

"In my seat." I shook my head, not meaning for that to come out so gruff. How could she have not noticed me? Salvatore must have engrossed her in one of his outlandish stories. "Did you check a bag?" I asked.

"No." She removed her suit jacket, exposing toned arms in a sleeveless top. "Just this bag right here."

My gentlemanly upbringing kicked in and I took the handle from her, our fingers tangled for a moment. "I got it."

"Thanks." She draped her jacket across her arm and followed closely as we made our way to the exit.

A few times, her hand rested on my back or tugged my suit jacket so we wouldn't become separated. After each touch, I turned to find a soft smile on her lips.

In the limo, Gwen huddled close and with every sharp turn, leaned against me. I could feel the moisture on her skin from the L.A. heat simmering beneath her blouse. It would have been cozy if Enrico and Thalia weren't there. Enrico's assistant drained her battery by taking pictures and posting to Facebook and Instagram, announcing all the *likes* she'd been getting.

Gwen snapped a few photos as well, but instead of sharing them with so-called 'friends' and 'followers,' she showed each one to me.

"Look!" she said with excitement and intimacy like I was the only person in the car. The only person who mattered. I'd not realized how I craved that type of attention. Getting it from Gwen felt...amazing.

The JW in Downtown L.A. was my favorite hotel of all the Marriotts. The side facing the Nokia Theater was sheathed in glass. Inside that wing, the ceilings were three stories high. And the roof deck beat the crap out of any chic Manhattan night spot. Some idiots on Yelp had remarked the decor looked *dated*, but I appreciated the *Old-Hollywood* glamorous feel.

With our sleek charcoal Prada suits, sunglasses, and high-end luggage, Gwen and I could have been mistaken for FBI agents. She sauntered to the line forming at the front desk, but I cupped her elbow.

"We have priority check-in," I said.

"I feel like a celebrity." She squeezed her shoulders and beamed.

"The way you'll get swarmed at the show, you'll probably decide you don't like it very much," I said.

Behind us, a raucous scene took shape. Someone ran away from the lobby bar with a pack of photographers yelling and snapping pictures. As the crowd rushed past us, I thrust myself in front of Gwen.

From over my shoulder, she rested her chin against my ear and said, "I think you're right."

♥ ♥ ♥ ♥

Gwen

I looked at my hotel room and let out a squeal of delight. OMG, it was a suite! I rushed to the full-length window and pressed my hands against the glass. The skyscrapers towered around me like columns in a cluster while the rest of the city was mostly flat. Many of the taller buildings had branding logos: Bank of America, Wells Fargo, and Citigroup. In the distance, a line of bronze mountains kissed the blue sky. The tips coated in white looked like they'd been topped with a scoop of vanilla ice cream.

My phone at last updated the time from New York to Los Angeles. I marveled at the disparity, not just from the distance and the temperature, I'd landed in a different world. Once my phone finished syncing, it vibrated with waiting texts and emails.

"Great," I grumbled, seeing how many messages had poured into my inbox while I'd been traveling. "It's five p.m. in New York. As far as I'm concerned, it's happy hour." I tucked my laptop under my arm and with my new expensive shades, I left the suite in search of a glass of wine and a better Wi-Fi signal.

An hour later, my half carafe of Sauvignon Blanc was empty, and I reduced my cheese and cracker platter to crumbs.

I read email after email, but paused on one and cried out, "No. No. *No*. This isn't happening." I grabbed my phone and called List LA.

"Kirsten, it's Gwen Foley at Prada. I just—Yes, my flight was fine. I want to—Yes, it's much warmer here than in New York. Can we discuss—" That was why I hated calling people. All they wanted to do was *talk*.

"Kirsten!" I ducked my head, embarrassed when others on the patio wrenched their necks in my direction. "*Please*. I got your email with the confirmed list of attendees. Is that number right?"

I listened in horror and thought for sure, my career was over.

My legs wobbled in the elevator and down the hall to Andrew's suite. He hadn't answered his phone or responded to texts and emails. My tears and business card had coaxed his room number out of the manager.

After frantic knocking, Andrew answered. He wore a tee-shirt that looked as if he'd taken a shower in it. The soaked fabric outlined his pecs deliciously.

"Sorry, I just got back from a run." He wiped his hands on his shorts.

God damn! I smoothed a shaky hand across my forehead and got myself in check. "I need to speak with you. I made a horrible mistake."

He stepped aside. "Come in."

"No," I answered, startled he'd so casually suggest it, given what happened the last time I entered one of his hotel rooms.

"What?" he said, looking clueless.

"I can't go into your hotel room. It's not appropriate. Especially, since we... Can we speak downstairs?"

"Gwen, we have suites for meetings like this." He tugged me by the wrist, his warm fingers easily wrapping around my hand. Commanding and powerful. "I promise, I can behave myself."

Glad you *can.*

His room at the W Hotel last year had also been a suite. We made out and had plenty of foreplay in the elevator. I'd had one orgasm on the sofa, and then he brought me to the bedroom, lowered me on his bed and took us both to another planet.

I padded inside the L.A. suite looking for something to distract me from that sizzling memory.

With Andrew going through his work bag, I snuck a look at his legs. Prada trousers hid those curved muscles. Bad, trousers. And, yikes. Those shorts he had on were...short. I prayed he wouldn't stretch and expose something I didn't think I could handle seeing again. Instead, he took a bottle of water into his hands.

Oh, please dump it on your head.

I did a doubletake when I realized he was talking to me. "Huh? What?"

"I said, do you want some water?" Andrew held the bottle out to me.

Only if I can lick it off your lips.

"No, thanks. Listen, Andrew." I held my stomach. I'd made so much progress with him and now it could all crumble. "I received the response count from List LA for the show."

"Really low?" He wrinkled his nose.

"No!" I waved off that ridiculous notion. "Just the

opposite. I never...I never gave them the ballroom's capacity."

"And?"

"We're overbooked by more than double."

Andrew relaxed. "It's fine."

"How can it be fine? We have three hundred people coming to jam their butts into one hundred and twenty seats."

"This is L.A. They won't all show up. List LA knew that."

Yes, the local publicity firm had to have known the capacity. I approved all the attendees, but hadn't done a count. "Has this ever happened to you before?"

"I never stressed over the headcounts to be honest with you." He moved closer to me. "I relied on the people I hired to manage all that. But I'm glad you'll be on top of things like that now. It *would* be a disaster if all those butts showed up." He smirked at me with an adorable grin.

I smiled back, but then got my serious face on. "Andrew, I'm sorry. I take full responsibility. This will never happen again."

After a long stare, he said, "That's certainly refreshing."

"What is?"

"To hear someone own up to a mistake." He lifted his arms over his head. "All I get are excuses and how it's someone else's fault."

I geared up to ask him if his workout went well, hoping that would lead to him letting me touch his biceps again, but the sound of a loud knock forced Andrew to open his door.

"Morgan." Salvatore glided in, moving right to Andrew's windows like he was checking to see if the view was better than the one from his suite. "Enrico wants to meet immediately. We've booked the private dining room."

"Signor Corella. Come in," Andrew said with annoyance lacing his tone.

"Ah, *bella.* You are *here.*" He cast a sideways glance at Andrew. "Saves me a trip to your suite."

"Let me get the rest of my papers," I said, noticing the scornful stare that had developed between the two men.

Sitting with Salvatore on the plane was a genius move. Still, I didn't want to professionally come between him and Andrew. Salvatore *was* a brilliant designer. The runway rehearsal and the media previews meant that collection would be spectacular. As the brand manager, Andrew should be proud of Salvatore's creations to enhance the Prada brand.

"I'll give you a hand, *bella.*" The designer followed me to the door.

"Salvatore, she's a big girl. She's managed a lot without you so far." Andrew caught his arm. "Besides, I have a few things to run by you."

Relieved to be getting out from between them before I started drooling, I clutched my laptop to my chest, calmed my hammering heartbeat, and said, "I'll see you both in a little while."

Not to mention, Andrew needed a shower. A long, hot one. Oh, to be a drop of Los Angeles County water.

I rushed out of the suite, wishing I had time to take a *cold* shower.

Later on, I marveled at the private dining room. It was the most beautiful and exquisitely decorated room I'd ever seen. I hadn't known rooms like that even existed in hotels. Like our suites, one wall was entirely made of glass. The sun had set, but a wavy line of deep blue speckled with pink and gold stretched over the horizon. The smog blurred all the tones like a Monet watercolor painting. North Fork residents enjoyed colorful sunsets over the Long Island Sound. That West Coast version took my breath away.

The beauty and elegance around me gave way, however, to the overpowering aroma of roasted garlic and sweet basil. On the back wall, a long sideboard held trays and trays of food. With a phone tucked into the curve of his shoulder, Salvatore filled a plate with folded slices of Italian prosciutto and salami. Thalia picked at an olive and cheese platter. Enrico swirled linguine onto a fork.

At a chrome tray, I lifted the cover and my stomach rumbled in delight. Raviolis in tomato-cream sauce were my favorite. On another sideboard were loaves of thickly sliced bread, and an assortment of oils for dipping. That was all Thalia's doing. And she was excellent at her job.

I made up a healthy plate instead of going back for seconds and thirds which would only draw attention to how much I was eating. I turned to take a seat at the elegant table, but where to sit perplexed me. I really wanted to sit next to Thalia. My role as a PR executive meant I needed to sit with management. Not gossip with an assistant.

The seat across from Andrew was the most inviting, with the panoramic scenery of Downtown L.A. behind him. As I sat, his carbon eyes locked on mine. *Much better view.* His dark eyebrows cinched together, sneaking a peek at my plate and the large amount of food. I would expect a man that handsome to snort in derision at how much I liked to eat. But he smiled and gave a slight nod, like my healthy appetite pleased him.

His wet hair was combed back and the shirt he wore was one of the more casual Prada dress shirts, pale yellow with a thin blue pinstripe running through it. No tie. On his plate, a half-eaten hamburger sat next to a pile of fries. He wiped his mouth and winked. *He doesn't like Italian food?*

Enrico brushed crumbs from his hands and wiped his mouth. "All right, the show is Friday, but before we discuss who, what, and where on that, Gwendolyn where are we with the events for tomorrow?"

With my mouth open ready to nibble on my first scrumptious steaming ravioli, I panicked seeing *all* eyes at the table were on me.

"Enrico, let her take *one* bite," Andrew interjected. "I'll start with the responses to some of the ads we ran earlier in the week." He detailed the results, and mentioned a radio contest to win a chance to meet Salvatore, who rolled his eyes. Andrew finished with the event he and I had planned together: a special preview for L.A. media and fashion bloggers.

"Salvatore, I assume everything made it here okay?" Andrew asked the designer.

"My team is going through the trunks now." He took a huge bite of bread. "I am not worried."

"I think we should include more of the ready-to-wear samples for the preview tomorrow," I added.

"Good call." Andrew nodded. "L.A. is not New York."

I wiped the corners of my mouth. "I can go over the other events if you're ready."

"Yes, *bella*." Salvatore snuck a look at Andrew. "I am yours to command this week."

"It's not really like that. This collection is your

vision. It's not just blouses, trousers, and dresses. It's you, Salvatore. You've put who you are into these clothes. You deserve to be celebrated."

"Salvatore likes to be *adorato*," Andrew quipped.

"Why shouldn't I be worshipped?" He leaned forward waving a fork.

Here we go. I forced down a few more raviolis while my rams banged horns.

CHAPTER ELEVEN

Andrew

I watched Gwen leave the private dining room while typing into her phone. She'd received her marching orders from Enrico and *whoosh*, off she went. Without even saying goodbye. I thought she would need hand-holding.

Nope.

The following day, she kept busy carting Salvatore around. At least she answered my texts. My day was also busy, meeting with corporate retailers and investors.

Things had calmed down enough that maybe I could take her out to dinner—to properly thank her for all she'd done for the show and our brand. Before I could ask her, I received a text from Enrico asking to meet him in the Mixing Room for a drink.

Barely seeing Gwen yesterday because of the flight, and not seeing her most of today, I suffered an emptiness I hadn't expected. Not having her around made me antsy and anxious. I missed her.

I stopped feeling like a widower in that startling moment. I'd licked my wounds, and now they were clean, ready to heal. Gwen did that. Before her, I'd locked my emotions away. Like live wires, if exposed, they were dangerous to be around.

I wanted to move my life forward and I wouldn't enter another relationship closed down and hidden. That's not what someone like Gwen deserved.

It'd been Gwen from the moment I first saw her. Then a month ago, she'd been brought back to me. She'd yanked me from the shell I'd been in and enticed me to laugh again, feel like it's okay to love again. She was entitled to see the man I *used* to be.

For so long, I considered a relationship between co-workers unwise. That was before I'd found someone worth the risk.

Now, I just needed to get to her before Salvatore drowned her with his over-the-top charm.

♥ ♥ ♥ ♥
Gwen

I'd kept in touch with Andrew all day, via texts. While getting Salvatore off to an interview that morning, I'd received the first message from Andrew:

And where are you right now?

I playfully responded: Wishing I were dead.

Ha! Another Salvatore interview?

He just drags them out.

Adorato. I warned you.

I see what you mean.

Good.

Back in my suite, I fell onto the elaborately made up bed where I squirmed and stretched. It felt so comfortable. *So* much better than my cheap twin mattress in Kelsey's spare bedroom.

I'd been on the go from sunrise, missed a gorgeous California sunset, and now was ready to call it a night.

I was exhausted and delighted to close my eyes.

Happy. Until I heard a knock at my door. *Grrr*. A spark shot through me, though, hoping it was Andrew.

I leapt off the bed in eager anticipation.

♥ ♥ ♥ ♥

Andrew

I entered the Mixing Room and my senses were thrown into overload. I'd been deep inside myself, thinking and musing, but now all the people, all the voices, the televisions above the bar made me feel open and exposed.

Hopefully, Enrico would be quick. I had enough of the roadblocks and interruptions. As soon as that meeting ended, I planned to see Gwen.

Enrico waved from a bulky leather sofa in the corner. The second I sat down, a tall server, almost taller than me, approached to take my drink order.

"Nothing for me," I said politely.

Kissing Gwen shouldn't be under the influence of alcohol. That thought stilled me cold. Had I planned to *kiss* her? Tonight?

"He'll have what I'm having," Enrico said, waving a short crystal glass filled with what looked like and smelled like vodka. A lime wedge had sunk to the bottom because he'd finished his drink. "And bring *me* another."

I crossed my long legs. "So, what's up?"

"I have no way to ease into this, Andrew. I need you to go back to Milan." My boss sounded stern, but a twang of guilt lingered in his accented voice. "I am not happy with how Marcello is progressing. If the creative director starts noticing…" He tipped his glass back.

Marcello had been Enrico's hire. The Milan brand manager typically reported to Stefania, the creative director in Italy. In a power-play, Enrico convinced

Stefania to have Marcello and his team report to the New York Marketing group. If Marcello failed, it would be on Enrico.

I hadn't made it any better. I'd trained Marcello while still in the throes of heartbreak and despair. The responsibility loosely rested in my lap as well.

"Sure." I didn't mind another brief trip, but couldn't the request have waited? "When?"

"After the show."

"*Straight* from L.A.?"

"We have all the clothes you need in Milan."

I stifled my irritation. "For how long?"

"Until the end of the year, at least."

My body froze. *End of the year? After tomorrow?* Tomorrow. That would be the last time I would see Gwen until *the end of the year.* Salvatore had stolen the day I wanted to spend with her and now Enrico was taking *the rest of the year?*

My boss sipped his drink and then rolled his eyes. "Fine, you can stop home to collect your things."

"It's not just things at my apartment. Don't you think there are things in my office that I need to take with me, too?" *Like Gwen.*

Enrico put his head down. "At least Gwendolyn has worked out."

She worked out, all right. It had taken less than a month for feelings of hope and happiness to bubble inside me. Could I wait two months to tell her how I felt?

Drinks turned into dinner, the dinner I wanted to have with Gwen. By the time I made it to her floor to speak to her, an unbearable tension settled in my shoulders. It rivaled any pain I'd felt the night before a show. That ache meant much more. My whole plan had been thwarted, hijacked. How could I do something like tell her how I felt or…kiss her, if I were leaving for Milan right after the show?

My legs still moved me forward, but I had no idea what I'd say when I got to her suite. It was a lot later than I would have preferred. And the box in my hand would be a sorry consolation for the fact that I would be leaving.

After a heavy knock, I couldn't shake that familiar bout of excitement sneaking into my bones from Gwen's bright smile.

When the door opened, my hands curled into tight fists. "Salvatore."

"Morgan. Come look."

I stepped in, wildly curious, but also afraid I'd see something that would upset me. Instead, a vision of elegant beauty made that pang of longing shoot through me. "Gwen?"

Her eyes lit up. "Andrew!"

She twirled in an emerald green full-length gown that cinched at her waist. Her body filled out the bodice perfectly and the upper swells of her full breasts peeked through the asymmetrical cutouts in the neckline.

"Isn't this the most gorgeous thing you've ever seen?" she asked.

Yes. But I wasn't thinking of the dress. "Salvatore, you've outdone yourself. I don't want to sound like a jerk, but why isn't this beautiful thing in the show?"

The designer rubbed a chin that hadn't seen a razor in a couple of days. "Do you know one of our models who could fill out a dress like this as well as our Gwendolyn?"

Our Gwendolyn?

"Salvatore, thank you." Gwen rushed to the designer to hug him, the gown giving way at the slit and showing her firm thighs.

My blood boiled when Salvatore's scandalous hands sat on her waist. She was *not* his. The tentative hesitation in her hug, however, cooled my fever. And the smile on her lips as she bounded in my direction reminded me of the woman she really was. Not all made up in a gown. Salvatore had tried to make her one of his models. A doll he could play dress-up with.

"Did you need something, Andrew?" she asked.

"Actually..." I could use a set of defibrillator paddles. "I have a gift for you, too." I swayed further into the room, my confidence returning with every step. From a linen sack, I removed a shoebox. "She should be in Prada from head to toe, should she not, Salvatore?"

The designer grumbled, appearing to regret he hadn't thought of the obvious accessory.

"Andrew, what have you done?" Gwen asked, resting her hands on her hips.

"Come here, Gwen," I commanded and pointed to her suite's desk chair. "Sit."

At the chair, she swept aside the long skirt made of raw silk and sat with her knees pinned together. My jaw trembled as I sank to one knee. The shoe I removed from the box was not a new design I could have swiped from the sample floor before we left. It was one of my favorites, a classic that had been around for years. The black suede gladiator sandal with satin nickel studs suited Gwen's edgy personality. It was the perfect complement to an elegant full-length gown. The moderate heel would also cushion her ankles as she moved through the show tomorrow.

I unfolded the soft tissue paper and held the shoe in front of Gwen.

"The Filettra sandal?" She looked at me, stunned.

"You know the name of this shoe?" Salvatore asked.

Before she could answer, I turned to the designer. "She obviously did her homework on our products."

"You boys really know how to make a girl feel like Cinderella." She slipped her foot into the insole while it sat in my hand.

I leaned forward to buckle the small strap around her ankle, my chest against her knee. After I repeated the same for the other foot, she stood. I'd worked for Prada long enough to know when a woman felt comfortable in one of our shoes. Her toes sat perfectly against the vamp without being crushed.

I sensed Gwen had stopped breathing. I lifted my chin slowly. On her face was a look of controlled satisfaction. Like maybe she would wait to show the depths of her gratitude for my gift when we were alone.

And why *weren't* we alone?

I licked my tongue against dry lips to speak, and for the first time, the obnoxious ring of Salvatore's phone was a welcome interruption.

"*Che cosa?*" he blurted. In Italian, he ranted into the phone for several seconds. Pulling the device from his face, he turned back to Gwen, who hadn't taken her eyes off me. "I have a situation to deal with."

The way Salvatore stomped to the door and slammed it shut, I knew *I'd* won.

♥ ♥ ♥ ♥

Gwen

Captivated was the only way I could describe how I felt at the moment. The dress was an amazing gift, but I saw right through Salvatore's motives. I'd been turning down his near-daily invitations, so giving me a dress must have been his way to see my curves. Pretty desperate.

While Salvatore had stormed in with his big personality, Andrew's quiet power commanded the room. *He* filled it with his masculinity. An honorable and loyal man, regardless of his beauty, was the right man. Any man who knew he could have anyone, but wanted *me*... That was the kind of man I wanted.

OMG, the Filettra sandal! Feet were so intimate. Given the length of the skirt, even with the slit, the shoes would be my secret to keep throughout the day tomorrow. A secret for me and Andrew to share.

"So, he takes up a lot of oxygen in the room, doesn't he?" Andrew pushed on one of his knees and stood.

"Salvatore's all showy though." I fingered the skirt and swooshed the fabric back and forth.

"Do you prefer a man who's more subtle?"

It was the first time he'd dared to get personal with me, and before he could retract his question or dilute it, I said firmly, "Yes, on the surface." *And smoldering underneath. Like you, Andrew.*

He stepped a few inches away. "I'm still concerned all the attention will be on *you* in that dress." He held his chin, smooth and fresh.

"I planned to wear my hair up." I gathered a handful of waves and swept them away from my face. When he stared at my bracelets as they clanged together, I let the bundle fall. "Or—"

"No. No." His fingers brushed past my cheek, lifting the hair off my shoulders again. "This is perfect."

Yes, it is perfect. He should have kissed me by now. His amazing lips, pink and full, should be on my mouth as well as other parts of my body. I wanted him to make me feel alive and give us both what we needed like that night.

How long could I wait for him before a crazy impulse to grab him took hold of me?

"I guess it's settled. I'm wearing my hair up tomorrow," I whispered, locking eyes with him.

He cleared his throat and stepped back, letting my hair fall. The weight of so many waves warmed my skin, even though I preferred the heat coming off his body.

I stepped back as well and slipped into co-worker mode. "Andrew, be honest. Is this dress...too much? I prefer my clothes simple and classic."

"I would call you classic, Gwen. But not simple. You wear our clothes beautifully." He ran his hand over the suit jacket I'd draped on a desk chair. "The way they sit on you tells a story of the woman we know other women want to be."

The compliment left me breathless. Prada had been in business for more than one hundred years. Andrew certainly made up for what he'd said about Starlight Elegance.

"Thank you, Andrew."

"No, Gwen. Thank *you*." His shoulders softened. "I need you to know, I couldn't have done this without you."

"That's not true." I blinked away the shiny tears I would never let fall. It was better if I were respected as an equal and not thought of as a weepy lightweight. "You've run plenty of these shows."

"Yes, and I know what it takes to pull this off. There was no way I could have done what you've done...for *this* show." He plowed a hand through his hair, his wedding band was—*gone*.

The sight took my breath away. I twisted my hair to the side to keep my hands busy. "Did you want to do one final walk through for tomorrow?"

"No. We're set." He bent down to the pick up the shoebox. His back straightened, emphasizing his dramatic height.

I hugged Andrew, loving how his touch felt vastly different from the night I'd hugged him on the street. The night when everything had turned around. And upside down. His fingers pressed into my bare shoulders and his body molded against mine.

Oh, the smell of him, musky and woodsy. Masculine. There it was, his heart, beating wildly. There was so much of the man, his heart must work so hard to pump his rich blood through so many veins.

The feel of his grip softening meant it was time for me to let go. "Have a good night, Andrew." I leaned upward for a kiss on his cheek. The edge of his warm and tender mouth caught the corner of my lips. *Tickle, tickle* went my stomach.

A strand of my long hair stuck in his collar, binding us together for a moment. Creating a bridge, if someone had enough courage to cross.

Andrew snagged the strand of my hair in his fingers. He held his gaze, breathed, and exhaled. "I believe this belongs to you."

It wasn't *exactly* what I wanted in my hand, but I took it from him and let it fall against my breasts, his eyes following. He looked hesitant, confused like he was holding back.

"Andrew, is something wrong?"

His fingers pulled at his collar. "No. I just... I feel..."

His indecisiveness sent a pang of alarm through me. If he didn't know for sure what he wanted, forcing the issue could have disastrous consequences.

"It's late, I guess, right?" I asked softly, drawing his

eyes back up to mine.

"I guess." He pressed his eyes closed and headed for the door.

After he turned around and another look passed between us, he nodded and the door closed, taking my breath with it.

CHAPTER TWELVE

Gwen

The next morning when everyone else seemed preoccupied, I snuck out on the runway. The folding chairs were being set up for the guests. Assistants were removing Salvatore's collection from black garment bags and hanging them up in the dressing rooms. The backstage area was twice the size of the room for the show.

The lighting team hadn't arrived yet and only yellow emergency lights poured down on the white ceramic platform. That was my only chance to goof off. I put my hands on my hips and glided down the runway. One foot crossed in front of the other just as the models did at the interviews and the rehearsals. The way a model moved down a runway wasn't how an ordinary human walked. After a few steps, my back had already cramped up.

Despite my cozy leggings, boxy sweatshirt, and sneakers, I felt beautiful tilting my hips and projecting my shoulders, right then left.

I wasn't a glitzy glamour girl. Or a model. I was real. Told it like it was. Even to my detriment. I was honest, raised by a cop and a housewife in a small town. It didn't get more real than that.

At the end of the platform, I did the quarter turns — one side, then the other — swung my hair in a dramatic swoop and sailed back up toward the AV screen in the front. I closed my eyes feeling elated.

Until I slammed into a wall. A wall of flesh and bone, tall and lean, and smelling like fresh cotton and spicy musk.

"Oh my gosh," I said, my hands splaying against Andrew's chest.

"I hope our models don't do that." He peeked at the two-foot drop just inches away from where I stood.

"Has that ever happened?" I asked, ignoring my body screaming in his delightful hold.

"A model sailing over the edge?" He shifted me back to the center of the platform, his hands firmly on my waist. "Not at any of my shows."

"I just wanted to walk this thing once. Was I not allowed to do that?" I wanted to know where *all* the boundaries were.

"Gwen..." He took the laminated card hanging around my neck in his strong hands, and my nipples tightened from how close he'd come to brushing against them. "You're an executive with Prada. This is a Prada fashion show. You have full venue access."

"Okay." Not wanting him to know how he made me feel, I repositioned my body.

"But please don't do that during the show," he joked.

"Can I do one more lap?" I tented my fingers in prayer.

"Why don't you practice walking out there and taking your bow?"

I tripped over my sneakers. "My *what?*"

"We all come out," Andrew said, smiling. "I usually go after Enrico. And with all the work you've put into the show, it wouldn't seem right to come out here without you."

"So, you mean I *have* to come out here later?" I swallowed. "In front of actual...people?"

"Yep, so practice." He winked and ducked back into the controlled chaos behind the large screen.

Several more seconds went by before I could move.

By noon, the viewing room was ready. The lighting team installed the spotlights and color filters. List LA's AV dudes conducted two rehearsals with the video and music. Security had their tables set up at the entrance for guests to check in.

I confidently carried my clipboard around the backstage area searching for disasters to mitigate. I never suspected I'd be one of them, until Enrico gave me a horrified glare.

"You are not wearing *that*, are you?" he asked, grimacing at my casual outfit.

"No, of course not." I self-consciously tucked a loose hair from a messy bun behind my ear. I'd seen first-hand what a crack hairstylist could do with unwashed hair. "I have a dress with me to change into."

"Better you go now." He gave me a concerned once-over. "Your makeover may take some time."

"Hey!" I protested.

Enrico shuffled away, but Thalia stuck around. "I saw the beautiful dress Salvatore made for you."

"You mean *designed* for me," I corrected her.

"I heard he sewed it himself," Thalia said, leaning in like it was a secret.

"I'm sure that's not the case." I bit my lower lip. Why would such a rumor be circulating? "Was it wrong of me to accept the dress? I mean, I'm not *interested* in him that way. Did I send the wrong message?"

"That's not a fair test, though." Thalia threw her hands in the air. "Who would turn down a dress from him?"

"Exactly." I led Thalia to a corner. "I don't want to hurt his feelings. But you don't think he's expecting anything in return?"

"Of course, he is," Thalia said. "He always expects something. There's no such thing as give and take with Salvatore. There's one give and then take, take, take, take."

I could not have articulated the man better. I squeezed the girl's shoulders. "Thank you, Thalia. You've done a great job this week. You've kept us all on track. We wouldn't be on schedule if it weren't for you."

Thalia blushed like no one had ever complimented her before. Andrew had found the time and the words to let me know *I'd* done a good job. It only seemed right to pay that forward. I smiled one last time as Thalia skipped away. I only wished I had told Andrew what I thought of the job *he'd* done.

Time had run out, though. An assistant on the hair and makeup team dragged me through a sea of bodies to a small corner dressing room. There, my dress hung on a velvet lined hanger. It looked steamed and smelled of pressing chemicals with a trace of…Salvatore's cologne. He had also made some last-minute adjustments. One of his minions had taken the dress from me the moment I'd arrived, bristling about having to shorten the hemline. Someone lowered the neckline and hiked the slit up even higher!

In the back of the dressing room, I took a seat at the makeup table. The ambient-colored round bulbs made my skin look flawless.

"I'm taking you home." I brushed my fingers along the lighted mirror.

"You read my mind." Salvatore's wicked smile reflecting back at me sent an uneasy chill up my spine.

"Excuse me?" I faced him. "Salvatore, I could have been dressing."

He stepped in, ignoring my concern. "I hope you

will give me the credit when people tell you how beautiful you look today."

"With all the models dressed up in your other clothes, I doubt anyone will notice what *I'm* wearing." The wash of grays and whites of Salvatore's collection, however, would make the bright green dress stand out. And me. My empty stomach flipped. "But now that you mention it," I began, but a tall thin man swooshed the black curtain aside and stepped in. I crossed my arms. "Doesn't anyone knock?"

"Check your modesty at the door, girlfriend," the man said, shaking a blond wave curled on the top of his head. "Cary is here to do you."

Do me? "Oh right, my hair and makeup." I ran my fingers on the table and touched the eye shadow palette. "I have done this before, you know. Don't you have models to tend to?"

"We always hire additional people, Gwen," Andrew said, holding the curtain away. The small dressing room started to feel like a clown car. "Signor Corella, there are people waiting to interview you." Andrew cast a furious glare at Salvatore hanging around my dressing room.

"Oh, right." I stepped away from the table. "Let me go find them."

"I got it, Gwen." Andrew spoke without glancing at me.

I tingled all over, sensing how much he wanted Salvatore away from me. Imagining Andrew as my protector gave me a warm and fuzzy buzz.

Salvatore strode briskly past Andrew and almost took the curtain with him. Looking victorious, Andrew winked at me and followed the designer through the crowd.

The stylist fanned himself. "What I wouldn't give to have those two specimens fighting over *me*."

"They're not *fighting* over me." I sat in the chair and faced the lighted mirror again. "Andrew is just making sure his designer doesn't get distracted before the show."

"Yeah, sure." Cary pulled my hair out of the bun and began brushing out the tangles.

I watched in amazement as he methodically captured every bent strand and smoothed it out. *I may take this guy home, too!*

"Girl, that man positively sizzled when he looked at you," Cary swooned.

"That's Salvatore's shtick."

"I was talking about the tall yummy one with hair as dark as a sinful night." Cary practically burst into a song.

Smirking, I wondered if my plan to make Andrew want me again worked, would I enjoy a *sinful* night of my own?

♥ ♥ ♥ ♥

Andrew

Once the guests arrived and were shown their seats, I relaxed. Gwen, wearing that stunning dress, had greeted everyone at the door with a look of welcome and comfort as if she knew everyone personally. She had even taken the time to sit with a few VIPs to make sure they were satisfied with their seats.

In other shows, I'd hired professional greeters dressed in black with headsets who robotically walked guests in and then dashed away for the next one. What a difference it made to have an actual Prada person do that. The room sang with a peaceful vibe and Gwen had made the guests feel privileged. Prada was a private company and didn't let many people behind its walls.

Gwen had floated through the room, crowded with the media, buyers, and celebrities with effortless grace and sophistication. She was gorgeous enough to have walked the red carpet out front.

Hmm. I didn't like the idea of *that* at all. Still, I raised my phone discreetly and took a few pictures of her. Zooming in on her face and then out, I captured all of her. In the shoes I gave her, she glided up and down the rows, elegantly whooshing the skirt from side to side. Each step made my shirt collar feel tighter and tighter. Not to mention my pants.

The bass of the opening music vibrated inside my chest. My production team operated like a well-oiled machine, but that didn't mean something couldn't go horribly wrong.

Runway models like Mira, who had been giving me *come hither* looks all day, were fragile. A meltdown could erupt any moment. They all lined up like North Korean soldiers, standing up straight and expressionless. The room, which moments earlier swirled with activity and voices, stilled, and all I heard was my heartbeat.

Next, the muffled sound of Salvatore's voice on stage rang in my ears. His accent always came out a little thicker when he addressed his fans. Prada never tried to hide its heritage and Salvatore was the best face for the design arm of the company. He liked to pretend he forgot certain words in English so he could slip in as much Italian as he could during his introductions.

I would have liked to see Salvatore be a more charitable person, give back to the industry that made him rich, mentor new designers, and not act like…well, like such an asshole.

In the monitors above, I caught a glimpse of Gwen sitting with *Vogue's* editor-in-chief. Smart. With her legs crossed, Gwen showed off shapely thighs. Salvatore cut that damn slit way too high. It looked even higher than last night. All I could think was how those legs felt wrapped around my waist last year as I thrust in and out of her.

Enrico sat next to *Vogue's* editor and behind them, sat Thalia, her eyes glued to her phone.

So why was I backstage alone?

In a minute, the entire line of models would take off, only to return and change into their next outfits. I'd rather not get trampled and preferred to be with Gwen.

In the viewing area, I noticed she had moved to the other side of the room. The way her head twisted from side to side suggested she was looking for someone. Couldn't have been Salvatore, he was on stage. Catching sight of me made her body language change. The curves of her face suggested she'd found what she'd been looking for.

Me.

I crossed the room with confidence, basking in her blue eyes. "Hey, I saw you sitting with Anna."

"Yeah, I couldn't get away from her fast enough. She scares the crap out of me."

Laughing, I bantered back, "Well, we want her to concentrate on the show."

"Where do you usually watch all this from?"

I squared my shoulders and took Gwen's hand. "Come with me. I'll show you the best seat in the house."

CHAPTER THIRTEEN

Gwen

"This is amazing!" I found it hard to breathe.

The view from the lighting designer's booth, although no bigger than a fireman's rescue bucket, really *was* the best seat in the house. The crowded space left me no choice but to pin myself up against Andrew for most of the show.

As the lighting team passed by again and again, my body fell further and further into his. Finally, I gave in and just rested the back of my head against his chest. My heart rate shot up when his hands pressed into her waist. The hold went from soft and gentle to a tighter sensation. Demanding.

Or maybe I imagined everything.

The heat from the lights raised the temperature in the booth and trickles of sweat beaded down my back. Andrew's breath, hot on my shoulder, sent tingles all over my skin. I feared my nipples had grown hard and the narrow cups Salvatore had sewn into the gown would not be enough fabric to camouflage how I felt at the moment.

During the show, Andrew's head bobbed in a rhythm that matched the beat-by-beat steps of the models. *He* should go back to modeling. Sales would soar. I loved how he usually skipped a jacket in the office. Prada's men's shirts were designed for his build. Wide shoulders and a broad chest tapered down to a narrow waist. He wore a lot of brick red which made his skin look pearly and accentuated his cheekbones.

Boy, that man could rock a pair of dress slacks, even if Prada's pants weren't made for his high round butt.

The fabric stretched tight across his delicious derrière. Andrew may still look like a top model, and his work persona was very professional, but I'd gotten to know the man behind the mask.

Salvatore's models began marching down the stage together—signaling the show was over. I sighed and erased all of the inappropriate thoughts from my mind. It had become a guilty pleasure to fantasize about Andrew.

"We'd better get down there," he whispered in my ear.

His breathy suggestion registered loud and clear, even over the roar of clapping from below. When he took my hand that time, his grip felt tighter.

I took a deep cleansing breath to get my libido in check, ready to go back to work.

We shared another look and once again the world fell away. The cozy moment either meant nothing or something. When would I find out?

"Ready?" he asked, smiling.

So ready. For what, I wasn't sure.

"Yep," I answered him anyway.

He acknowledged people hooked up at work and seemed open to the idea if it were the right person.

Was I the right person?

Hand in hand, Andrew and I crossed behind the crowd as Salvatore walked the runway with Mira.

Enrico's voice came over the loudspeaker. He thanked Salvatore and kissed some media ass, finishing with a few embarrassing jabs at some of the celebs.

Andrew gripped my hand tighter. "Here we go," he said like he knew Enrico's routine.

"And finally, I want to present the two people who made this event happen," Enrico said into his mic. "Our

U.S. brand manager, Andrew Morgan and PR Executive, a woman new to Prada, Gwendolyn Foley!"

Zipping around the seating area earlier in the day, I'd blushed at the remarks about my dress, my shoes, and my hair. I'd laughed off the compliments that I could have been a model. Now, with the full lighting package shining down on me, every step I took, I felt more and more beautiful. With a former model at my side, one who knew how to waltz down a runway, any feeling of awkwardness that I didn't belong in that world vanished.

I slowed down and loved the feel of Andrew leading me. At the end of the platform, we waved with our free hands, but Andrew let go completely to whistle at me, commanding more applause.

People stood up and clapped. I recognized all the faces I'd said hello to earlier. The admiration felt exhilarating, topped only by the feel of Andrew's hand in mine again. He whisked me away like I was his and he wanted me all to himself.

Just as we escaped to the backstage area, almost everyone out front teemed in behind us. I struggled to breathe, taking in the madness all around me. So many faces, everywhere, like a swarm, made me dizzy. Andrew's beautiful eyes anchored me, though.

"Are you okay?" He gripped my hand tighter. "You look worried."

"What..." I swallowed. "What do I do now? I hadn't anticipated all this." I pointed to the swelling crowd. No one had ever wanted to meet a Starlight designer.

"I tried organizing this craziness once. We have to let this part of the show flow. Don't worry, security will do their job." He glanced around. "And Salvatore loves this. Remember I said he wants to be worshipped? Let it happen. All of these people will upload tons of pictures. It's the best free publicity we can hope for."

"Okay. Um, I'll let you do what you need to do." I tried to let go of his hand.

The grip felt rock solid, though.

♥ ♥ ♥ ♥

Andrew

I couldn't bring myself to let go of Gwen's hand. Perhaps the assignment in Milan wasn't the deal-breaker I'd originally made it out to be.

I wanted Gwen. Period. Exactly how, beyond another amazing night in her arms, I had no idea. I'd let nature take its course. I'd let destiny guide me. If she were *the one*, and I hoped to hell she was, it would happen.

"What do you...what do you want to do now, Andrew?" she asked, her head tilted in a seductive way.

"I'd rather show you than tell you." Squeezing her hand, I said, "Come with me."

In her dressing room, I finally let go of her hand. She took a few steps inside, and then turned around. She straightened her back, projecting those amazing breasts. They looked so perfect in that damn dress, and I was ready to become reacquainted with everything underneath. My arm wound around her waist, tugging her body against mine. Soft against hard. The fingers of my free hand cradled her chin, gently pulling it to a more upright angle.

"Is this okay?" I asked and held my breath.

"So okay," she answered, letting her own breath go.

As I bent down to kiss her, our eyes connected, her lids lowered, and her mouth widened to a smile.

My lips brushed against hers, gentle at first, but

eagerness ate through me. My tongue slid slowly into her mouth and found hers, soft, wet, and equally ready for me. Every cell in my body came alive.

"Gwen," I said. "Oh, Gwen." I opened my mouth for air, but didn't want to waste the time away from her lips. *I missed you.*

I backed up into the makeup chair, and without coaxing, she fell into my lap, her legs spread wide.

"Oh!" she cried out.

"What?"

"The chair's arm handles, they're cold."

I glanced down. The backs of her thighs rested on the metal edges. Smiling, I slid both hands under her knees, lifting her so she wouldn't cool off before I made her hotter than hell. With my hands occupied at the moment, I kissed her neck and ran my lips under her jawline. Her fingers threaded through the back of my hair. I settled her on my lap and put her down just enough to rub against my fired-up erection.

"My, my, Mr. Morgan." Her voice deepened to a husky drawl.

"*My, my* is right, boys and girls," a voice from the front of the dressing room clucked. "What *have* I interrupted?"

Gwen jerked around. "Oh hi, Cary."

Breathless and stunned, I couldn't push the words *get out* fast enough.

"I'm just getting my bags. You two kids have fun." Cary grabbed a black suitcase and winked at Gwen. "Told ya!"

I caught her chin. "Told you what?"

"That you wanted me."

"Was I that obvious?"

"To him. I wasn't placing any bets on the matter."

I looked down. "Because I was a jerk when you first started?"

"That. The whole working together thing. Our one night together." She smiled and ran a finger across my cheek. The edge of her fingernail teased me, reminding me what else she could do with those nails to my body. "Mostly, I wasn't sure if you were ready. I have a feeling that first time you weren't."

I released a breath. "To go beyond the night we had? No. No matter how amazing it was, and what it did for me physically, and even mentally. Emotionally, I wasn't ready to take that further. And I wouldn't string someone along. But I'm ready now. For what exactly, I don't know. But I want *you*, and I want to try." My one hand crept up into the back of her hair, while the other slid under her skirt.

The soft, wet skin I found waiting for me meant Gwen was also quite ready.

CHAPTER FOURTEEN

Gwen

Having sex in a makeup chair with only a thin black curtain to separate my writhing body from hordes of people—people with whom I'd shaken hands and seated earlier—wasn't the wisest move. Not to mention terribly unprofessional.

Andrew sliding a finger inside me made it impossible to stop. It felt too damn good.

"We should stop," he said, winded, his eyes dark and wild.

"What? Why?"

"Because you're moaning a little too loud." He kissed my neck.

"Was I?"

He nodded and lifted me off the chair, whispering, "Let's go someplace where you can scream my name as loud as you want."

Dizzy, I twirled around the dressing room ready to grab everything I'd brought with me.

"I can't wait much longer." Andrew's lips nuzzled against my ear. His warm body and the way he held me from behind made it easy to leave everything behind.

"I have to collect my stuff," I said.

He looked down and with one swoop, everything settled neatly in his massive arms. "Got it. Let's go!"

I checked my appearance in the lighted mirror and made sure my dress wasn't tucked into my thong. Salvatore's dress hung on me perfectly, but I looked a little on the disheveled side. With so much going on for the show, no one would notice a few of my hairs out of place.

After a quick peek, as I'd suspected, no one's eyes were on my dressing room. I was a nobody. Andrew and I slipped out the closest exit.

Andrew followed close behind until we were in the lobby then his free hand took mine. Just like on the runway, he walked ahead, leading me. Taking me.

The mass of people waiting for the elevators killed my buzz, but a faint ding in the distance caught my attention. A bellhop pushed a rolling luggage cart down the hall to a maintenance area of the hotel.

"Freight elevator?" I said.

"Whatever gets us upstairs faster." Andrew spun in a half circle and charged in that direction.

Around the corner, utility aluminum doors closed, but he used his body to stop them. Once they opened up, I slipped in and jammed my fingers against the panel to close the doors.

A stack of banquet chairs in the corner gave me pause. "I hope that guy wasn't coming back for these."

"He's gonna have to wait," Andrew said and slid my pile of things on the top chair. He took another and sat, pulling me back on his lap. "Get over here."

I released a low, throaty laugh. Girls giggle. Women do not. Andrew held me like in those romantic movies. His strong hands wrapped around my ribcage, his thumbs brushing against the sides of my breasts. I lowered my head to kiss him. His lips were so full, I couldn't get enough. As each minute passed, my hidden, sensual side emerged. Just for him.

I slowly slid a finger in and out of his mouth. His wolfish white teeth closed around my knuckle and playfully bit down. "Touch me again," I whispered.

"Where?" he teased, kissing my neck.

"You know where."

He smiled, but the doors opened up.

"Who took this elevator?" a different bellhop huffed, but turned white when Andrew stood up. "Sorry to disturb you, but we need this elevator to accommodate our guests, sir."

"No problem." Andrew scooped my things back up and stepped out onto my floor.

We were whisper quiet as we walked to my room. In the dressing room and even in the elevator, I felt Andrew had held back. I knew what he could do behind closed doors. Inside the walls of my hotel suite, I had a feeling he'd fulfill my every desire—like a genie granting not just three wishes, but all of them. What does a woman pick first?

My hands trembled sliding the key card into the reader at my suite's door. Nerves made me shake, and Andrew's body no longer jammed against mine made me cold. It was a toss-up.

Inside the room, he placed my things on the dining table then turned around. Holy crap, was he beautiful. He crept slowly toward me, his head dipped as if I were his prey.

I had no intention of running away.

His hands reached me first, his fingers gliding across the neckline of my dress. As his thumb slid into one of the cutouts, he said, "There are so many reasons I want to rip this dress off of you."

"Go ahead," I said, dotting small kisses on his face.

"I have faith in Salvatore's sewing that it won't separate at the seams too easily." He gently squeezed my heavy breasts, filling his open palms.

"Then here." I turned my back to him.

As the zipper skated down, the gathered shoulder straps parted and slid away. Andrew ran a knuckle across my exposed skin. I turned, holding the fabric against my body, waiting for his nod to release it. When he did, I let the fabric fall.

Andrew staggered back. "Jesus, Gwen. You are as goddamn beautiful as I remembered."

I kicked the dress away from my ankles, and in nothing but a thong and his black sandals, I strode toward him. He dropped to his knees and kissed my stomach, his fingers tickling my oblique muscles. For someone else, I may have covered myself up. Not with Andrew.

He fingered the sides of my thong and slid the fabric past my hips. His eyes following the fabric made me feel more desirable than I could have ever imagined.

"No teeth this time?" I joked wryly.

He smirked. "I was way hungrier that night. This past month being with you was our foreplay. My appetizer."

"I like the sound of that."

Slow and measured, he watched me. My body burned with every inch his eyes touched. "God, I love your body. I wanted to see it and feel it so bad."

I ran my hands through his hair. "Oh, yeah, and when did you want all that?"

"In my office, that first Friday night." He cleared his throat. "I didn't realize it was you at first, but when I did, damn woman, I got hard immediately. Which means I wanted *you*, and not just any beautiful woman."

"I don't know what to say." I soaked in his words.

"Gwendolyn, you've had such a profound effect on me. I almost want to say thank you."

I fought the short-circuited confidence from a husband who'd ended our marriage with no explanation. No post-mortem.

"Gwen?" Andrew's tone, hesitant and troubled, pulled me together.

I crossed my arms. "You're behind by a few layers, Mister."

"I thought you'd never notice." He undid his belt and slid the beautiful leather out of his trousers, but before he tossed it aside, I caught it.

I held the ends together, reduced the slack, and snapped the sides, creating a *crack* sound. Andrew's eyes widened.

"That's what you're gonna get if you're a bad boy again," I said playfully.

He scooped me back in his arms. "That kind of makes me want to be a little bad." He kissed me rougher, his lips harder against mine.

"Let me help you with this." I unzipped his fly and his trousers slid down long muscular legs. Everything about Andrew screamed male, heat, and power. "It seems you just don't want to get undressed."

He splayed his hands across my bare breasts. "With your beauty lighting up this room, I—" His hand jerked away as if something bit him. When I glanced down, his mouth hung open. "Gwen, what's that scar?"

Uh-oh. My hands shot up to cover my right breast and the recent puncture mark, courtesy of Dr. Sage.

Perhaps I should have mentioned the issues I'd been having weeks ago when the subject of both Cate *and* my mom had come up. Andrew and I had been getting to know each other again, professionally. An abnormal mammogram didn't seem to be an 'officey' subject. With a male, no less.

"Gwendolyn, what's going on here?" He pointed, staggering back.

I regretfully gazed down at my skin, joining Andrew's stare.

"I had a breast biopsy," I choked out.

"A biopsy?" He moved his beautiful body away.

I tried to stop him. "Andrew, wait, listen."

"I'm listening, Gwen." But his touch was gone.

"My last mammogram came back abnormal."

"Abnormal?" he asked with sheer panic in his voice. "Do you have breast cancer in your family?"

I bit the inside of my mouth, choosing not to respond to his question. "I'm fine. The biopsy came back...okay. Sort of."

"Sort of?"

"I have to see a specialist. They told me I'm fine. But I may need more...monitoring. Just to be sure. Andrew, please, I'm fine."

The rich color in his skin from his arousal faded. "You didn't answer me, Gwen. You told me weeks ago your mother passed away. How did she die?" He glared at me.

"That was a long time ago," I snapped.

"She died of breast cancer, didn't she?" Andrew asked pulling up his pants.

"She was a busy mother of three. My father's a cop and worked a lot of overtime. Okay? She missed her regular screenings. She had lumps, the size of golf balls in both breasts for years. She just did nothing about it."

"But Gwen, you know what that means." The man stood frozen watching me.

"I *know* what it means. And I'll deal with it." I bent down to pick up my dress. I wasn't having that conversation naked.

"I...I went through so much, Gwen. I may not be able to do all that again." Andrew didn't appear to have the patience to wait for the right place and time to have a rational discussion.

"But *I* am *fine*, damn it." I spun around and faced the lights of Downtown L.A.

From the outside, the tinted windows wouldn't reveal my bare body. Only the inner reflection caught the glistening of a tear starting to roll down my cheek.

"Gwen, I'm sorry."

A stark picture of my life with Andrew came into focus. I hadn't connected any dots of what his experience and what *I'd* been going through meant if we... The concept of me and Andrew had only sharpened a few days ago.

The photos of Cate from her blog flashed through my mind. What the disease had done to her. How it mangled her body. Poor Andrew had to watch it all happen. When I'd said losing a mother differed from a spouse, I meant it. Yes, I'd watched my mother wither away, too, but my father had been there to bathe her, to hold her head when she vomited. I also had Greg and Skye to help when Dad needed a break.

There had been no break for Andrew.

And he looked like he was getting out now before it even came to that.

"It's late." I wiped my eyes and pulled the dress against my body tighter. Bravely facing him, I said, "This was a mistake."

"Gwen, *I*-" He waved his hands, but dropped them to his side. After a few more seconds of silence, he rubbed his face. "Okay. Maybe you're right."

My breath clipped like I'd been hoping for more of a fight from him. Sighing, I nodded. "I'm sorry."

When he didn't acknowledge my apology, I ambled to my bathroom and slammed the door shut.

♥ ♥ ♥ ♥
Andrew

I inched toward Gwen's bathroom door and rested my palm against the smooth satiny wood. How could something that felt so right turn out so bad? So fast?

I lifted my hand to knock on the door. I had to tell her about Milan. The extended trip had sat in the corner of my mind while we were getting naked. *No, by all means, continue with your fun.*

I'd planned to gently break it to her after we made love.

Life was short—I'd learned that the hard way. I had no intention of letting the coming weeks apart derail what could be my second chance.

What if Gwen got sick like Cate? The horrors I'd witnessed with Cate still burned deep inside me. What if I committed to Gwen and something happened? Could I see it through?

Unable to find the answer at that moment, I buckled my pants and reluctantly left her suite. What a mess.

By the time I made it back to my room, anger crept into the mix. Gwen had shut me down, refused to talk to me. *She* let *me* go.

At two a.m., I held my phone with Gwen's number on the screen. Would she even pick up? My clouded head had too many thoughts running through it, the loudest being my flight to Milan tomorrow night.

Frustrated, I put the phone on the charger. If Marcello couldn't get up to speed by the end of the year, I would be trapped in Milan permanently. With a half-stray cat and a full-blown heartache.

CHAPTER FIFTEEN

Gwen

I waited for Andrew at the airport gate the next afternoon. We were on that flight together, but alone. Enrico and Thalia had plans to stay until Sunday. And Salvatore needed to stay until the following week. I left the designer in the hands of List LA to finish his interviews, and his personal assistant could get him to his meetings.

Nerves pooled in my stomach. I'd hoped Andrew would have tried to make contact, either last night, or that morning.

If things between us got settled and went somewhere, there had to be a clear understanding that my health was *my* business. When and if I came across something to worry about, I would let him know.

I gasped at that thought. *Something.* Something real. A real problem. Could I do that to him? How could I have not seen that conflict?

Slowly, I backed away from the gate and took off to find another flight home.

♥ ♥ ♥ ♥

Andrew

I checked my phone after the attendant said, "We're boarding, sir."

Gwen never showed up for the flight. How was that possible? I'd summoned the courage to go back to her suite that morning, but all I'd found was a cleaning cart outside an empty span of rooms. Gwen had already checked out. And instead of waiting for me to share a taxi, she got herself to the airport. Strong independent women could be infuriating at times.

So, how did she miss our flight?

I cursed under my breath and got on the plane.

To sit in that damn middle seat sucked. I considered getting plastered, except I had approximately six hours to go to my apartment, pack up enough clothes for two months, go to the office, pack that whole mess up, and get back to the airport for a red-eye to Milan. *Meelano.*

The jet stream got me to New York in less than five hours, and in my office if I had enough time, I would stare at Gwen's desk for another five. It was so neat, not a paper out of place.

I scanned my messy desk and made sure I had everything. All those trips back and forth were now routine *and* irritating. My office in Milan had plenty of supplies. My eyes fell upon one item I didn't have in Italy.

Huffing, I swiped it and stuck it into my canvas bag.

Maybe it was for the best as Gwen had said.

♥ ♥ ♥ ♥

Gwen

Walking into my apartment in the harsh Sunday morning light, I felt like I'd *walked* home from L.A. Exhaustion passed me doing ninety hours ago. I was on fumes at that point.

Ditching my flight with Andrew was cowardly, I admitted that to myself…eventually. Paying a crazy amount of money out of my own pocket—money I couldn't spare—to take a flight that made *two* additional stops was evidence I'd screwed up.

As soon as I got two steps into my apartment Skye rang my cell phone.

"Well finally you're picking up!" My sister croaked into the phone. "So, how was L.A.? Did you see Miles? Did you kick him in the balls for me?"

If I closed my eyes to roll them, I would have fallen asleep. She was asking me if I saw her rockstar ex-boyfriend. "The fashion show was good. No, I didn't see Miles. And I'm guessing if I did, I wouldn't have been able to get near him to get a good kick in." Although, something told me, if I had explained to Andrew what happened to Skye, he'd punch the guy out for me.

"What's wrong with you?" my sister asked.

"I'm just tired." I wiped my eyes. "I didn't sleep on the plane."

"Hmmm," Skye grumbled into the phone. My attorney sister could spot a lie a mile away. "I know when you're tired. Did something happen?"

Unlike the seams of Salvatore's dress, I busted open and easily let go of the tears I'd been holding back for eighteen hours. "I messed up."

Dragging myself onto three different planes made that abundantly clear.

"Okay. How so? Talk to me."

"Can we talk about it when I come home?"

"And when will that be?"

"I don't know." Days like those I wished I lived closer to my family. Going to school at FIT gave me a thirst for Manhattan that never got fully quenched. I'd outgrown my North Fork hometown. I just hadn't admitted that to my family. "Let me put on a pot of coffee and I'll call you back." I wiped my nose, wishing I could open a bottle of wine instead.

Ten minutes later, I called Skye back and described the beautiful hotel and how it felt to sleep in that fantastic suite. How it felt when Salvatore surprised me with a gorgeous dress, but Andrew one-upped him with those amazing shoes. How I felt that intense moment when he slipped the sandals on my feet.

Even serious Skye gasped at the gesture. "Okay. And did something *happen* with Andrew again?"

I drew a sharp breath and had to end the story there. My family didn't know about the abnormal mammogram or the biopsy. I couldn't bear worrying them.

"Um, but I realized with us working together now, sex would be a big mistake."

Ben and Jerry and I would cry over the real reason. Later.

"Uh, huh," Skye responded to my entire recap. I waited for words of brilliance from the *Columbia School of Law Top of her Class Smarty Pants*.

Instead, Skye asked, "What size are those shoes?"

"Really?" I bit out while rubbing my eyes again. "That's all you got?"

"Okay," Skye finally said in a smooth even tone. "You'll see him in the office tomorrow. You need to be strong and just pretend it all didn't happen. You won't be able to work with him otherwise."

God, she was right. But how would I face him? If I thought it'd been hard to stare at him, feel him stare back, knowing he'd seen me naked a year ago when I'd been a random stranger… How could I deal with those gray eyes basking in a memory so fresh?

I stared at my luggage hoping I had clean underwear for work tomorrow. "Maybe I should just call in sick."

"Coward," Skye said, exhaling. "Want me to ask Greg to drive to the city and pick you up?"

"God, no!" My brother would get in his cop car and hunt Andrew down.

Skye laughed. "Well, call Dad. I'm sure he wants to hear your voice. You sure you'll be all right by yourself?"

I always am. "Kelsey will be home soon. But thanks, I love you."

"Same here, kid." Skye kissed me through the phone.

Hours later, I sat in my tiny kitchen and forced down some take-out food. Kelsey came home, but she and her boyfriend went back out. They'd asked me to join them. I wouldn't hang out with a lovey-dovey couple on a good day.

After thinking more about Andrew, about the possible explosion in the office, I swallowed my pride and made the ice-breaker call.

Put your big-girl pants on, Gwendolyn.

For now, it was nothing more than a *let's get the awkwardness out of the way* call about how to work together going forward. Again. *Ugh.*

Every call went right to voicemail, though.

Hello and Ciao. You've reached Andrew Morgan at Prada. I can't take your call right now, but please... He repeated the message in Italian. His deep sexy voice drove me mad. When had he created that greeting? Which Andrew was I listening to? The man who still had a wife? The recent widower? The man who'd just met me?

I called the number again and again just to analyze the damn message, listening to voices in the background to give me a clue.

At four a.m., I gave up.

CHAPTER SIXTEEN

Gwen

The next morning, I walked to work with wet hair I was too lazy to blow-dry and avoided the smell of the subway. With every city street I passed, I turned more and more numb.

With my phone clutched in my palm, I wished a call or even a text from Andrew would make the phone buzz. The nothing, the silence, made it hard to breathe.

Then several emails from Enrico poured in. He laid out my next assignment: *Work with the advertising team for a holiday campaign and set up the promotional VIP parties and other events.* While Starlight gave those tasks to the greenest employees, at Prada, no event or campaign was unimportant. I imagined Prada's holiday marketing budgets were huge.

Enrico had also put me in charge of Salvatore's new collection. My experience qualified me to develop a strategic marketing plan. Andrew hadn't been copied on any of the emails. Enrico hadn't mentioned Andrew at all. No, *work with Andrew on this*, or *get with Andrew for that*.

Good God! Had he told Enrico what happened between us in L.A.? I'd be mortified to face Enrico now.

On the elevator to the marketing floor, my stomach churned, but anger took over. I planned to walk in that office, give Andrew a stiff nod, and not speak to him after all.

My legs wobbled as I swayed in that direction gearing up for the confrontation. The stainless-steel lever felt colder than I remembered. Andrew must have already iced it over.

"Gwendolyn."

I blinked and turned around. "Hi, Enrico. I'm sorry I'm late. I'm still jet-lagged."

"You look like you flew home on the wings of the plane," he said.

Which one of the *three*, I wondered? Probably all of them, based on how I felt at the moment. The muted steel-blue sweater dress and dark stockings I'd put on that morning fit my somber mood. To make that the perfect start of a new week, my period had arrived and the pain bordered on unbearable.

With Enrico there, a small dose of relief crept through me. I wouldn't be facing Andrew alone. It would be too jarring, after all. Searching for something to say out of stress made people do and say stupid shit.

"Do you need something, Enrico?" I asked with inviting eyes. *Please don't go.*

"Yes, I want to talk to you about Andrew." Unless Enrico wasn't neutral.

Andrew *did* say something. *Son of a bitch*, I screamed in my head, but in a calm voice, said, "Okay. Let's go to your office."

"No, your office is fine." He tapped on the wood, encouraging me to open the door.

Oh. Dear. God. He wanted a face-to-face intervention.

I gripped the door handle again, and my heart rate lowered. A locked office meant Andrew hadn't arrived yet and wouldn't be sitting in his chair with a pissed-off look on his face. I had time to get my shit together.

Inside the office, his familiar scent made my stomach flip. It wasn't even cologne. It turned out to be a combination of his soap, fresh laundered shirts, and his intense masculinity that left a taste of him in the air.

Oh God! I missed him.

I got my control in check and turned to my boss. "What did you want to talk to me about?"

"Sit down, Gwendolyn."

The fear that something might have happened to Andrew hit me so swiftly I *had* to sit down. If I didn't get a grip on my emotions, the terrible Chinese food from last night would end up all over my desk.

"I'm sitting," I managed through clenched teeth.

Enrico took Andrew's chair from his desk and glided it next to me. "Unfortunately, Marcello in Milan has not been working out the way we had hoped."

I swallowed. "We?"

"Andrew and I." Enrico pressed his lips together. "I have sent him back to Milan."

Andrew was in Italy. He wasn't even *on the same continent.* "For," I stumbled, "for...how long?"

"This may be good news for you, Gwendolyn."

"How can *any of this* be good news for me?" My eyes shot open wide. *Did I just yell at my boss?*

"Scusa?" Enrico stared at me with a wrinkle above his nose.

Exhausted, I swiped at eyes I hadn't bothered loading up with my usual heavy mascara and eyeliner that morning. "I'm sorry. I'm just not feeling well."

"If Marcello does not work out and we have to let him go, Andrew will have to assume the position." He studied my face. "I have given him until the end of the year."

The end of the year. I glanced at the puppy calendar tacked to the corkboard next to my desk. Thanksgiving was the following week. I wouldn't see Andrew until next year? Or... A choking sensation tickled the back of my throat. Or not at all if that Marcello didn't get his

Italian act together.

I'd been biting my lip so hard I feared I'd break the skin and draw blood. "So *why* is this good news for me?"

"You have far exceeded our expectations. On Thursday night, Andrew and I had dinner and we spoke about you at length."

Thursday night. The night before the show. The night before we almost made love. "What did he say exactly?"

"He said the work you have been doing showed him you could handle both yours and his position here in New York, if he were to remain in Milan permanently."

"On *Thursday* you asked him to go to Milan?"

"*Si.*" Enrico nodded. "It was a last-minute request, but Andrew was happy to accommodate me."

My stomach turned over again. *Happy*. He was *happy* to take off. All with the intention of making love to me. *Before*.

"You and I will talk more about the new position for you if it becomes necessary," Enrico said. "We have not made any final decisions."

"Enrico, these photos of the show were just dropped off." Thalia came into the office and placed a thick stack on my desk.

"Ah, yes. Thank you, Thalia," Enrico said.

I couldn't make eye contact with the girl. We'd been talking about how Salvatore may or may not have expected something for the dress. Then I left with Andrew, who had escaped to Milan. That was why people shouldn't shit where they eat!

"What are these for, Enrico?" I tapped the photos.

"For today, we would like you to review these proofs and work with the art department to create the media kits for Salvatore's collection."

The 'we' cut deep into my heart, but I pushed out a strong, "Okay. I'll get that done today."

"Then go home if you are still not feeling well." He stood and smiled, suggesting he had nothing further to say and didn't know Andrew and I had fooled around after the show.

"I'll be fine." I closed the door behind Enrico and spun around the office.

Andrew had to work in Milan until the end of the year. *And* he knew all of that when he went back to my hotel suite. Even though he wouldn't be strolling in any moment, his absence left a gaping void greater than his presence. A part of Andrew lingered, watching me.

I picked up the stack of photos, carelessly letting pictures of model after model slide past my fingers. Then I came across one of me. The green dress stood out from all the neutral colors in the other pictures. I yanked that photo out. Behind it, a photo of me and Andrew made my heart pound. I studied his face for the truth he'd kept from me. I hoped to see a man hiding a secret and planning a massive getaway.

No, all I saw was adoration. *Adorato.*

So why didn't he tell me?

In a burst of frustration, I threw the photos in the air. I wanted to forget that day. The glossy prints rained down around me with flashes of white from the backs fluttering like doves released at a wedding. That felt more like a funeral, though.

My hands shook, rolling Andrew's chair back to his side of the office. I slammed the executive swivel so hard into the desk, a small glass container of paper clips fell over. After debating whether or not to leave the mess, I took the high road and cleaned them up. The empty space in front of Andrew's phone jarred the hell out of me.

The picture of Andrew and Cate was gone.

I braced my body against the desk, staring at where the photo had been. Just the week before, Andrew had moved the frame to make room for art layouts we'd been looking at. It had struck me how he picked it up with no emotion as if it were his stapler.

Now that stupid frame, the one *I* purchased, was in Milan. With Andrew.

♥ ♥ ♥ ♥

Andrew

In my Milan office, I sat with my chin leaning against my wrists as I listened to the rain pounding against the windows.

I stared at the photo of me and Cate, but all I saw was my reflection in the glass. Cate's eyes seemed to narrow at me, disapproving how I'd just left.

It ate at me how Enrico had to tell Gwen I'd gone to Milan. It ached to think about how she'd take the news. My phone lay on my desk, dark, cold, and dead, only coming back to life since I'd plugged it into my laptop.

Somewhere in the twelve thousand miles I traveled— including the multiple stops I made—my charger went missing. I clicked on my laptop to do some work, and the auto-play icon popped open. I took a breath. Managing my photos from the show was normally delegated to my Milan assistant. Knowing she would sort and upload them to Dropbox, accessible to the entire department for use on the company's website and other materials, I brought the pictures up to view them first.

With a few more clicks, thumbnails dotted the screen one by one. The size of the files made the process crawl. I passed the monitor several times while getting resituated as the last set of photos materialized.

Gwen's face appeared in one small box after another. My jaw quivered as they came into focus. They weren't just pictures of a colleague at an event, smiling or pointing. Many were ones I'd snapped as I watched her from the shadows. Her face, her hair, her shoulders swallowed up the frames. Those photos were all I had of her, now.

Her smile reminded me how much she had wanted me. For most of my adult life, I felt not just wanted, but *hunted*. Gwen hadn't made me feel like a prize, though. With her, being desired felt different. Natural.

I'd have trouble shaking the feel of her in my arms. How she held me. Powerful yet supple. Her combination of curves and strength brought out another side of my passion. Wild. Dominant. Last year in bed, she'd taken every ounce of what I had to give and gave back just as much. I was myself with her, the old me.

Gwen could handle the *real* me.

Yet, I couldn't ignore feeling blindsided by the news of her health. While it would have been startling to hear, she should have been upfront with me. She'd made it seem like no big deal. Either she was being careless with her health or she hadn't intended on opening up to me. Even if we were in a relationship?

I'd felt so ready to take that step forward with Gwen. Now my hopes for a new start evaporated.

With little hope in my heart, I highlighted the ones of Gwen and created a new folder: *My Gwen*. Those photos I kept just for me.

The rain hadn't let up and by the time I made it back to my building, my clothes were soaked. In the center of the hallway on the cold tile floor, the black cat sat, also wet from the rain.

I glanced around, curious why my furry friend was just sitting there. The mischief on the fuzzy little face made me smile for the first time since leaving Gwen. I tapped the owner's door, but the one across the hall opened up instead.

The attractive older woman who always watched me with intensity called out in her broken English. "Signora Morelli pass away last week."

I glanced down at the soggy feline. "I'm sorry."

"My daughter...she is allergy to cats."

"Allergic," I corrected. And now I owned a cat.

"I have been feeding him out here, and I think he likes to sleep outside anyways." She disappeared into her apartment, the black lacquered door slamming behind her.

When it opened again, she came out balancing two dishes and a small bag of dry cat food. I rushed to help her and caught a glimpse of smooth olive skin under her silk robe.

Her dark eyes met mine. "*Scusa,*" she murmured.

The moment hit me like I'd been slammed into a wall. That beautiful woman had hinted all along she wanted me. I was technically a single man. I could have dropped the bag of food and pulled her into my apartment.

That's not what I wanted. That woman wasn't *who* I wanted. I cleared my throat and moved my eyes away. Fast.

"I'll do my best to take care of him. But I live in America. I'm only here until the end of the year."

"I will see if another neighbor can take him after that. But he is looking, how you say...lonely right now?"

The cat looked lonely indeed. I knew the look. It's what I saw in my mirror. "*Grazie.*"

Without a formal invitation, the cat scampered into my flat. I followed him in and grabbed a small towel to dry him off. The cat purred happily at my touch.

I set up the two bowls under the window my friend liked to climb through. While placing the nuggets down, the writing on the side of the food bowl caught my attention. "Your name is Casper?"

He purred loudly, his body stretching up to get the food.

I pet his back while Casper crunched on little fish-shaped nuggets. "That's a strange name for a black cat."

CHAPTER SEVENTEEN

Gwen

My mother used to make the stuffing for the Thanksgiving Day turkey the night before. Her unique recipe with onions, sausage, sage, and raisins gave the house a scent embedded in my amygdala, the part of my nose that triggered my heartbreak.

Every year, Skye and I attempted to recreate the stuffing to bring the Thanksgiving Day scent back into our house. And with it our mom.

Greg stabbed into the pile I put on his plate with excited force. But the look he slid me and the quiet gentleness in the way he chewed, suggested Skye and I had failed. Again.

That day could have been very different for me thanks to Salvatore's invitation to watch the Macy's parade in the city from his expensive high-rise apartment. But that'd been an easy invite to turn down.

I had something special to be thankful for. Dad's physical therapy was going well and he'd been cleared to go back to work. While Skye chatted away about one of her cases, I watched my brother. Even without his cop uniform, Greg with his six-foot build, a full head of golden-brown hair, and bright green eyes, he still turned plenty heads in my small town. I felt bad for the women in Manhattan if he got into the FBI and strutted around New York City all dressed up to the nines.

I had to get him into a Prada suit, ASAP.

Behind his eyes, I knew my brother was hiding how lonely he really was. His wedding had been scheduled for Thanksgiving weekend, so that holiday always hit him hard. He'd been so in love with Faith Copeland and everyone remained puzzled why she ran off. Especially me since Faith and I had been best friends since grade school.

"Who was that man playing Santa?" Skye asked about the yearly Darling Cove Fire Department parade. A small but satisfying substitute to the Macy's circus. "Even with that fake beard, I could tell he was hot, hot, hot."

"Makes sense if he's one of the volunteer firemen," I said, pouring gravy on my lumpy mashed potatoes.

"He's the new fire chief," my dad said, hobbling back to the table with another beer.

"Oh right, I saw that on the Darling Cove Moms Facebook page. Edward…something," I announced.

"Mendelsohn," Greg chimed in. "Why are you on Darling Cove Moms? You don't live here anymore."

"And you're not a mom," Skye added, smiling.

"Leave your sister alone," Dad jumped in to protect me.

"I can talk for myself, Dad."

"Sorry, pumpkin. Habit." He brushed my hand and his eyes lingered across the table to where my mother should have been sitting. I watched his smile fall and it broke my heart. Sure, I missed her, too, but my mom was my dad's sweetheart, his…everything.

She was everything to me. Andrew's words tore through me.

"Edward Mendelsohn," I mused out loud to push the thought of Andrew out of my head and grabbed my phone. Edward even *sounded* hot. "Holy smokes."

"Appropriate," Skye said. "Being a fireman and all."

"Take a look." I showed her my phone.

"Holy shit." Skye didn't have her sensor button on

and my dad just shook his head. "*This* guy lives in our town?"

My sister's eyes turned gooey taking in the dark auburn hair, cerulean blue eyes, sculpted cheekbones, and full lips. Edward wore a white chief's cap and a dress uniform on the webpage that said: *The Darling Cove Volunteer Fire Department announces its new chief.*

I was surprised the website hadn't gone down.

"Oh shoot," my dad said, looking back at the kitchen. "I never picked up the pie."

"I'm on it, Dad." Skye threw down her napkin. "Greg, go to Sadie's and get us the pie."

He grunted. "I'm still eating. I'll go when I'm finished." He pointed his fork at Skye. "Why don't you come with me and fake a fainting spell. Your fireman may show up."

"Oh, good idea." Skye checked for food in her teeth with her butter knife. "Pie *and* some hot mouth to mouth with—"

"I'm glad you two are joking," My dad snapped at Greg and Skye. "What the heck are you two doing with your lives, anyway?" He pointed to me. "At least your sister's been married. Which is more than I can say for the two of you."

"Dad, I'm still getting over this thing with Miles," Skye quickly defended herself. "Besides, my law practice is keeping me busy."

"Oh, save it. You do real estate closings. I drive by your office at night and it's dark."

Dad's eyes drifted to Greg, who kept his face focused on his plate. "Don't either of you want kids someday?"

"I was *supposed* to be married," Greg said bitterly. "In case you all have forgotten."

Maybe not.

"You were left at the altar years ago, Gregory." Dad waved his hands, dismissively. "Get over it. I never thought my youngest would be my best chance to have a grandchild."

"Me?" I gasped, feeling the furthest away from having a baby since my heart was aching over Andrew.

At least Greg and Skye had clear-enough heads to find love again.

The way my love life had been going, I was certain to be the last to give my dad grandkids. Greg had a better shot with his runaway bride. And Skye and the hottest fireman I'd ever seen may be strangers, but I bet they'd make the world's most beautiful baby.

Not me and Andrew.

♥ ♥ ♥ ♥

Andrew

Thanksgiving Day meant nothing in Italy, but after going through reports with Marcello all morning, I ate lunch and left work early.

Casper had been coming and going at his own leisure. With no one to eat dinner with, I chose to walk the streets of Milan's shopping district. Anything to fill the hours.

In Italy, it was just another Thursday. But for *Black Friday*, even the smallest of merchants were gearing up.

Every day felt black without Gwen.

I jammed my chilled hands in my pockets. I played a daily game of watching New York's temperature, looking out for snow. My gut twisted, waiting for Gwen to experience the magical New York City holiday weather without me. Italy felt like forty thousand miles away, not four thousand.

My cell phone ringing drew out a long sigh. "Hi,

Ma."

"Happy Thanksgiving!" Ma sounded chipper calling from Bermuda.

When I'd told my parents I'd be in Italy for the holiday, Ma pouted for a week. She'd gotten over the sting, though, and dragged my father out of town for a long weekend.

"Is Dad at least enjoying the pool?" I asked.

"No. He's playing golf. I'm in the room by myself," Ma said wryly.

I sat on a bench facing a park. School had let out, and kids were playing. Their delicate voices tolled in Italian, relaxing me. "Can I talk to you for a moment, Ma?"

"Of course, my handsome boy. Do you need something? Do you need me to ship anything to you over there?" She said *over there* like Enrico had sent me to a military base in Kabul, Afghanistan.

"No. I assure you Milan has stores and I have everything I need." Except Gwen. "So..." *I can't believe I'm going to say this.* "I met someone, Ma." The intake of air in Ma's lungs was shockingly audible. "Ma, are you all right?"

"Hang on. I'm checking my phone to make sure I have the best signal possible. I don't want to miss a word of this." She huffed, and said, "Hmm, it looks like three bars is the best this five-star resort can offer. Go!"

"Okay, *met* someone is probably not correct." I took a breath. "There's a woman I work with. She—"

"In Milan? Andrew Michael Morgan, you can't be thinking of moving to that country. I want grandkids and I want them *here*. In New York."

My fingers gripped the phone tighter, my mother was already talking about *grandkids*. "I meant a woman in the New York office."

"Oh!" She squealed in delight then released an, "*Oh-h-h*. How's that working, long-distance and all?"

"Distance isn't the problem at the moment." I chose to leave out the near-sex in L.A. details *and* that wild romp last year. "She's the woman who sits in my New York office. You were looking at her pictures."

"Oh, her. The girl from 'No.'" She laughed, and I laughed with her remembering my mother's smart-ass comment in my office looking at Gwen's photos. "Okay, and?"

"She had a scar. A biopsy scar. Her mother died of breast cancer. Gwen doesn't have it. But I started to panic and asked a bunch of invasive questions. She got very defensive and when I pushed her, she asked me to leave and I haven't spoken to her since."

My mother said nothing for a moment. We were fiercely alike, in looks *and* mindset. I inherited my father's sense of business, but when it came to matters of the heart, I was all my mother. Yet Cate had driven a sharp wedge between us. I loved my wife and proudly stood by her side in the face of being isolated from my parents. But I'd hated those dark days and couldn't bear to go through it again.

If Ma couldn't support me this time around, I'd rather know now.

Finally, my mother said, "Well then, you have to fight for her."

Relieved, I asked, "How do I do that from Italy?"

"You're in the country of love. Put her on a plane and show her how you feel."

CHAPTER EIGHTEEN

Andrew

I remained silent for a moment after Ma's startling suggestion. In the past two weeks since I'd seen Gwen, I brought up her number on my phone so many times and just stared at it. My fingers hovered above the call icon, but I never pressed it. Several emails I'd written sat in my draft folder.

What stopped me every time? Wondering if I could do the right thing by Gwen if she were to get sick. Could I stick around to watch the horror of someone wasting away, *again*? Those questions completely dumbfounded me, and I didn't trust myself to make the right decision. The scars from losing Cate had healed and made my heart tougher now. But deep inside, losing another woman I loved would utterly destroy me.

"What if I'm not really the best man for Gwen, considering what I've gone through?" I asked Ma.

My mother cleared her throat.

Here it comes.

"Andrew, if you even had the notion to talk to me about this woman after all the *other* women in your life I've never met..."

"Okay, Ma." I huffed, pissed off she'd throw my roaring whoring days that overshadowed much of my twenties at me. As Lanvin's top male model I'd had my pick of women. Plenty of beauties had fallen at my feet and in my bed. "But you make a good point."

"Of course, I do!" she chirped proudly. "You're so like me. You know that, don't you?"

"Yeah. Ma, I gotta go. I have..."

"Work? You've been hiding behind your job for two years now." Ma finally got the timeframe correct.

"I have some serious thinking to do."

"Call back if you need me. I love you, my handsome boy." My mom cleared her throat after I grumbled. "Oh, Andrew, you'll always be my handsome boy. But you *are* a man now. Whatever you decide this time, I trust you, and I will *never* abandon you again." Her voice drifted off at the end, hiding the regret of how she'd once alienated herself from me.

Opening up to her lifted an enormous weight off my shoulders. It sounded like a blessing to pursue Gwen even with the risks. Life had no meaning without risks.

When I settled into my office on Monday morning, Enrico's reminder for the monthly branding team meeting popped up in my inbox. *Uh-oh.* The other attendee made my heart pound: Gwendolyn Foley.

I swallowed. Hard. Most of Western Europe and an ocean would dissolve the moment her voice came over the phone. I suspected Enrico chose to monitor the call to further gauge Gwen's performance.

If only Enrico knew the truth about what almost happened in L.A.

"Okay, okay," I said, calming down as I read through my notes for the meeting. "It's just a phone call. I can do this. It's not like she'll see how nervous I am."

I attempted to eat lunch, but the update sent by Enrico, changing the meeting to a Zoom teleconference made me toss the rest of my panini in the trash.

I barely prepared to hear Gwen's voice, even though I had all day to stress over the matter, thanks to a time difference not in my favor.

I'd faced Gwen after we'd slept together. Even

though we didn't have sex in L.A., the connection to her felt deeper. I'd gotten to know her on another level and she meant so much more to me.

My shaking hands logged into Prada's Zoom account. With excruciating anticipation, I watched the buffering icon spin and spin.

"Andrew!" Enrico's face filled one rectangle box. "How are you? We miss you."

Immediately, my throat tingled. *We?* "Hi there. Yeah. I miss New York, too."

"I'll bring Gwendolyn in," Enrico said and tapped a few buttons.

I swallowed a few more breaths, preparing to see her face. When she came into view, Gwen's eyes were focused on her lap. Her hair, pulled back into a tight bun, looked glossy as usual, but her cheeks had lost some volume. It pained me to see how thin she looked. That was not the same woman I left two weeks ago.

"Hello," I said hesitantly. "Um, Gwendolyn."

It hurt to say her name out loud. I'd been calling her Gwen because she asked me to. I wasn't sure I still had that right.

Her lids lifted to the camera, and it felt like an entire colony of butterflies hatched at the same time in my stomach.

"Hello, Andrew," she said with caution. She began her status updates, staring at a yellow legal pad. "I collected progress reports from Gus, Stephan, and Antonia for the menswear lines. They'll have at least a dozen prototypes ready to ship to Milan for review by the end of the month. The new jewelry line, however, has had some issues. Their schedule's been set back, I'm afraid." Her head lifted briefly. "Enrico and I have been trying to mitigate the effect it would have on their deadline, but a shortage in the non-corrosive, environmentally-friendly metals we specified have been more of a problem to source than the team's initial estimates."

Enrico jumped in. "Without assigning blame, we think one of the production assistants did not provide the manufacturer with our exact volumes and specifications. But Gwendolyn here is on it. I have her working with the strategic sourcing group in Paris to find another vendor."

"Okay, but..." I paused. "I was part of the initial negotiation. I'd like to be on any calls you or she arranges."

"I would like this matter addressed immediately." Enrico shifted in his seat.

I crumpled the paper in my fingertips and heard my mother's voice. *Put that woman on a plane.* "Perhaps it would be best to do the call together in person."

"In person?" Gwen asked.

"Sono d'accordo" Enrico agreed. "Gwendolyn, I know this is short notice, but *could* you fly out to Milan tonight?"

"Tonight?" Gwen shrieked.

"*Sì.* And Andrew, when she is there, perhaps she could meet with Marcello. Have her sit with him...give him a hand."

Gwen glanced at the calendar she kept tacked up behind her desk, leaving only her profile visible. My fingers touched the monitor outlining her face, but pulled my hands away when she looked back into the screen camera.

"Gwendolyn, are you okay with this?" Enrico asked her again.

I swallowed, waiting for her to reply.

"Sure," she released on a long breath."

Enrico took a call on his cell. *"Prego,"* he said into the phone and looked back at the camera. "I'll let you two work out the details. I am needed on the designer floor."

My boss's screen went black and the look on Gwen's face could only be described as panic-stricken.

♥♥♥♥

Gwen

My gaping mouth hung open as I stared into Andrew's dark gray eyes. In the last two minutes, I'd been told to go to Italy. *Tonight.* To fix a jewelry mess I could have easily taken care of with one phone call from New York. Alone. And what was that meeting with Marcello really about?

"So…" Andrew said, shoving a hand through his hair. The ring was still gone. "Hi."

"Hi," I replied back, preferring to keep my voice even to gauge *his* reaction.

"Um. How are you?"

God, I hated that question. *Great. Never better.* "Okay. You? How is Milan?"

"Cold. Make sure you bring your winter coat."

And we're gonna talk about the weather now. My nerves had my stomach in knots. I drew in a ragged breath. "Listen, Andrew—"

"Gwen, I went back to your room Saturday morning."

The air trapped in my lungs escaped in a slow ragged exhale. And…he called me Gwen. "You did?"

"I wanted to tell you myself I was coming back here."

"Oh." Not to smooth things out. To deliver the news that either way, we wouldn't be together in any meaningful way. Right. Message received.

"And why weren't you on our flight?" he asked.

Our. That little detail stabbed at me. I looked down, guilt creeping in. "I ended up taking a different flight home."

The way he pursed his lips meant he understood why. He looked down as well, clearly agitated. "Okay."

"Andrew, I'm sorry I—"

"No! *I'm* sorry. You didn't do anything wrong. I came at you with a bunch of invasive questions about something obviously personal and sensitive. I know I overreacted." His large hands, hands that had been all over my body, covered his beautiful face. I stroked the monitor mentally willing him to lower them. "It's because of what happened...to me, with Cate. I just freaked out. I'm sorry."

"So am I." The explanations might be out of the way, but ugly and gritty residue like tea leaves at the bottom of a saucer, told me Andrew and I may be at some kind of an impasse. "Hey, we're adults."

"I wanted more than one night with you, this time." His voice came out just above a whisper.

He tossed the ball in my court with his response, though. Last time, I dropped it by shutting him out and hiding. Too many thoughts fought for position in my head, from *run to that airport, now,* to *run away.* I searched somewhere in between for the right response, but the words caught in my throat.

"I guess..." Andrew said when I hesitated. "I guess you just didn't feel the same way." He sat back, sounding sorrier than I was prepared for.

"I don't know how to do this," I groaned.

"Do what?"

My hands pointed back and forth between us.

"This. A relationship, like this."

"But you were married."

"Yes, to the second man I ever slept with. I met him the first week after I graduated college."

Andrew's lips widened into a smile and his body shook from a laughing fit.

"What's so funny?"

"You have a lot to make up for," he said.

"Was I that bad last year?" I asked, appalled.

He coughed. "Are you kidding, you—" He cut his words short as his eyes drifted over my shoulder. "Um, can you call me back on your phone?"

I looked outside our office. A group of women had gathered by the sidelight, holding papers, but watched Andrew on my monitor through the glass. Their flushed faces and puckered lips gave me a glimpse of what being with Andrew Morgan would look like. The man could have anyone. And they would line up for him.

I smirked. *Step aside bitches. He's mine.*

I turned back and sat up straight. "We can finish this when I see you tomorrow."

"We better." His bold confidence sent a rush of heat through me.

He wanted me. Still.

"There's an 11 p.m. out of JFK, by the way," he said. "It's usually full, so you'd better call now to make sure you get a seat." His eyebrows dipped with a seductive promise that made me almost slide off my damn seat.

"Okay then. I have to go. Apparently, I've got a plane to catch."

CHAPTER NINETEEN

Andrew

"Andrew Morgan," I answered my desk phone the following day hoping it would be Gwen saying she was waiting for me in the lobby.

"Can you speak for a few minutes, Andrew?" Enrico's voice killed that wish.

I glanced at my clock. It'd been excruciating waiting for Gwen to arrive. Her plane landed two hours ago. Every call I made to her cell went straight to voicemail. Even the driver who'd gone to pick her up wasn't responding. I had an overblown visualization she'd been kidnapped. Or some Gucci agent had spotted her and lured Gwen away.

"Sure. What's up?" I answered Enrico.

"I have been doing some thinking."

Uh-oh. Enrico's 'thinking' had landed me in Milan in the first place, training Marcello. "What about?"

"I haven't said anything to Gwendolyn. She is doing a great job here, but I need you in New York, Andrew."

"I need to be there, too. Being here for extended periods of time..." I didn't want to sound petulant.

"*Lo so, lo so.*"

"I know you know, Enrico. What's your idea?"

"What do you think of Gwendolyn replacing Marcello if he does not work out?"

I thought about that for a moment. "I think she can do the job. But having Marcello report to us was already a gift from Stefania. Now you want to move that position to New York all together?"

"No, no. You misunderstand. We will transfer

Gwendolyn there."

I froze. *Fuck!* The words *Gwen, you may have to move here to Italy* would have a hard time coming out of my mouth, fearing she may run me over to get a work visa.

No, that wasn't an option. At all. If Gwen were there in Milan and I was in New York…

That would be a disaster.

"Andrew?" Enrico prodded me for a response.

"Yeah. I don't think putting a New York person in that position will go over so well. I can't see the creative director agreeing to that."

"You let me worry about Stefania."

I held my head.

"Why so glum?" a soft voice echoed from the doorway.

My head shot up and my throat suddenly went tight. "Gwen!"

"Ah, she is there," Enrico said into the phone. "I will leave you to it then. *Caio. In bocca al lupo.*"

"I'm gonna need it," I said under my breath as I hung up.

It took me another moment to look back at Gwen. Before I said anything, she swayed into the office. A short wool coat hung on her shoulders. Underneath, she wore the winter-white sleeveless dress I'd seen on her desk last month. The wool frock sat on her body as nicely as I thought it would.

"Everything all right?" she asked.

It is now. "Yeah, that was our boss."

"Oh." She pulled off brown leather gloves. "Did you need to finish speaking to him?"

"No, he said enough."

"Ha! I bet you don't miss him," Gwen said, smirking.

"No, I miss you."

Her body froze. "Andrew, I..." She slowly lifted her eyes to me.

"I mean, I miss working with you." The way she looked at me made me wonder if I had to start back at square one with her.

Her shoulders softened. "Oh. Okay. Yeah, it's not the same without you in the office."

"Enjoying all the space?"

"That, and now I can work without faces pressed against the glass gawking at you."

"Stop it. That didn't happen." I turned and looked out my open door to the rest of the department. A woman stared at Gwen with a frown. "Anyway...let me show you around." I stood to slide my suit jacket over my shoulders. "I dress more formally here in Milan. You know, Miuccia's here."

Gwen smiled and moved further into the office with her luggage. When she glanced down to situate it, our bodies collided. "Oops, sorry."

I'm not. "It's okay," I said, instead. Feeling her body sent a tidal wave of emotion through me. I could lift her up right now, lay her on the desk, and penetrate her easily.

The way she held the stare felt like she didn't want to let go. In her eyes, were the answers I wanted. The longing and the need I'd once seen had returned.

I hadn't expected to be so close to her so soon into the visit. If I only knew how she felt. *Ask her, you dummy.* A little voice that sounded oddly like my mother's rang in my ear.

"Gwen?"

"Yeah?" Her body inched closer.

I loved her height compared to mine. It brought out

the protective side in me. Before I could consider whether her replacing Marcello was something I should keep to myself, my mouth opened, and the words tumbled out.

"One of the reasons you're here is because Enrico may want *you* to take over for Marcello if we have to fire him." I snuck a look through my lashes. "And Gwen, I'm sorry, but that's looking like a real possibility."

Gwen's chest heaved taking in the news. "That means you're back in New York." When I nodded, she quickly gave voice to my worst fear. "But I'll be here."

"Those would be the logistics."

She turned away. "Either way we'll be...in two different offices," came out in a delicate whisper laced with sadness.

I released a sharp breath and spun her back around, my fingers gripping her shoulders. "I want..."

Her body softened against mine. "You want what?"

We were in the land of *amore,* but still in the office. As much as I wanted to kiss her — and I suspected she wanted that too — I couldn't, and put distance between us or I'd go crazy.

It was too soon.

♥ ♥ ♥ ♥

Gwen

Only when Andrew's hand found my body had the knot from the last few weeks inside my stomach loosened. It stung when he let go, but we were in the office.

"Right now, I want to show you around." Andrew held his door open. "Let's take a walk. It's almost the end of the day, but I think Marcello should still be here."

"Should I leave my things here?"

"Sure. I'll lock the door." Andrew fiddled with the

handle. "Of course, you could have just packed a toothbrush and hopped on the plane. If you think there are plenty of clothes lying around New York, wait till you see the production floor here."

"Show me." I let my excitement shine through. "I can't wait to see the world you've been a part of for so many months."

"This isn't my world. My world is home in New York." Andrew bit his tongue as if he wanted to say more, but kept his lips firmly shut.

Strolling through the corridors of Prada's Milan headquarters felt surreal. Italian purred all around me. That was where it all began. The new campus had been built in the Largo Isarco section south of the city and it was *stunning*. It looked more like a museum, but not in a stuffy, cold way.

The large concrete entrance ended with a tower of glass, and while it only rose up two or three stories, it sprawled out for acres behind me. There were several wings, each with classic red tiled rooftops, one of which spanned an entire city block. The line of arch-shaped windows down the corridor reminded me of a church.

"You look like you belong here." Andrew tugged on the curled ends of my long dark hair. "Stop it."

I smiled behind my gold-rimmed shades. "Does Marcello know I'm here?"

"*Sì, lo fa*. I mean, yes, he does. But as far as Enrico's little scheme? Let's just say you're still getting familiar with the company, and you want to share some ideas."

I resisted an eye roll and instead gave an encouraging nod, thinking: *The man works for Prada, he can't be that dumb.*

"I'm sure there were subtle hints of what's wrong that you missed." I followed Andrew into Marcello's office.

The man's chin rested on a phone while he spoke Italian. By the look on Andrew's face, it must have been a personal call.

After Marcello hung up the phone, he stood and faced me. "*Scusa.*"

Marcello was tall, but lankier than Andrew. His body hadn't bulked up yet, the way a man's body filled out when he reached his thirties. Dark brown curls flopped on a thin and bony forehead and his cheekbones cast a shadow on the lower half of his face.

"Marcello, this is Gwendolyn from the New York office." Andrew rested his hand against the small of my back, sending sparks up my spine.

I leaned across the desk, piled up with papers and folders. Worse than Andrew's used to be. "It's nice to meet you," I said.

"*Così meraviglioso di conoscerla.*" He cleared his throat. "I mean, it is wonderful to meet you…Gwendolyn."

His eyes lingered on mine for a moment, but he dragged them away with the sound of Andrew's voice. They conversed in Italian for a few moments. Hearing Andrew speak Italian in person again, I knew I was a goner.

♥♥♥♥
Andrew

After work, I hoped for some kind of flinching objection when I suggested Gwen check into her hotel.

Nope.

She'd been up in that damn room for an hour getting settled and ready for dinner. I sipped my third cocktail at the lobby bar, wondering what the hell I was doing there and not up in the room getting her ready…for me. The way I wanted her.

"*Sono pronto, Signor Morgan,*" Gwen purred. "Did I get that right?"

I looked up, and my throat tightened. Christ, now I knew how she felt when I spoke Italian. I listened to the language all day, but Gwen saying it, turned me hard as steel.

"*Sì, perfetto,*" I said, nodding.

She looked like a cat who had swallowed an entire pet store of canaries as she twirled to show off her first clothing score from the Milan production floor.

"Good?" she asked with a smile that was going to kill me.

"*Bello.*" Except the red and black wrap dress she changed into was too low cut, and too damn tight. It showed every luscious curve of her body.

I tossed a wad of Euros on the bar and steered her out of the hotel. My hand rested on her back and I had no plans to stop touching her until we got to work tomorrow. On the walk to the restaurant, she stayed silent.

But the chatty Gwen that drew me in the night I met her, had finally arrived. She would not shut up and I loved listening to every word that came out of her mouth. Mostly, I loved watching her mouth. And considered how those lips would look wrapped around my cock.

The baked apple crisp I fed her after the dinner we shared, had me going crazy watching the fork slide past those lips.

"We need to get out of here," I said, signaling for the check.

Walking back to her hotel, I should have paced my steps slower to let her enjoy a view of the city.

I wanted, no *needed,* to be with Gwen. In her hotel room. In her bed. I'd been given a second chance and I wouldn't let anything mess that up. That included not letting her turn away or give into doubts.

Before we reached the hotel marquis, I gently pushed her against the brick wall in a spot between the lampposts' amber lighting.

"I'm sorry," I breathed into her mouth, watching her lips sip my apology. "Can we start over?"

"By start over do you mean—"

I answered her with my lips and she hungrily took my kiss. The waiting storm from a year earlier swelled up and crested over. A year ago, I took a gorgeous stranger to bed. Now, I wanted the woman I'd fallen for.

Gwen pulled her mouth away. "We just *can't* pick up where we left off in L.A."

"Why not?"

"Why not?" She blinked in astonishment.

"Because there never should have been this stupid gap of time." My face felt pinched and contorted, filled with tension. "L.A. should have been a new beginning for us. Not the end."

"Either way, we have to re-set this whole thing to base it on reality. That night was a fairy tale." After she pulled the collar of her coat closer, she drew a fist to her mouth. "I was a princess and you were—"

"Look at me." I lifted her hand away and leaned it against my lips. "Gwen, I don't want a princess. *Or* a model. I want *you.* The real you and everything you are."

"Even with my...issues?" The vulnerability in her eyes killed me. She may have blown off my concerns about her health in L.A., but now she let me in to share her fears.

Cate had stayed closed off. Never let me in. If Gwen let me in…

I set my lips against the curtain of smooth chocolate brown hair and whispered in her ear. "I can't stop thinking about what you did to me in L.A." When she released a slight nod, I said, "Just trust me, please."

When she said nothing more or didn't move, I worried there were other emotions lurking under the surface. Perhaps they would come out in time. I didn't have time. Didn't want any more time…to think…to wonder. I wanted to move forward with my life. *With* Gwen.

I exhaled and stepped back. "Fine, let's do this. Let's get this ugly part out of the way so we can get on with our life together. I don't want anything festering."

"Okay." She took a deep breath. "Did you even consider that I wanted to wait to tell you about what had been going on with me *after* I got to know you better? *After* I figured out that night in L.A. wasn't going to be another one-night-stand?"

I crossed my arms, certain there was more. And I had to let her get it *all* out.

"Meanwhile," she continued. "You climbed into my bed harboring your own secret. You were leaving me either way. When were you going to tell me, you weren't coming back to New York?"

"Oh, you were allowed to withhold information until after we had sex, but my doing it meant I was purposely keeping something from you?"

"That night in L.A. was a big deal to me, Andrew. Last year you disappeared, and I never heard from you again. How could you run off to Milan after leading me to believe I meant something to you this time?"

"You left my hotel room in New York last year

without even giving me your name. How was I supposed to find you?"

"I thought you were resourceful." She crossed her arms.

I sawed out a harsh breath. "I told you, I wasn't ready last year, I'm sorry. Yes, I wanted you then, badly. I saw you and I had to have you. But I couldn't give you anything else. Now I can. Now I'm ready." I pulled her against my chest, possession storming through me.

She sniffed and pressed against my coat. I could be intimidating with my height and my bulk. She also needed to know I could protect her.

"Please, don't shut me out, Gwen." My voice cracked as if a wall burst. "You've done that twice now, and I wasn't strong enough to stop you."

"What's changed?" She gripped my arms.

"I was miserable without you. With you, every day I laughed and felt happy and excited. Do you know I hadn't smiled, or at least it didn't feel like I had since that night in New York?" When she drew a breath, I moved a lock of hair out of her eyes. "And without you, I couldn't breathe. Sometimes you don't realize what a hole you have in your life until someone shows up and fills it."

"That means so much. But…" She flicked away the loose tear skidding down her cheek. "I can't promise you I'll *never* get sick."

"No matter what happens, I'm here for you." I held her tight. "This can only work if we open up to each other."

"I'm trying," she said, lowering her chin.

"We're in this together. This was meant to be. It has to be. You had a choice in L.A. Salvatore clearly wanted you. But you left the show with *me*. I was the one who ended up in your suite."

When her shameful eyes looked away, a burning sensation lit my throat on fire.

"Wait a minute." With a hand over my mouth, I asked, "Did you hook up with him while I was away?"

"He invited me to his apartment to watch the parade." She threaded her hands together.

"Yeah, okay, I guess I don't need to hear any more." I stepped back. Mentioning Salvatore flushed me with so much fury I could set the hotel on fire.

"Andrew! I didn't go. I'm not seeing him. I'm not *anything* with him."

I took a cleansing breath, fucking relieved. "Why?"

"Because I want *you*, you *jerk!* And I couldn't bear another man's hands on me after you. I didn't want it after New York, if we're being honest. Even if I didn't think I'd ever see you, or be with you again." She swallowed.

I smoothed my thumbs across her burning cheeks, and when the slightest hint of resistance from her body vanished, I lowered my head to claim a much-needed kiss. She met me more than halfway and kissed me back. Hard. I tugged her by the waist, drawing my hips against her stomach. Even through layers of cashmere and merino wool, she could feel my arousal, I was so big and hard at the moment.

Her kiss scorched my lips and tasted sweet. Her tongue felt so soft, yet powerful. Demanding, yet hesitant. The total and complete ease mixing with raw anticipation from what her body could do to me was an enthralling paradox.

We stopped kissing, but I kept my head bent close to hers, my eyes fixed on the blue pools of light I missed. I didn't want to sleep in that hotel after all.

"Gwen, what do I have to do to get you to come back to my flat tonight?"

She let go of a cool exhale and smiled. "Ask me."

CHAPTER TWENTY

Andrew

I paused at the door to my flat. Once I got Gwen on the other side, I wasn't sure what would happen. I collected my dirty thoughts spilling over like a pot of boiled water.

The months I'd spent alone in Milan before finding Gwen again had flown by, days melting into each other. Those two weeks apart, however, had scraped along like metal on concrete—smoking and clanging, leaving nothing but a piercing shrill.

Gwen grasped at me, clawed under my coat, her nails digging into my Prada dress shirt. I didn't care if she tore right through the damn thing. When her fingers repeatedly slipped inside my trousers, I couldn't keep a clear head. I hungered for her to the point we would both lose control.

I opened the door and the look on Gwen's face taking in the simple, but authentic Italian flat warmed me. If things didn't work out with Marcello, that place would be hers. Prada had flats all over the city. If she had to live in Milan, I wanted her here. I'd hire a bodyguard for her, too, even though the safe and secure building had many great neighbors. All hard-working, decent people.

And my new roommate would watch over her.

"Who's this?" she squealed, pointing to the cat sitting on the floor in the middle of the living room.

"That's Casper."

"That's exactly what I would name a black cat." She lifted the tiny bundle of fur into her arms. Cradled like a baby, Casper patted her cheeks with white-tipped paws.

"Yeah, I thought the same thing." I laughed, gently twisting a white foot around my fingers. "I think he likes you."

"I love cats. Dan was allergic." Gwen pressed her face against the small patch of white above Casper's nose. "How old is he?"

"I don't know. He belonged to a neighbor. But she died recently. Now he's mine." I smiled. "*Ours.*"

Her eyes rose cautiously after my comment. That simple word held a wealth of meaning. I hugged her and kissed her to relieve the fierce passion building up inside me. A gentle whine from between us interrupted the moment.

"Are you done with him?" I asked, sliding my hand under Casper's back.

"For now."

The cat's long body stretched as I released him to the floor. Casper pranced across the parquet squares and curled into a ball on a new bed filled with plush toys.

"He's as happy that you're here as I am," I said.

Gwen's mouth crashed hard against mine. Agreeing with that enthusiasm, I lifted her up. The way her legs immediately wrapped around my waist sent me into a fit of lust.

I carried Gwen to the bed I'd slept in alone for weeks wishing she were next to me.

♥ ♥ ♥ ♥

Gwen

Andrew's long strong arms surrounded my ribcage like a caveman carrying his woman. I even detected a grunt.

He put me down and twisted me around. Being

kissed on the nape of my neck made my legs rubbery. The man was so intoxicating. I couldn't hold back anymore. I turned around and slid my fingers into his thick hair. His arms came up, engulfing me as he kissed me with a sense of urgency, bringing a rush of heat to my face.

His tongue pushed past my lips, softly enveloping me in a deeper, more passionate kiss. My body softened with the sense of relief and warmth, even though I was still a little ball of need.

Sometimes half-dressed sex got me so hot, but I wanted to be naked and exposed. Andrew must have had the same thought. He ripped off his tie, undid a few buttons on his shirt, and then wrenched it over his head.

I reached back to slide the dress zipper down, but my arms weren't long enough. "Need. Help."

"Got it," he said robotically, duck-walking with his trousers around his ankles to reach me.

He unzipped the dress and kicked his slacks away at the same time. Someone else would have paid six hundred dollars for the pants he just chucked in a corner.

The same went for my dress. It was still a prototype, but others like it were topping twelve hundred dollars. I couldn't get it off my body fast enough. The soft jersey fabric slid down my legs and Andrew's hot furnace of a body leaned against me, clutching me from behind again. Oh, the heat and the power. The sense of him. He was so large, yet he moved so elegantly. Those modeling years went to good use. His form didn't belong to anyone else. It was mine. *He* was mine.

His arousal raged and pressed into my back. Begging for attention. Release. He bit and nipped at me while his hands roamed across my breasts. My bra straps slid down my upper arms, but I twisted around, letting him see the fabric drop away.

Andrew fell to his knees and I glided my hands along shoulders that went on for miles. What a specimen. He kissed my stomach like he worshipped me. After every press of his lips, he released a soft pant and then a moan. Relief in his breath.

He gripped the sides of my satin cheeky panties in his manly hands and slid them down my hips. He buried his face in every inch he exposed. Kissing, nuzzling, smelling, and tasting. He dragged the panties all the way past my ankles, and he gasped when I lifted one leg onto the edge of the bed. His fingers trailed back up, curving into the heat between my thighs.

My head fell back, the pleasure soaring through me. Andrew rubbed the sensitive nip of flesh that drove me to dream about that man. "Mmm. There, yes," I cried out, even though I had trouble breathing.

He may have lifted me up and put me on the bed, or I fell into his arms. I'd tumbled into a trance, a spell cast by his fingers. Circling, dipping, withdrawing my wetness and heat then massaging my throbbing center again. And again, until I was mindless, blanked out from the pleasure.

"Lay back," he whispered.

"No," I protested, rearing up on my elbows. "I want to watch you do this to me."

He kneeled on the floor and after a sly smirk, his tongue hit my skin. Scorching. I grabbed his hair, noticing he'd let it grow in since Los Angeles. So much of it tangled around my fingers. His tongue worked up and down, in and out, and along the sides of my aching need, slow and then fast. He clearly had no intention of stopping until I finished.

The thought of Andrew completing me that way sent rocket waves through me. A man who wanted to give me pleasure to the point of madness felt too good to be true.

"Andrew, yes. Right there. Like that. Don't stop. Keep—" My mind shattered into a thousand pieces.

Blood rushed through my ears. He didn't let up even after my orgasm. Any man who'd been with enough women knew how sensitive a clit was right after climax. While I pulsed and shook, Andrew kept feasting on me, even harder. More.

"I want you to come again for me," he rasped in between breaths.

Lost and wound up, I slammed back into the mattress. I was a short, half-lit fuse five minutes ago. Ready to blow, but now I needed time and he seemed to recognize that. He kissed the insides of my thighs, his fingers massaging my swollen nub again.

He pulled my butt closer to the edge of the bed and spread my legs wide. I wished I'd stuck with ballet to be more flexible. Cupping my ass, he tilted it toward him. He laid a full open-mouth kiss over my entire throbbing slit. His tongue flicked at the opening, swirling around sensitive skin.

I'm a dead woman!

All the while, his fingers massaged me with the same intoxicating pace he started with. Deep thrusts in, and then smooth swirls.

"Andrew," I cried out, biting my own fingers.

"Gwen, you're incredible. You feel so good. So hot, so tight." His tongue curled around the rim of my belly button, while his fingers did all the work. "I don't know how long I can wait. I *need* to feel you come again."

A man who didn't want to wait. Couldn't wait.

Needed it. It was too much. And for the first time *ever*, I came again, deeper and stronger than the first climax.

Holy shit! I'd been denied *that* all these years. My voice cracked and all I could get out was, "Yes. Yes, yes!"

After the second time he did stop and next his body blanketed mine.

"You're sweaty," I said.

"That's you, my dear."

"I have to do that to you. Please let me." I reached for his boxers.

"Wait." He treated me to an open-mouth kiss. The salty sweetness tasted so delicious.

My hand skidded down a long and sculpted torso. I'd futz with his nipples another time, I wanted to touch his hardness, feel what had been inside me last year, he'd been too eager to sink himself deep inside me.

Andrew roughly tugged down the fabric of his boxers until a massive erection sprang free. The startling proof of his desire.

Seeing his biceps earlier and not being able to touch them had left me aching to feel Andrew's skin again. I had every right to touch his muscles again now. Several dark beauty marks dotted the velvety texture of his skin. Yes, they marked him well.

The boxers clung to his hips. My nose trailed down his body, smelling him, kissing him. Woodsy and musk and fresh soap.

I bit at the tiny patch of hair sitting above his magnificent length, while my fingers massaged him.

"God, Gwen," he groaned.

"You better think of other deities to call out to." My tongue circled the tip which had already released a dab of translucent salty goodness. I lapped it right up and then in one quick movement, I took him entirely into my mouth.

His legs buckled as he groaned, "You're gonna kill me."

I released him in a slow torturous trail, trading my tongue for my lips. I stopped to say, "I can't kill you. I need you."

I repeated soft licks and swirls of my tongue, until my hair was being pulled so tight, it hurt. Hurt so good, though. He was so strong. Such a man. A real man. My palms took hold of him, my mouth made him so wet and slick.

He jerked again. "Gwen, unless this is how you want this to end, I suggest you stop." Bending down, he kissed my mouth roughly. "I want to be inside you when I come." He twisted toward his nightstand and removed a shiny foil packet from the top drawer.

While he bit it open, a move which made me gasp, I asked, "And when did you buy those?"

"Yesterday." He removed the condom. "After our call."

The idea of him leaving work to buy condoms gave me an erotic thrill. "You expected this to happen?"

He lurched forward—his large body made the bed scrape along the hardwood floor. "Do you always shave your legs and keep this soft goodness waxed?" His fingers slid along the smooth folds.

"Maybe," I laughed.

"I plan to spend a lot of time here." He kneeled against me and with the condom fastened, he settled at the base of my wet waiting notch.

At first, only the massive bulbous tip slipped past my knotted nerves. I still quivered from his mouth and hands. He leaned forward resting on an elbow to keep his face close to mine. His breath felt hot, and I loved dragging it deep into my lungs.

"Ready?" he asked with devilish humorous tone.

The short break brought things back into perspective. And reminded me we'd made it past a hurdle Andrew couldn't climb in L.A.

"You'd think this was our first time."

He drew me near. "I want New York to be *our* last first time."

"I want you, Andrew. All of you. *Please.*"

A tingling sensation rushed through me as he filled me, quick, and rough.

"God," he groaned into my hair. "You're gonna think I'm terrible at this."

"Why?" I panted, my chest falling as his rose up to meet mine.

"I feel so close the moment I'm inside you." His hips rolled in a perfect sweet rhythm.

"That's because it's been a while."

He kissed my lips. "No. I take care of myself daily. This..." He gasped for air. "This is you."

"*Daily*, huh?"

"It's how I'm built. It's always been that way."

"I'd like to see that sometime."

"That would be a waste."

"I'll bring you back to life."

"You already have, honey." He buried his face in my shoulder, his teeth gliding along the collarbone, nipping at my skin. "Oh God, Gwen. I'm coming."

He was so massive, his pulses felt like a vibrator. I slipped into my own orgasm. My third! I ran my nails down his back and yelled his name.

I took his orgasm and raised him one, my hips curling and circling to maximize his pleasure.

Increasing my own. Our tongues locked as our bodies spun out of control together in harmony.

When Andrew stopped shuddering, his head lifted, and his eyes squinted. *Daily.* I implanted that sight in my head to take back to New York.

He slid out, and I jerked again.

"Let me go toss this. Don't move." He kissed my cheek before he rolled off the bed.

"I'm not sure I can move." I stretched and propped up on my elbows to catch a glimpse of that Adonis of a man walking around naked. The sight of his tall lean body was as good as I remembered. With the lights coming in from the window, a halo shimmered against his pristine figure. Even from several feet away I saw him blush.

Out of curiosity, I leaned forward to peek into the nightstand that condom came from. I gasped. Gold foil packages as far as the eye could see.

"Holy shit, I'm in trouble."

CHAPTER TWENTY-ONE

Andrew

I woke Gwen up the next morning by climbing on top of her.

"What time is it," she moaned, holding my ass as I eased inside her. So hot. So tight.

"It's early," I whispered, taking long glides in and out of her. Slow and deep.

"Is this how I can expect to wake up all week?" she asked in between soft pants.

"If you let me. I warned you, this is who I am." I took a hardened nipple between my wet lips. "I think this is who you are, too. You just didn't know it."

"I wouldn't have wanted to be like this with anyone else."

"Good." That swelling, falling over the edge feeling came on again. I lasted a little longer that time. Each dive into her glorious heat, my self-control grew stronger. "*Ah-h-h*," I released, and properly kissed her good morning.

"Is there coffee?" She stretched, her pale body luminous against the faint morning light outside.

"Yeah, but we have to get your stuff from the hotel." My fingers ran across her stomach.

"Oh, right. Can't keep showing up in the same dress, can I?"

"Don't think of me as a pervert." I snapped off the condom, *wet*. God, she was soaked. "I would like nothing more than to walk you through that building, your hair all fucked up, your mascara smeared, your dress wrinkled—"

"Don't forget the limp from you riding me so hard."

"Oh, I didn't think of that."

"That will get me a lot of respect if I *do* become the brand manager here. Thanks," she commented wryly.

That reality bit into me. I didn't want to hold her back from her career. I'd rather see her rise the ladder in New York, so I'd be there to look under her skirt.

Just that thought made me hard. Again.

An hour later, I grumbled at the time. "We're gonna be *really* late. We still have to stop at your hotel."

Damn, why had I anxiously dragged her here last night? I hadn't even let her go up to her room to get her suitcase.

"And whose fault is that, Mr. *I-love-shower-sex*?" Gwen asked, combing her wet hair.

Instead of answering, I looked away, embarrassed. I was getting out of control with her. Was there a line I wouldn't cross? Could I push her too far, too soon? Of course, I could. That's what happened when I was in love. I went all in.

That reality stopped me cold. Made me shudder. Animalistic possession overtaking me.

Mine.

She stepped toward me and stroked my chin. "What's the matter?"

I cleared my throat and said, "Even if Marcello is gone and one of us has to live here, Gwen, I'm not giving up on the idea of us." I glanced around the flat. "We can make this work."

Gwen looked away and exhaled, considering my words. "I'm already drowning in debt from being out of work for so long. This job is helping. I don't know if I can add thousands of dollars in airplane tickets to my monthly expenses."

"I'll take care of all that. I have plenty of money.

Most people don't know…Cate…well she was very wealthy. Her share of the Reese family trust is now mine." I waited for her to flinch from my confession.

Nope.

"And you want to pay for everything because you're the man?"

Boldly, I answered, "Do you have a problem with me wanting to be strong for us and take care of you? The way you deserve to be pampered?"

She brushed my cheek. "When you put it like that, no."

"Money can buy private jets, but it can't buy time. I have more seniority at Prada. I have more autonomy to travel. Especially here." I sat on the edge of my bed. "We can do this. Trust me."

♥ ♥ ♥ ♥

Gwen

After leaving Andrew's flat, we walked one block north to get two steaming mocha lattes. Even the milk tasted extra fresh.

In the taxi, Andrew chatted about how the public transportation was fairly reliable, but he put an Uber app on my phone linked to his account for me. Then he put his head down to hide his frustration. Like it troubled him to think about me being in that city all by myself. It gave me pause as well. My family was an hour train ride out to Darling Cove. Anyone I needed and loved was just an hour away. Could I live so far from everyone?

After checking me out of the hotel, resisting a quickie on my unmade bed, we reached the office in time for Andrew's first meeting. He didn't let go of my hand, though. He strode through the Prada corridors with strong shoulders, proud that I belonged to him. If he were a new man now, it showed more than ever. He introduced me to everyone we passed. Everyone greeted me in Italian. I simply replied with warm nods and lots of *grazies*.

Andrew chuckled walking away from the creative director.

"What?" I poked his ribs.

"Stefania asked how the weather was in New York. She's going there next week. You said, '*thank you.*'"

The rest of the morning, Andrew whispered in my ear all the Italian I struggled to recall. For every word I got right, he treated me to a kiss. Talk about positive reinforcement!

All delight, enjoyment, and out-of-this-world sex aside, that was still a business trip.

Andrew parked me in his office and booted up his laptop. "I got an email back from the Paris team. They can do a call tomorrow morning."

"Right." From my work bag, I pulled out a spiral notebook.

"Um, ever hear about this thing called the computer?" he mocked me adorably.

I tugged his laptop and tapped on the keys the way he did, a series of one-finger slams. "When you learn to type properly—" I halted mid-sentence, my breath sucked in by a startled gasp.

Slapping the keys had opened a folder chock-full of photos of *me*.

The name on the folder shocked me even more. *My Gwen*.

I stared up at him. "What's this?"

"I took those in L.A," he said softly.

I checked the file folder to read the date stamp. "You'd just gotten back here and even though we didn't make love, you still considered me yours?"

"Does that scare you?" he asked quickly.

Without Andrew, the days in New York after L.A. had been suffocating and dark. Being with him now, that dead feeling got flipped on its side, cartwheeled, and split apart into a thousand unrecognizable pieces.

Thank God! Andrew had brought me back to life, too.

"It takes a lot more than that to scare me, Mister."

"Good."

After work, I settled in Andrew's flat, taking over most of the closet. He sat on the velvet sofa looking at dinner menus from local *trattorias*. I considered sitting next to him to have a look as well, but a wild burst of passion overtook me.

I stood and treated him to a strip-tease. I planned to give my body to him, so it wasn't really much of a tease.

"You're wearing Prada, woman. You can't be that uncomfortable." Andrew's jaw dropped watching me.

Stupid, adorable man, he thought an itchy dress made me want to be nude around him.

I sat on the opposite side of the sofa and spread my legs, wanting to feel the velvet upholstery against my body when he took me hard and good. If he got around to it.

"You can keep looking at those menus if you want. I'll be right here," I purred, touching myself.

Andrew tossed the menus in the air and loosened his tie.

"No," I cried out and covered his hand. "Keep it on. Keep it *all* on and take me."

Andrew's massive body sprang off the sofa and into the bedroom. He came out with a condom wrapper in his mouth and he lowered his zipper with anxious hands.

With his Prada slacks lowered just under his beautiful ass, he cupped my bottom and started a slow rhythm that exploded into blinding ecstasy. Twice.

♥ ♥ ♥ ♥

Andrew

During the conference call with Paris on Thursday, I kept shifting in my seat. Being with Gwen all day had a vicious downside. I'd been walking around half erect most of the time because I couldn't stop thinking about her. If there were a way to brand Gwen, I would.

By noon, her perfume had dissolved from my clothes and I needed to be on top of her again. Soon.

She stood and addressed the Paris sourcing team, pacing, like it was easier for her to think. I'd seen her do that back in New York. She commanded the conversation and drove me crazy while she did it. The tight pencil skirt showed off her figure a little too nicely. Damn, her curves made me melt. I wanted to sink my teeth into every rounded edge. She offered me an easy smile and a wink. Her soft demeanor, and the languid way she moved her hands as she spoke ate away at all rational thinking.

Watching her interact with others in that Milan office, other men, *Italian* men who clearly wanted her, unnerved the hell out of me. If she had to work in Milan, *alone*, she'd be hounded non-stop.

I pulled at my collar for air, watching her. Every breath she took and every rise and fall in the tone of her voice spelled her out perfectly to me.

I also got a handle on what I'd been feeling. The angst. The excitement. The craving. Love. I *was* in love. I recognized how love made me feel. What it did to my body and my mind. I'd been in love before, but with

Gwen it was different. It felt more complete. I had my family's back, too.

Yep, I was hooked. By the cattle prod sticking out of my pants, it was also clear I was branded. For life.

♥ ♥ ♥ ♥

Gwen

The fingernail splitting sex from holding the bed sheets so tight had been dinner *and* dessert that night for me and Andrew. Knowing we'd be apart soon made him feel like a meal I needed to shove in my mouth before the plate got taken away. He tasted like a deep soothing gulp of wine needed to melt the ache of our pending separation.

Before I got to Milan, I only imagined his life here, that flat, that bed. Now I had memories, real and raw to bring home and obsess over. The sight before me now — Andrew lying in that bed, face down, still naked with the top sheet resting just above his ass, stilled me. He made me lose my breath again and again. It hurt *not* to touch him.

I tugged the sheet away and ran my fingernails along the entire length of his body. Up his rock-hard calf, over his perfectly round butt, and across his back.

"Hey!" He squirmed and rolled over. "That tickles."

Much better view.

I straddled his hips and danced my fingers up his torso. His skin glowed with a sheen of sweat from our lovemaking moments earlier.

I loved how the hair around his navel darkened when it became wet. "Better?" I asked.

"No. You're going in the wrong direction."

Pressing my bare chest into his, I stroked his cheek. "Are you sure?" I smoothed the skin under his eyes.

"I like that."

I'd been ready to respond where else I wanted to put my fingers, but the sound of his cell phone cut me off. Understanding sometimes Prada came first, I unwedged his phone from between the pillows.

"It's your mother," I said, reading 'Ma' on the screen.

He swiped the call to voicemail and stopped the clatter. "I'll call her back tomorrow."

I had mixed feelings about him blowing off his mother for me. But we were naked with sweat still dripping from our bodies. My nipples were still hard, and Andrew's hungry gaze meant he was getting ready for another go at me. "Does she know about me?"

"Yes." Andrew smiled.

"And does she know I'm in the middle of a divorce?"

"I'm not sure I mentioned that. Only because it's not important."

I brought my hair to one side, the curled tips tickling my sensitive nipple. "I'm sure a woman who's been married so long might think of me as a failure."

Andrew sat up. "Your husband *divorced* you." He kissed me with an urgent passion I'd not felt before, then said, "You didn't fail."

Relaxing, I rested my head against his chest and asked the question burning inside me. "Did your mother like Cate?"

"No," he said, leaning back as his foot dangled over the side of the bed.

The answer floored me. How could he be so direct about something that had to be an issue in his marriage? Mrs. Morgan not liking Cate amped up the stakes for me. I had to make sure Andrew's mother would be on my side.

"If I had one complaint about Cate," Andrew began, without further prompting, "it was that she didn't even try to make my parents like her."

"Do you think they would like me? I mean, you went from a beautiful successful model to a…"

"To a what?" He looked confounded. "How exactly do you see yourself?"

"Just a small-town girl from the North Fork trying to make it in the big city." I watched in amusement as Andrew pondered where the hell the North Fork was. "Never mind. We're just getting started here. Who even knows—"

"I know. I know what I want. And I know what my mother and my father want in a…a wife for me."

"When you find her, let me know."

"I'm gonna ignore that." He pitched his body forward hooking my legs around his waist as raw sexual fury overtook him.

With a soft thud, I landed on my back. From the nightstand, he grabbed at the mountain of condoms. God, it was amazing to watch him roll one on. He was so long and thick. It was a miracle they fit. After several sweet licks of a tongue anxious to please me, he drove deep inside me, rhythmically rolling his hips.

The sex got better and better. He'd learned a lot about my body those nights in Milan, and I figured out all the secret spots that made him shiver. Running my hands from his navel to the pelvis drove him wild. I didn't even have to move further down. Oh, when I did, Andrew responded like he'd been lit on fire.

All week, I'd stolen delicate touches in the Uber and under his desk. He'd gone crazy when *I* decided I needed sex and stroked him to life.

There was so much of his body to study and enjoy.

God, how he filled me. Touched every inch of me. Ignited every nerve. His precise and measured moves were slow and torturous. That man knew what he was doing. Knew how to take me, to please me.

The rest of the night, we lay awake touching, caressing, and kissing. It was still early according to my body clock. I let Andrew eventually drift off into an easy sleep so I could watch him delicately snore. The covers tangled in his long muscular legs. Yes, he would be strong for me, for us. It was primitive, but very powerful.

As far as the confession about his money? So what? Dan had money, look where that got me. My career was my ticket to success. Not a man's bank account.

Andrew's chest rose and fell in dramatic high and low swells. I rested my fingers above his heart. The smooth easy beats pleasing to my touch.

Andrew rolled over, my body molding against his, our legs locking beneath the covers.

So, this is what forever feels like…

CHAPTER TWENTY-TWO

Andrew

In front of my office on Friday morning, I battled Gwen over who could tear ourselves away first. We played the in-person game equivalent of: *No, you hang up.* Except it was: *No, you walk in first.*

Finally, I placed a soft kiss on her lips, nudged her body inside my office, and closed the door.

I had work to do with Marcello. The guy had to get up to speed so Enrico wouldn't fire his skinny ass. A big hurdle was coming up. The yearly report of all the brands' activities and a projection for the following year was due by December thirty-first. That report had taken me months to put together my first year. Marcello didn't have months.

I'd have to spend the next two weeks drinking espresso well into the night using my old report as a template. After I showed it to Marcello, I was relieved to hear he planned to work throughout the weekend to get started on the report.

As for me, I had a better plan for *my* Saturday.

♥ ♥ ♥ ♥

Gwen

My body hurt on Saturday morning. Everywhere. Every muscle got stretched and challenged the night before the way Andrew had gone at me.

I'd arrived in Milan cautious and curious. Now when I left, I'd be heartbroken and in love. In love?

"Hey," Andrew whispered, smelling my hair. "I want to show you around Milan today."

I processed his words with two conflicting emotions. Relief. I needed a break. Soon, I'd start to disappoint him. Selfishness. I wanted to stay right there. Keep him to myself and not share him with a whole city.

My guttural instincts won when Andrew got out of bed and I clawed at him like a hungry lion.

"I created a monster!" he said.

"Are you kidding me?" I crushed him with my pillow. "I can barely move."

He pushed me down. "This is who I am. I love sex. I'll want a lot of it." He kissed my mouth and lowered to my bare breast. "Can you handle that?"

"Physically, I'm gonna need to start working out or something." My mind blanked as he moved further south. "Mentally? Yeah-boy!"

Sipping coffees from the corner café an hour later, I let Andrew lead me through his charming neighborhood. A stone church caught my eye and I considered stopping to light a candle for my mom. I wondered if that would make Andrew think about his wife. Was it still proper to consider Cate his wife?

Passing the church, Andrew grew tense and quiet, squeezing my hand to the point of pain. The way his head dipped squashed the idea of stopping there.

"I have to ask," I said to fill the silence. "If I'm leaving tomorrow, why are we spending my last day outside and away from your bed?" I nuzzled against his neck.

"I'm usually here alone," Andrew explained. "I always knew I would rather experience this city with someone special."

My heart squeezed when he said, *special*.

"I also want a life with you that goes beyond sex." His short and succinct answer left no room for follow-up or a discussion. His eyebrows dipped down, creating that dramatic expression he liked to lay on people to get what he wanted. "And I'm willing to sacrifice my pleasure, even in the limited moments we have to share things with you. That's the relationship I want, Gwen."

"Me too."

A sidewalk café still had tables outside even in the brisk weather. Andrew ordered pastries and espresso. Listening to him speak Italian still turned me on to the point I pulled at my jeans.

Drenched in winter sunlight, I eagerly scooped up the tiny cup and sipped the espresso. "Holy crap, *that* is so rich."

"Enjoy. Refills are free here." He leaned back and crossed his legs, watching cars going by. His square jaw and taut mouth made him look like he was posing in a photo shoot.

Short trees lined the quaint street. We could have easily been sitting on Center Street in Darling Cove. Andrew looking out at the simple neighborhood with ease and pleasure filled me with hope. Perhaps the tall, gorgeous, Prada-wearing ex-model wouldn't mind coming with me on my weekend trips to the laid-back North Fork. My dad's neighbors, however, would have a heart attack. I could hear the whispers: *Did you see the handsome man from New York City yet?* They really said, 'New York City' like in that old salsa commercial. I chuckled into my cup.

"Something funny?" asked the handsome man.

"No, but can I ask you a personal question?" I leaned forward. When a startled look crossed his face, I backpedaled. "Never mind."

He reached for my hand. "Of course, you can. I'm just surprised you prefaced it that way. After what you've done to my body all week, there's very little personal information I have left." He glanced down and cleared his throat. "Do you want to ask me about Cate?"

I bit my lip. He still didn't know I'd stalked Cate's blog and had all the info I needed. I'd been dying to know something else. "No, not right now."

"Okay." He took a relaxed sip and resumed his pose. "You can always ask me anything. So, what then?"

I tilted my head and asked, "I have to know... How did the whole modeling thing come about for you?"

Andrew's eyes flickered and he pursed his lips, suggesting I could ask anything, *but* that.

My chest tightened. "I'm sorry. I don't need to know."

"It's fine." He put his cup down. "But Gwen, is that all you see when you look at me? A model?"

"Of course not," I said, dumping my hands in my lap. After so much time studying his face, I saw beyond the crushing good looks and appreciated the man underneath. Small flaws made him real like the faded scar on his chin and the way his left eye tended to drift when he was tired. "I just suspect it's an interesting story."

He studied me for a moment and a small smile formed. I wanted to know why he made that career choice, and wanted to peel back the layers to prove my interest went beneath the beautiful surface.

"I was working in my father's law firm when I was in my junior year at NYU. Yes, my father had expected me to go to law school, and yes, he expected me to become a lawyer just like him. He was actually very cool with my career choice, though. Anyway, I'd been in the law library looking for something when one of the partners in charge of the entertainment side of the firm introduced me to one of his clients. He gave me his card and told me to call him."

"Which modeling agency?"

"Ford. What he proposed sounded interesting enough. I had the height and I was thin. My hair was a little longer then, too. The look was in demand at the time. I got a portfolio together and I started working almost immediately. Mostly runway stuff, some catalogs. The agent tried to push me to do commercials, but that included trips to L.A. for auditions. I liked the runway work. Then it got tedious. And the scrutiny... If you think this business objectifies women, wrap your pretty head around this one. The ratio of women to male models is six hundred to one. To say *male* modeling is competitive is an understatement."

What a journey, I thought. "So how did you end up at Prada?"

"I was in a show for Lanvin, and I met Enrico. We bumped into each other at other shows after that, and one day he asked me to lunch to talk about working for him." Andrew checked his phone for the time. "Enrico asked me brand-related questions. My major in college was marketing, so he must have done some research on me. I didn't realize he was looking for a brand specialist. But he wanted my take on Lanvin. I'd been modeling for them almost exclusively and knew the creative director well."

The mention of Lanvin made my heart spike. Cate had modeled for them. That must be how they'd met. Two married models. Wow. What a fairy tale *that* must have looked like. I swallowed and self-consciously touched my face, knowing I wasn't model-material. My follow-up question got lost in the back of my mind.

After a throat clearing, I found it. "Was it hard adjusting?"

He blew a large puff of air from his cheeks. "You

have no idea."

I'd only known Andrew in his brand manager role, and he owned the position with command and power. It showed in every facet of his marketing campaigns and strategies.

Before I could respond, Andrew looked lost in his thoughts. "Is something wrong?" I asked him.

"You're better at all of this than I am. You realize that, don't you?"

The unexpected compliment set me back. "I don't know if I would say 'better.' Maybe just different. We basically had the same education, and we both worked in fashion our whole careers."

A thought tickled me deliciously. Andrew and I could be a fashion power couple. *Prada's most beautiful couple behind the scenes.*

"Enrico wouldn't give you Marcello's job, if you weren't…"

The idea that I'd be the Milan brand manager had taken a backseat to the whirlwind romantic week with Andrew. What a boon for me. The whole point of walking away from Starlight Elegance was to propel forward and have the career I'd worked so hard for.

But what if getting the job I'd always wanted made me lose a man I never knew I needed?

♥ ♥ ♥ ♥

Andrew

I held Gwen's hand as we walked through the shopping district of Milan. I could feel her happiness and excitement. I loved how I could read her thoughts and what every curve of her face meant.

Her natural beauty and fresh even skin tone gave her face a warm shimmer. What frightened me was the striking beauty who emerged when she spent more than five minutes on her appearance. Part of her charm was that quiet beauty. I wanted to keep her that way.

Her golden highlights gleamed in the sunshine. I loved her hair...so long, rich, and thick. I adored how it felt in my hands, how it felt on my body when we made love. Gwen fit me perfectly. Like she'd been built for me. The way she easily snuggled against me, leaned into me, touched me without hesitation or concern if someone was watching got to me—drove me crazy. It had only been a few days, but I was convinced now that I'd fallen hopelessly in love with her. That should have scared the crap out of me. It didn't.

On Piazza Castello, I cupped Gwen's cheek. "I have a question for you."

"Okay." She secured her scarf. "Shoot."

I steered her to a bench. "Tell me about your mother."

At first, she delicately touched her lips. I studied the shape of her fingers, the smoothness of her skin. I didn't like that they were empty. Single women were targets in my opinion.

I stirred in my seat waiting for a response. "Gwen, if it's too difficult to talk—"

"No. Not at all. I just realized when I think of my *mom*, I think of how much she loved my father. I know that's boring and corny. But she adored him. She wasn't from the North Fork. They met in Chicago. She was a city girl. Her parents had money, but I'm not sure what happened. I think they didn't want her to move away. I don't recall having a relationship with my grandparents on that side." She stopped to take a breath. Her face reddened, and her eyes grew heavy.

I unfolded myself from the bench and stood next to her. "It's okay." The story bore some similarity to what had happened to me. How my parents had turned their back on me when I married someone they didn't like.

Gwen stroked my hand. "But my mom loved our town. I guess because it was so different from where she grew up. She was the typical strong, dedicated cop's wife. I already told you my dad worked all kinds of shifts. I never knew if he was coming or going, but my mom managed our schedules and his flawlessly."

So much that the woman had neglected herself. I'd make sure that didn't happen to Gwen. I kept those thoughts to myself, as she continued.

"Even when I was older and at the age where your parents being all lovey-dovey is kind of gross., what moved me was how her body just came alive when he drove by in his patrol car and blew his sirens just for her. She'd take whatever was in her hands and wave to him."

"That's amazing, Gwen." I smoothed the skin on the hand she'd been using to clutch her scarf.

"Are your parents happy?" she asked, returning the touch on my arm. "You're such a decent, honorable man. Your father must have had a strong influence on you."

Smiling at the warmth in her voice speaking about my dad, I said, "It wasn't as sugary as all that. Attorneys are serious and work long hours. My dad doesn't have much of a sense of humor. But my mother wasn't looking for a comedian. He gave her the life she wanted, and as far as I know, he's always been faithful."

"Everyone has their own definition of happiness, but it sounds like you grew up with two great role models."

"Now there's a modeling job I wouldn't mind having, right now." My words were meant to amuse her, but my serious tone made Gwen shuffle back a few steps. She'd been ready to respond, but I cupped her chin. "Why don't we get some lunch."

CHAPTER TWENTY-THREE

Andrew

I held Gwen by the waist as we walked to a quaint *trattoria*. Its dark paneled walls, the mosaic-tiled floor, and red patent-leather booths made me feel as if we'd been propelled back into the fifties.

I ordered wine while Gwen glanced at the menu. The serving girl with her short skirt and low-cut shirt gave me lustful looks, irritating me.

She brought the wine then ambled away from the table, still looking at me, making me uncomfortable.

Not Gwen. She sounded pissed when she said, "I think she purposely spilled the water on herself to have her own wet tee-shirt contest."

I didn't pay attention to women dressed provocatively. Especially in the presence of another woman. I felt it wise to note, "I hope she realizes dressing that way will get her attention she probably doesn't want."

"Or looks of disdain from your date," Gwen countered.

"Is that what you think you are? My date?"

Gwen responded with fire. "That's just it. She doesn't know that. I could be your *wife*."

I wished I had a mirror. I could only imagine what expression sat on my face. The 'wife' remark had fallen on my head like a hammer.

Gwen bit her lip as if she regretted her comment.

I reached across the table, and my heart spiked when she tucked her hand in her lap. "Gwen?"

Her other hand clutched the wine glass as she swallowed another long sip. Now I'd have to get that server's attention sooner rather than later for a refill.

"I have another question," Gwen said softly.

I sucked in a breath. "Sure."

A dark expression took over her features, and it alarmed the hell out of me. "Have you considered we may *not* be able to work this out?"

The weight of the words and the serious pout on her face forced me to actually consider it. "Okay," I said in a scratchy voice deprived of oxygen.

Gwen's face contorted, taking in the changes of my features. "What happens then?"

I swallowed a hard lump in my throat. "Happens?"

"The likely scenario is that I'm here. And that *occasionally* you'll travel here." Out of nowhere, Gwen fell apart in front of my eyes.

"Gwen, stop. Just stop this right now." My stomach twisted watching her.

"No!" She wiped her eyes. "How do I look at you then? I'm not making any promises—"

"I *am*."

"Don't expect a brave soldier sitting here on the other side of the world. You and Enrico think Marcello is doing a shitty job?" She finished her wine and collected her scarf. "Don't expect too much from me." She sprang from the table and rushed out through the door behind her.

I lunged across the table to grab her. My legs tightened ready to go after her, but I paused.

The inappropriately dressed server reappeared. *"Are you all right?"* she asked in Italian.

I clenched my jaw and took out a credit card. *"Bene."*

I paid the bill and stepped outside. The sun's sharp angle stung my eyes. Adjusting, I didn't see the blurry figure in a tan coat materialize.

"Gwen!" I wiped my eyes. "Honey, are you okay?"

She rushed into my arms, her head sliding under my jaw. "I'm sorry. I didn't mean to pressure you."

"That was hardly pressure." I cupped her chin to see her face. "You can always tell me what you're feeling or thinking. That's the relationship I want."

I kissed her lightly, but her tongue tickled my lower lip. I opened my mouth and took a full and thorough kiss that overwhelmed me with passion. Needing a breath of air, I rested my cheek against her forehead.

Before I could think, I said, "I've changed my mind, Gwen."

Her body hardened and she jerked away. "About what?"

"You'll see." I smiled and folded her hand back into mine. "*Taxi!*"

♥ ♥ ♥ ♥

Gwen

I leaned my head against Andrew's shoulder while riding back to his flat. Casper greeted us at the door and after treating him to a double dose of head scratching, Andrew and I charged into his bedroom.

Unbuttoning his coat for him, I breathed and spoke while kissing him. "We can see the rest of Milan another time, I guess."

"I've seen enough. I need to see you. All of you." He reached into his nightstand and took out a shiny gold square. "This is my last one. Let's make this count."

"I love how you think." I slid my coat off.

"I love—" He choked. "Um…"

I covered his mouth gently with my fingertips. "We'll find our way there."

"I love how *you* think." He wound his arm around

my waist, and he carried me to the bed.

After several more kisses, I stripped and dragged the covers aside to slip beneath the cool sheets.

Sigh.

As fashionable as Andrew always looked, watching him remove his clothes slammed me with a desire I'd never known. His coat eased down his long arms, and when his sweater was no longer in the way, I sat up to run my hands across tight stomach muscles.

I may have taken too long caressing the upper part his body because he shoved his pants down and stepped out of the puddle they created at his feet. Every inch of skin he exposed rushed me with more heat. His erection bulged through clingy boxers.

"Can I put the condom on you?" Without even touching him, I knew he was ready.

"God, I would love that." Andrew possessed my eager mouth and kissed me.

"You open it, though," I whispered. "I get so turned on watching you slice into these things with your teeth, like you can't wait."

"I usually can't," he mumbled with the packet in his mouth. He turned it over. "It goes on like this."

I snatched it from his hands. "I know how a condom works."

"Kiss me while you put it on." His command enthralled me.

Telling me what he wanted affected me in a way I didn't think I could ever shake. He groaned as I slid the thin piece of latex over his magnificent length.

There was no time for foreplay tonight. My body sizzled hot when he entered me. Fire spread through my veins when we became one. We connected as never before, sharing our passion for the act and the act alone.

"Oh, Andrew," I cried out, muffled against his shoulder.

"I know, Gwen," he said, caught between a sigh and a moan.

When he kissed me, I tasted the wine on his lips and his skin smelled like the fresh cold air from being outside all day. He lifted my leg to get the maximum depth. His long legs and strong thighs gave him the power to pull all the way out and slide back in. He teased me, running his hard, thick length across my aching flesh before sinking back deep inside me, hitting the end of me.

That was certainly the end. The end of any rational thinking about anything. I'd go back in debt for my man. Gladly. He was so worth it.

My body went wild, as a burst of energy soared through me. "I want to be on top."

"Are you sure? I'm close."

"So am I. I want to take you, make you mine."

"I am so yours, you have no idea." He rolled over, but his bulky body forced us to disconnect.

I leaned back, my greedy hands feeling for him. He felt slick in my hands and I slid him back into my aching, needy center, ready to throb and pulse at any moment.

"Wait," Andrew said, reaching down.

"It's fine. You're inside me." Sitting back, I spread my thighs wide, my body ready to tingle.

He grabbed my hips and rocked me back and forth. "Gwen, that is so unbelievably good."

My hands flew over my head, my fingers tangled in my messy hair. His palms roamed my body, holding my breasts, squeezing hard nipples in between anxious fingers.

"Yes. There. Right there," I moaned. "That's it. Yes.

Yes."

His back arched in a steep curve, sending him even deeper inside me. Andrew's orgasm reduced him to moans and groans. When my pulsing stopped, I fell onto him. His long arms came up and pressed my body into his. Tight.

He found my mouth and kissed me hard. "Oh, my God. That was incredible."

I dragged a deep whiff of his cologne into my nose. He smelled differently when we made love. A scent of pure satisfied male drifted gently from him.

A loud meow from the end of the bed drew our heads together.

"Someone wants dinner," Andrew said with a chuckle.

"That certainly worked up my appetite."

"I'll feed him and get the menus." He leaned forward and kissed my nose.

I gripped the mattress for a firm hold in order to climb down from Mount Morgan.

"Uh-oh," he said, staring at the bed.

I spun around. "What?

He bent down and from the center of the sheets, he picked up the condom. "It must have fallen off when you moved."

Feeling warmth between my legs didn't shock me. Or how wet, very wet I felt… "Oh," was all I could respond.

I snuck a peek under my lashes, thinking he'd be looking the other way. His eyes focused firmly on mine. The girl who only had three sexual partners was no condom expert. I'd been so caught in the moment, and so loved the idea of putting it on him, I didn't want to wait for a damn lesson.

"Is this a…" He swallowed.

"Is this a bad time for me, you mean?"

"Yeah."

I gave a dismissive wave. "No. It should be fine. I doubt I'd be …" I couldn't say the word.

"Oh, okay. Good. I guess." He closed his hand around the condom and took off toward his bathroom.

Once he was out of the room, I ripped my phone out of my purse. I kept track of my cycle in the online calendar. I found the little X from last month and counted to find what my *unsafe* days would be.

Oh no.

I wore a brave unconcerned face the rest of the night, the gloom of my departure the next morning overshadowed any worry of a sexual slip-up.

After a light dinner and a shower, where Andrew made me come with his mouth, we settled back in his bed.

My eyes were heavy, but I didn't close them. Couldn't close them. My head leaned against Andrew's shoulder while our fingers locked at the knuckles. He never let go of my hand. I focused on the silver lining in the situation: his return home in a couple of weeks.

He said he'd work day and night if he had to, to make sure Marcello's annual report would show Enrico he could do the job.

And if that didn't work…

We would think of something. We would make our relationship work. Somehow.

Andrew and I fell asleep that night in a tangle of sheets, legs, arms, and a happy, well-fed cat.

In the airport the next morning, I reached the line for security, but Andrew pulled me aside and kissed me gently while stroking my cheek.

"Gwen..." His face blanked, searching for a way to finish.

I swallowed hard, my throat dry. "Me, too." I had no idea what he couldn't tell me, but surely my face looked the same as his did. Sad. At that moment, *I* was the strong one. "I'll text you when I'm on the plane."

He nodded, tamping down his emotion. "I really want this to work, Gwen."

I smiled and kissed him softly. But in my mind, I thought, it just may *have* to work.

CHAPTER TWENTY-FOUR

Gwen

It'd been almost two weeks since I'd seen Andrew...and my period should have arrived three days ago.

I hadn't put additional worry on him, though. Andrew had enough stress with Marcello, but that night had been the worst possible time to have unprotected sex.

One slip-up had me in my bathroom for the last twenty minutes, peeing on pregnancy sticks.

"Give me another one." I stuck my hand around the bathroom door and waved impatiently to Kelsey. "The other brand. I can't believe this."

"Here you go." My roomie handed me a wrapped stick that reminded me of a popsicle.

The others rested on the edge of the sink, all positive. I stuck the new test between my aching thighs, set it beside the others on the counter, and waited.

Sitting on the edge of the tub, I clasped my hands together, a horrid memory attacking me. When Dan and I were first married, I became pregnant right away, but after two months, I'd lost the baby. The weeks prior had been a shit-show of morning sickness and headaches.

When I woke up that December morning with a churning stomach, the thought of telling Andrew I was pregnant gave me an even bigger headache.

My nervous fingers picked up the latest stick. *Just like the others.* Two little pink lines winked at me. I slapped them all off the sink, shooting them into the shower, cheap plastic echoing off the tiles.

"Am I opening another box?" Kelsey asked from

the hallway.

"No." I scooped up the sticks and opened the door.

"I hope you're going to throw those away." Kelsey scrunched her face at the five wet sticks in my hand. "They have urine on them."

"If these are accurate, I'm having a baby." I ambled into my bedroom and let the sticks fall into the trash one by one. "And I'll have more than urine all over me soon."

"All those pink lines and you're still not convinced?" Kelsey asked.

The last hour rocked my emotions all over the Richter scale. Andrew and I had spent an amazing week together with the promise of a great relationship on the horizon. Now, his hand would be forced. And I only had myself to blame for being so anxious and not letting him put the damn condom on himself.

I glanced down into the trash bin. "Oh, I'm convinced all right."

"Are you done being melodramatic? Come here." Kelsey hugged me. "A baby. You're having a little baby!"

"Andrew is six-foot-four. I don't know how *little* this baby will be." As if there weren't enough to worry about.

Kelsey released me. "When are you going to tell him?"

I dropped onto my bed face first. "He's four thousand miles away. Should I text him the good news?" I'd heard the term *Expectant Father*. What about an unexpectant one?

"I agree, you should tell him in person." Kelsey sat on the edge of my bed and bit her nails. "When is he coming home?"

"Christmas Eve."

"That's some present, Gwen."

"Surprise!" I mocked.

Kelsey sighed and dropped her head. Good grief, she thought there'd be a screaming baby in that apartment now. The woman was a saint for letting me stay there for free. I wouldn't cramp her and her boyfriend's naked Sundays with an infant.

"Um, Kelsey, I'll arrange to live with my dad," I offered.

She gave me an odd look. "Why? I mean…" Her head shook. "It's just that, Brian and I have been talking about…living together."

What better place than a free awesome apartment on the cool and trendy Upper East Side of Manhattan.

My cheek ticked up. "Me getting pregnant was sort of meant to be then, huh?"

"There you go. That's positive thinking."

Only, the commute to my office every day from the North Fork was ridiculous. Nothing positive about that.

Still the news was overwhelming and I needed my sister. She'd put a different spin on everything.

"What?" Skye blurted into the phone, sounding definitely *spun*.

After a short and sweet and *clean* version of Andrew and I *kissing and making up*, I said, "You're gonna be an aunt."

"Cool. Did you tell him?"

"No. We just worked things out." I stared at my ceiling. "Now I'll never know."

"Know what?" my sister asked.

"How he really feels about me."

"What do you mean?"

"This will force his hand," I pointed out.

"I don't think guys think like that anymore," she said.

Not wanting to get into a women's lib debate, I strained to look at my alarm clock. "So that's the latest. I'm getting hungry."

"You're eating for two!"

"Great." I felt like an elephant in my office already. No one there was pregnant. It was all size-two stick figures. If anyone was pregnant, I couldn't tell.

"When you come home Christmas Eve, I'll give you some TLC. Casey's good for kisses."

I smiled thinking of getting licked to death by a Golden Retriever. "Sounds good. I'll call you toward the end of the week."

"Okay. I assume I'm not telling Dad or Greg?"

"Do you want to see our brother lose his chance to get in the FBI when he tries to strangle Andrew?"

"Our brother is gonna strangle *someone* because Faith has been back in town for three months and it has the big dope on edge. He's painful to be around." Skye's passion on the subject shocked me.

"Maybe we need to figure out how to get those two in a room together," I said, thinking it'd be great to put Greg and Faith under the spotlight so I could quietly have my baby out of wedlock.

"Maybe hell will freeze over first." Skye scoffed. "Okay, Casey needs a good walk. Talk to you soon. Love you."

"Love you, too," I said and hung up.

Christmas Eve was in a few days and Andrew arranged to fly home for the holiday. He needed the week to work on his report. His and Marcello's projections were due on the thirty-first. He initially sounded optimistic about Marcello's progress.

Andrew's tone, however, had since turned grim.

I mashed my wet face in my pillow. Wrapped up in Andrew's arms that week and making love again and again, the distance had been easy to dismiss. Reality had been a cruel bitch since I'd been back in New York.

Nine-hour flights made weekend getaways impossible and U.S. and Italian holidays rarely lined up. If I moved to Milan, it would be completely unreasonable to maintain a relationship or expect we could ever grow into a real couple.

Now I added a dense, sticky layer of complication. How in the world would we raise a baby together living on two different continents?

A whiff of cigarette smoke drifted under my door. I'd smelled it before. Brian's one and only flaw was a doozy. Kelsey must love the man to invite a smoker to move in. Or he was a stallion in bed.

My stomach violently rolled at the smell, though. I dashed for the bathroom. And I wasn't sure what time I'd fallen asleep, but it was on the cold tile floor.

"You sound so exhausted," Andrew said to me the next morning, when I called him from the office.

"The smoke just makes me queasy," I'd told him the Brian smoking story. Many people were nauseated by cigarette smoke.

And not just from being pregnant.

"I, um, don't like the idea of you being around a smoker, to be honest. You know, second-hand smoke, could um…"

He was probably thinking of my mammogram scare. I'd give Andrew the scare of a lifetime if I told him the *real* reason I shouldn't be around a lighted Lucky Strike. His concern for me, though, was sweet.

I'd been stressed all morning about how it would

feel to talk to Andrew, knowing I was pregnant and *not* tell him. That melted away when I found I needed him. Needed to talk to him. Hear his voice. Being hit with so many impending changes, the possible job in Italy, the baby, having to move out of my apartment, Andrew listening to me with concern in his voice, calmed my shredded nerves.

"Hey, um, are you in our office?" he asked, breaking me away from my thoughts.

"Yeah." And I loved how he still called it *our* office.

"Go to my desk and sit in my chair."

I'd resisted that. My basic black mesh task chair felt impersonal. Andrew's executive swivel had a high back, curved sides, and yummy leather.

I wiggled my butt against his seat trying to absorb any long-lost heat. Then I remembered Enrico had technically sat in it last. *Ugh.*

"Hello?" Andrew called out to me. "Open my top desk drawer."

"Okay." I slid it open. Messy. Shocker. "What am I looking for?"

"My spare keys."

Tucked in the back sat a batch of keys on a single stainless ring that made my jaw drop. "What are all these for?"

"They're for everything. My building, my mailbox, my apartment, my bike lock, my car, and my parents' apartment on Fifth. I want you to stay in my apartment until I get home."

I'd heard a major movement in a relationship was when a man gave a woman a key. *A* key. Andrew was handing over his life. "I don't know what to say. This is very trusting of you."

"You sound surprised."

"With great power comes great responsibility," I joked, closing my fingers around the heavy key ring.

Andrew chuckled. "Call me tonight when you get there, okay, honey?"

I sighed at his endearments.

Greg and Dad's overprotectiveness grated on my last nerve, but Andrew's robust sheltering felt different. It felt primal and dominant and he made me feel...cherished.

"But you'll be asleep," I pointed out the flaw in his plan.

"That doesn't matter. Call me. Okay, Ms. Foley?"

"Mallory."

"What?"

"I signed my divorce papers. In a few months, I'll be Gwendolyn Mallory again."

After a brief silence, Andrew gave his usual response, "Good."

I stirred, wondering if those keys meant I'd have to change my name...*again*.

The keys unlocked more than Andrew's apartment. I already knew that wasn't where he'd lived with Cate. In the blog, she'd mentioned a snazzy midtown duplex. Andrew's new apartment was downtown. It was a typical pre-war layout with a narrow galley kitchen, white ceramic tiles, and an open countertop overlooking the living room. On it, I placed the dinner I'd picked up on the way, as well as an overnight bag I'd packed up from my place at lunch time.

I wasn't sure how long I'd stay there. Just that...I wanted to be there. Have that piece of Andrew. I had my own anchor now.

On the far wall, a row of windows overlooked Seventh Avenue South. My gaze wandered down the dark hallway that led to his bedroom. I'd save that for last.

Take-out menus under magnets were neatly lined up on the refrigerator door. Sure, his desk looked like it had been grabbed by Godzilla, shaken, and put back, but that place was immaculate.

Thank goodness, though.

His scent lingered in every room, but the strongest traces were in his bedroom. Without wondering if Andrew would mind, I opened one of his bureau drawers and fingered through the pile of clothes.

The colors drew my attention. "Jets and Yankees, huh?"

While those weren't my favorite teams, Dad would love my man. "I hope he doesn't mind me putting some Mets and Giants colors in here."

I smiled and closed the drawer. He had to know I would snoop. He'd not just started dating women. Where to look next. Hmm.

Andrew's closet was filled with Prada shirts, pressed and lined up, organized by color. Very little white. Burgundy mostly. That looked best on him. My fingers glided along every piece of fabric. All those clothes had been on his body and they just sat there now waiting.

"I know how you feel," I said to a pair of pants. "You'll be on him soon. And me, too, hopefully."

Wanting to get a better look, I pulled on a silver chain to turn on the light. A splash of color on a shelf way up high caught my attention. A pink and lavender floral hat box wasn't very manly. It must have belonged to Cate. What could be in there?

Maybe Andrew just kept the box.

Curiosity burned through me. Looking up to figure

out how to maneuver that box down, my eyes were stung by the thousand-watt bulb he screwed into the fixture. *Okay, that's the first sign this was wrong.*

"I guess it doesn't matter how I get it down," I mumbled to myself, dragging his desk chair from the living room. The box sat so high up, I bet he just slid it in no problem. The chair wobbled as I jumped, trying to touch the box. "Great. Someone will find me dead right here, and he'll know what I did."

I huffed and reached up one more time, dislodging the box. It hit my head on the way down, popped open, and dozens of pictures rained down on me.

"Son of a bitch." I scrambled off the chair and gathered everything that had spilled out, checking under the bed so a year from now, he wouldn't find an old photo there, too.

Looking at the photographs, I watched the man I loved grow up. There were even some headshots from his modeling days. How young he looked! How *thin* he looked made me catch my breath. He'd been reedy as well when I'd met him, both times. Now his face had filled out and the muscles on his shoulders no longer looked like they'd been strangled tight. In my hands, was the old Andrew. Thin and unhappy.

Way at the bottom of the pile were the pictures I really risked my life to see. The ones of him and Cate. That pile didn't match the chronological order of his life. The heartbroken Andrew tucked *those* photos away.

A brown envelope sat in the middle of the batch. I peeked inside. "Yikes." My hands shook, going through images of Andrew undressed and in a compromising position with another woman.

It should have bothered me, him keeping these pictures of Cate, but I understood that throwing out reminders of someone he once loved must have been difficult.

Going back to the more *respectable* photos, I saw how Andrew had matured during that relationship. Cate was as beautiful as I remembered from the blog. The evidence of the ideal couple I'd conjured sat in my hands. Lanvin's top models. Fashion's original power couple. A tall, stunning blonde next to an even taller, gorgeous, dark-haired man. They looked happy. Natural. Like they *belonged* together.

Sifting through photos where Cate looked absolutely fabulous begged the question, why had Andrew chosen one of her looking so sick to keep on his desk? Why remember her like that?

It was one flawless picture after the other. *Ho hum.* Where did I fit in the equation? I'd known my whole life I was pretty. Cate Morgan was another level. *This* was beyond me.

I shook my head and placed everything back in the box. Tomorrow, I'd get a forklift and put it back. Back where it belonged. Cate's memory had been tucked away in a box. Stored up so high, even Andrew needed a ladder to look back.

I'm here in his bed, and I'm having his baby.

Did Andrew even *want* kids? There *were* people out there who didn't. I was pretty sure Skye was one of those people. And men, too. There were men who didn't do the right thing by pregnant girlfriends.

What if everything I thought I knew about Andrew was wrong?

Burning on that last thought, I tossed and turned in Andrew's bed until dawn, too many horrible *what-if* questions taunting me, fracturing me, my mind racing and running away with my sanity.

The anchor yanked out...

Every passing day until Christmas Eve, I drifted further and further from the idea that Andrew would want to raise a baby with me.

CHAPTER TWENTY-FIVE

Andrew

I had to run to make that damn plane to New York. Grinding holiday traffic delayed my transport van to the Milan airport. I'd have run all the way back to Gwen if I could. Being without her those past two weeks made the hours crawl by. She'd gotten under my skin. Over it *and* under it. In the best way possible. I didn't think I was capable of connecting to her the way I had.

On the plane, I settled into my seat and thought back to those past few days. I sensed something was wrong with Gwen. The distance must have been hard on her as well. It troubled me how the days apart may have torn her down. She'd brought out the best of me, bringing back the man I used to be. I wanted to do the same for her. I looked forward to hours of getting under *her* skin…and over it…and inside it.

While I had no idea what would happen with the Milan brand manager position, one thing was certain, Gwen and I *were* going to be together, one way or another. I'd fallen hopelessly in love with her. There was only one thing to do when that happened…

When I got off the plane in New York, I checked my messages and breathed a sigh of relief when Marcello confirmed he'd seen the marked-up draft of his year-end report on his desk. I only hoped the red ink wouldn't frighten him: *Change this. Research this better. Spell this correctly.* It would come down to a razor-thin wire, whether or not I'd gotten through to him enough to make the proper projections for the coming year.

What would Marcello have done if I hadn't been there to help him? That thought stopped me from running to JFK's baggage claim.

"What if I weren't *here*? What if there was no brand manager in New York?" I asked myself, fumbling with my zipper in the men's room.

Enrico had tipped his hand: *I need you in New York.* If I quit, my boss would *have* to keep Gwen in New York. Being unemployed wasn't the best Christmas present I could offer Gwen, but I hoped my grandmother's engagement ring would make up for it.

And I had plenty of money.

My mother's support mattered so much. In Sarah Morgan's usual style, she'd planned the whole thing for me. She'd told me to bring Gwen to their apartment and on the Christmas tree there would be a little mini stocking with her name on it. Inside, Ma had hidden the ring.

"You'll have to change the setting," she'd suggested. "Today's woman needs something more sophisticated."

If I didn't get home in time, Ma would have that all picked out, too. That made me smile, being caught in between two strong women.

The airport buzzed about a blizzard coming to New York. As usual, the weather models varied. Some said it would hit tonight, some said tomorrow. Others said not an inch would fall. Still, if all went according to plan, I'd get to Prada just when the holiday party was winding down. After a brief chat with Enrico, I'd take Gwen to meet my parents.

I chose not to tell her anything about my plan and kept it a surprise.

Oh, I couldn't wait to see the look on her face.

♥ ♥ ♥ ♥

Gwen

I frowned at the flurries of snow while the Prada holiday festivities went on behind me. My face hurt thanks to all the European style kisses, especially from Italian men with thick, overgrown five o'clock shadows. The virgin eggnog I'd been nursing tasted too sweet and left a fuzzy feeling in my mouth. I'd poured it right from the container since the bowl reeked of alcohol.

The party showed no signs of winding down. By seven p.m., most people were hammered because they'd started drinking after lunch.

Big fluffy chunks of snow swirled outside the window of the second-floor lobby. A white Christmas had always excited me. Except, I had a long train ride to the North Fork after the party. The two feet predicted for tomorrow on Christmas Day would bring the suburban line to its knees. Unlike New York City, which didn't shut down. Mostly. It took a terrorist attack, a blackout, and a hurricane so bad-ass it was called a superstorm, to bring my city to a halt.

Andrew's plane had landed according to Alitalia's website. He'd been tight-lipped the past couple of days about his plans for the holiday. I couldn't find any real intimacy with him over the phone, either.

Perhaps if I'd told him about the baby. He'd been so preoccupied with Marcello's report, sometimes it'd been hard to get a word in.

I came up empty in the planning department for how to tell him I was pregnant. I considered putting the pee-sticks in a box, but that seemed cold. And gross. Every other idea of how and when to tell him ended up as crumpled pieces of paper in a wastebasket.

His plan included getting to the office, meeting with Enrico...and nothing else. He hadn't even asked me what my Christmas plans were, so I assumed he'd be spending it with his parents. As far as I could tell, he had no intention of being with me for the holiday.

And why should he? Who *was* I? No one, except the mother of his child. But he didn't know that. I left Milan with a promise we'd be something, some day. No rush. And I'd been okay with that. Heck, I didn't even know if I'd still be living in New York.

A thought violently shot through me like a knife in the chest. What if Enrico *already* planned to fire Marcello and Andrew knew that? That meant my boss would offer me the position in Milan. Andrew had been in the fashion business and worked for Prada long enough to know I would be insane to turn it down. Perhaps not mentioning plans for the holiday suggested he chose to distance himself from me. Maybe he had a change of heart after thinking things through. And in his mind, he probably thought he was doing what was best for *me*. Plus, the last two weeks of separation may have convinced him the distance was just too hard.

Or perhaps…I wasn't worth it. Not worth the trouble. Or the money to travel, even though he had so proudly offered to bear the brunt of the expenses with his new found wealth.

Fear, doubt, and anxiety circled me like the drifts of snow outside, creating a vortex of panic so strong that before I could stop it, I began to sob.

How could I face Andrew like that? A dab under my eyes confirmed my mascara had smeared. No. I couldn't handle seeing him. I needed to leave. *Right now.*

I turned from the window, but the elevator opening stopped me in my tracks. The arrival bell sounded louder than I would have expected with a lobby full of voices and laughter. It rung out with an extra metallic shrill. Daunting and foreboding. A sensation crawled down my spine, leaving my extremities cold. The doors opened, and Andrew stepped out of the car.

My heart splash-landed into the milky eggnog sitting at the bottom of my sour stomach. I stood on the other side of the lobby with at least a dozen people in between. Yet I saw him as if everyone else had dissolved away.

He hadn't noticed me, though. His head pitched downward like he wanted to wander in unnoticed. *As if* a gorgeous man of six-foot-four could ever pull that off. Even at Prada. Perhaps he didn't even want to see me...at all.

Feeling frantic, I slid behind a rack of coats, peeking through a dark gray trench and a fuzzy fur coat that looked like it'd been made from a litter of Cavalier King Charles Spaniels. A line had formed for Andrew, mostly female. The way they all smoothed their hair and checked their teeth made me sick.

Andrew's chin rose when Enrico waved to him from the other side of the room. His tall body moved with grace and elegance. Even after a nine-goddamn-hour plane ride.

He and Enrico chatted briefly. Andrew mostly listened, his head bobbing at whatever Enrico said to him. A moment later they marched down the corridor and toward Enrico's office.

In a flash, I raced to my office and gathered my things. I slipped back into the corridor and raced to the west staircase, not wanting to wait for an elevator.

Steps away from the stairwell door, a voice called out to me, making me spin around.

CHAPTER TWENTY-SIX

Andrew

I sat in Enrico's office, antsy and full of concern. Where was Gwen?

I'd played it out in my mind. I would step off the elevator, and she would be there in the middle of the holiday party. I would rush to her, pull her into my arms, and kiss her senseless in front of everyone.

She was nowhere to be found. It wouldn't have been surprising if she'd been in our office, working away. Her impressive commitment turned me the hell on.

I'd tried to make it to our office, but got swarmed by other women. Then Enrico found me. Hopefully, he wouldn't take too much more of my time.

I had a woman to propose to!

"*Bene.*" Enrico closed his office door. "So, now we are alone, tell me, how is our friend Marcello doing?"

"He's coming along. His report will be on time. And so will mine."

"Andrew, *you* I am not worried about." Enrico waved his hand. "Your report will be stellar. I am certain. You are irreplaceable to me, Andrew. Please do not ever let anything that happens make you feel otherwise."

The sentiment swelled me with guilt, considering I was now scheming to quit in my own power-play if the Prada gods dragged me away from Gwen.

"Enrico, Marcello *is* doing better." I leaned forward. "He's not where I think he should be. Perhaps if you give him more time. Give *me* more time with him. Maybe another month?"

"But Andrew, this has been dragging out long enough, yes? Let's wait to see what his report shows. That will tell me if he has a full grasp of his job or not. And whether or not we need to replace him."

I swallowed a bitter lump. "With Gwen? Is that still the plan?"

"She has proven herself extremely capable. With the Milan position not operating at its fullest potential, do you think we have time to vet another candidate? That would mean more trips for you. And do you want to train someone from scratch all over again?"

"What if…" I cleared my throat. "What if the position went back under the creative director? Maybe we bit off more than we could chew."

Enrico leaned back, his chair squeaking. He tented his fingers and looked away. Even though I'd thrown in the "we", Marcello reporting to New York had been Enrico's doing.

I'd just insinuated my boss had made a massive blunder. Maybe I wouldn't have to quit. Maybe I'd get fired. My jaw clenched, and I prepared to backpedal.

Enrico narrowed his eyes across the hall to my and Gwen's office. Had he seen her? I glanced in that direction and exhaled. Nothing. I tapped at my phone hoping to see a text or call from her. Nothing.

"All right," Enrico finally said. "I will take everything into consideration, and *we* will make a decision by the end of next week."

I shot to my feet. "Good. I think in the end it will all work out. For everyone."

"You like her, don't you?" Enrico stood as well.

"Um, Gwen? Yeah. Sure." I loved her, but kept that to myself.

"I knew you would like her." Enrico waved a finger

at me and smiled. "I may be an old man, but I can tell what's best for you."

My heart fluttered. Did Enrico know what'd been going on? Before I left, Enrico added, "She has done well for us here at Prada. She has a bright future. I thank you for working with her and showing her what it means to have our standard of excellence."

I released a sharp breath. Business… Enrico was talking about business. Now I needed to get to my *pleasure*. "Merry Christmas, Enrico."

"Same to you. Give your mother my best." Enrico winked.

I narrowed my eyes, but smiled back.

While standing in front of Thalia's desk, I called Gwen. *Pleasure*. That's what I needed tonight. Deep, sweaty, grinding, fingernails-scraping-down-my-back pleasure with the woman who hopefully would agree to be my future.

♥ ♥ ♥ ♥

Gwen

"Salvatore?" I turned at the sound of the designer's voice.

"*Bella*, you are leaving so soon?"

I exhaled. "Yes, I have a long train ride to the Island. And my *name* is Gwen."

After a grunt, he said, "American women are too hung up on such formalities."

"It's called respect," I said, backing up closer to the stairs.

"You know, I am going to my house on Lake Como for New Year's Eve. Perhaps you would like to join me, yes?"

The hand on my arm may have blazed with Salvatore's heat, but a man other than Andrew touching me made my stomach heave.

Since I hadn't answered, Salvatore must have assumed I considered it. "At midnight, the lights in the sky burn brighter and with more brilliant *colores* than your Fourth of July. Come with me…Gwendolyn."

Lake Como. *Really?* Many women would kill for a tumble with Salvatore on one of the world's most beautiful lakes, but I released a snort of laughter at the absurd notion I'd run off with him.

"The idea makes you giddy, Gwendolyn?"

I smiled and put my hands on my hips. "I'm sorry. I can't go to Lake Como with you." I turned around and initially thought I didn't need to respond further. To make sure he never propositioned me again, though, I added, "I'm in love with Andrew Morgan."

Running down the stairs, I stifled a new choking sob, thinking Andrew may not feel the same way about me after all. My boot heels clicked against the concrete, sending an eerie echo all the way down to the main floor. When I got to the street level and fled out the service entrance, my phone blew up. *Andrew.*

"What am I doing?" I asked myself, my heart pounding.

With shaking hands, I answered the call, but sloshed down the street to catch a taxi on the West Side Highway.

♥ ♥ ♥ ♥
Andrew

"Gwen! Where are you?" I cried into the phone, ecstatic to hear her voice.

"I'm on my way home," she said over muffled street sounds in the background.

"What?" I spun around and headed to our office.

"What do you mean you're going home?"

"The party was winding down. When I didn't hear from you, I thought maybe your plane was delayed."

A shudder soared through me, but a sense of calm relaxed me. "Oh, you're going back to my apartment?" I hoped that's what she meant by *home*.

"Oh, no, sorry. Home, to my dad's house on Long Island," she said firmly.

Startled, I snapped, "Gwen, it's Christmas Eve. I just got back into town."

"Uh, yeah. I figured you'd be with your family."

Stunned, I couldn't think of how to respond. I covered my mouth with my free hand.

Gwen then said, "You didn't say anything about us getting together, so I figured I would just see you on Wednesday." She sounded even further away.

I fell against my office door slamming it shut. I hadn't said anything. She was right. How stupid of me to assume *she* would assume we'd be together. It didn't matter if I'd had a whole damn surprise waiting. That's the fucking nature of a surprise. Still, I should have made it clear I expected to *be* with her. The ring was enough of a surprise.

It occurred to me, however, if Gwen hadn't expected to see me for the holiday, how would a ring go over?

"Hello? Andrew, are you still there? Do you need to get going?"

I shook my head. "No. I mean yes. I need to get going." *To the North Fork to be with you.*

"Okay, I'll see you in a couple of days," she said through harsh breaths and then the phone went dark.

"Not exactly, Gwen," I said, getting to my feet, but I faced the window and cringed. The blizzard. *Fuck!*

CHAPTER TWENTY-SEVEN

Gwen

I could hear a pin drop in Darling Cove. The twenty inches of snow that had already fallen sound-proofed the whole town. The train had stopped at so many additional stations along the way, I'd lost track of the time, I just knew it was very late.

Center Street's lamp posts sparkled in gold and green lights and the houses on the side streets also glistened brightly with twinkling colorful beams. Small town charm.

My boot heels crunched under the fresh snow as I passed on a taxi in favor of walking. The place I wanted to be was only a few blocks from the train station.

Midnight mass at St. Mary's always drew a big crowd. The man waiting outside the church drew me in. Seeing Greg pacing on the sidewalk, I smiled until I realized I was keeping a secret from him and my dad. "Why are you waiting out here? The mass has already started, right?" If Skye told Greg I was pregnant, I'd march into that firehouse and tell gorgeous *Santa* my sister had the hots for him.

"I wanted to wait for you. Is that wrong?"

"No, not at all." I could use the pampering for one night.

"Let's get inside, it's—" My brother froze and his eyes glazed over my shoulder.

"Mom, I'll go get us seats," a sweet voice called out from behind me.

The voice registered. Loud and frighteningly clear. I turned around slowly. "Faith?"

Faith Copeland, Greg's ex-fiancé and runaway

bride stood there looking pale against her green swing coat. Her jaw slacked open staring at my brother. Her first love.

I spun around to him. "*Talk* to her."

He just stared at Faith, his mouth tight, and it pained me to see how hard he was breathing.

I spun around to Faith. "*Talk* to him." Gazing between them, I said, "One of you, *please*, say something." Facing Andrew in Milan and being brave enough to ask for what I wanted from him after everything we'd gone through gave me the courage and hope that Greg and Faith could get out of their damn way after the dark hole of the last five years.

Faith opened her mouth. *Finally!* It figured the woman would be brave enough, but she'd been the one to leave in the first place. "I have to go." Greg's ex turned around and staggered away.

Maybe not.

Mr. and Mrs. Copeland were off in the distance, Mr. Copeland clutching a walker, Mrs. Copeland clutching him.

Faith reached her parents and steered them into another entrance of the church.

That was small town for you. You could escape your ex all week, but then Sunday… Or Christmas…

"Greg, I'm sorry." I pulled on my brother's sleeve. "You know where she lives. Go to her house. Later. Tomorrow. Knock on her door. Do *something*. I hate seeing you like this."

Greg took a ragged breath and choked out, "I hate it, too."

My heart broke for him all over again. I pushed my way into his arms. "I love you."

"I love you, too, kid." He squeezed me and I could

tell he did everything he could not to look in the direction Faith had gone into the church. "Let's get in before the whole service is over."

He gripped my hand to keep me steady. My brother was the best man I knew, besides my dad. I nodded and wiped away a tear, every little damn thing made me weepy. I had my own love life drama and right now a Greg and Faith episode needed to be put on pause.

Every seat in the church was swallowed up by people I only saw on Christmas and Easter.

You know we do this every Sunday, the priest needled the hordes who filled up the vestibule and lined up against the wall under the *Stations of the Cross* figurines. His snarky comment always got a laugh.

Dad waved to us from a seat in the left section just past the break. With Greg behind me, I squeezed between the two men I loved. The men who meant the world to me. My throat went tight, thinking of where Andrew fit into the picture now.

"Where's Skye?" I whispered to Dad, touching his hand.

He pointed to the line of singers in front of the altar. Skye's face lit up when I found her. Many faces stared at my stunning sister. Most notably, a shine from blue eyes standing against the wall. Edward Mendelsohn! In the yummy flesh. He looked every bit as powerful and gorgeous as a fire chief should be.

Skye zeroed in on one heck of a hunk. God, in person Edward was breathtaking. Tall with dark auburn hair, full and rumpled. A little boy with the same color hair leaned against Edward, but I didn't spot a woman with them. Was he a single dad?

That's what I got for moving away. All the hidden gems sparkling in a small town.

The choir finished their hymn. My reveries drifted in and out of time. Greg's hand brushing against mine made me think of him and Faith, and what would have been, *should have been.* Edward watching Skye made me think of what could be someday.

Threaded in between, mine and Andrew's uncertain future blinked like a yellow traffic light. *Proceed with caution.*

The songs were about hope. I *hoped* with the ghosts of love past, present, and future, I too could find my way to happy ever after.

After the mass, Greg shifted on his heels outside the church, his cop eyes combing the place. For Faith, no doubt. I hoped the jolt would loosen his anchor and he'd get off the damn sandbar already.

He'd bought his own house several years ago and mumbling about an early shift tomorrow, he said goodnight.

His hug felt tight and yummy. "Merry Christmas, handsome." I touched his face, round with cheeks that curved so nicely when he smiled.

"I'll stop by Dad's in the morning during my shift." My brother pecked my forehead. "Good night, Dad." Greg hugged my father and shuffled to the parking lot.

"'Night, Gregory." Dad watched him go, shaking his head with the same sense of heartbreak we all felt for him, especially during the holidays.

"Dad, I'm exhausted." I fumbled with my overnight bag, which he took from me.

"Let's get you home then."

Home. I felt so unclear about where home was for me. My apartment. Andrew's apartment. My childhood home.

No matter what, though, my dad always gave me

comfort. I looped my arm in his and we weaved through the parking lot until we reached his car.

We drove home in the new falling snow and on the front porch of the house, Dad kicked the snow off his boots. "Another year, pumpkin…"

A pang of sadness drew my hand to my chest. "I know, Dad. But she's with us."

I closed the front door and stared at the Christmas tree. Sighing, I switched the twinkling lights on. Mom had always kept them on all night for Christmas Eve. The only night the tree had been allowed to stay lit until dawn in the Mallory house.

I used my Christmas wish and hoped Greg had driven to Faith's house. Even if he were just staring at her bedroom window. It would take small steps to face the woman who'd devastated him.

A sob built in my throat, feeling their heartache and emptiness because it consumed me, too.

When I sniffed, Dad said, "Anything you want to tell me, pumpkin?"

I froze, fear constricting my chest. "Okay." I didn't need to be afraid. I was with my dad. The man who'd always love me no matter what. My lips parted, but the words caught in my throat.

Dad came up next to me and gripped my shoulder. "So, when *is* this baby due?"

I looked down and grunted. "How do you feel about having only two children?" More gifts for me.

He laughed and cupped my cheek. "Your sister was concerned about you, that's all. We all love you, Gwen. We want to protect you and make sure you have everything you need."

"You said at Thanksgiving I'd be your best shot at grandkids. But are you disappointed in me having one like this?"

"Of course not. And the father?" When I knocked my head from side to side he added, "He doesn't know, does he?"

"And you know that from years of detective work?"

"No. I can't imagine if a man knew you were carrying his child that he wouldn't want to be here with you now."

I took my overnight bag from him. "I'm afraid to tell him."

"Afraid he won't live up to his obligations?"

"I'll never know how he really feels about me."

"Is he a nice man?" Dad asked, looking hopeful.

"He is." I sighed, absorbing the reality of the situation. "I just don't know how he'll feel about this."

"You have to give him a chance."

"I know," I muttered as more and more tears built up.

Those intimate moments with Andrew had lulled me into feeling like we were the perfect couple. I didn't know how to navigate the confusing waters where I worried people might judge us harshly. *Oh no, they don't belong together.*

The sneering thought that might stream through people's minds when they learned Andrew was *staying* with me, committing to me because I was pregnant. *Oh, he's just doing the right thing.*

Dad broke the silence. "No matter what, pumpkin, I'm here for you. You can always count on me."

"I always have, and you've never let me down." I pressed my face into his chest, his familiar musk filling me, calming me.

"And don't you trust you would choose to be with

a man who has the same values?"

I thought about that. Women tended to pick men who had the same qualities as their fathers. Martin Mallory was a decent, loyal man. A man who showered his family with love. In Milan, I'd seen those qualities in Andrew and even commented on them. How could I let my insecurities make me think I'd been wrong about him? *Damn hormones!*

"You're right." My voice cracked.

"It's late. Let's get you and my grandchild to bed." Dad steered me to the staircase.

At my bedroom door, I gave him one more hug. He cupped my chin and said, "I'm working a morning shift with Greg then covering for a few of my guys later on so they can be with their families. But we'll talk at one point and figure this out. You're welcome to come home. There's plenty of room for you and a baby."

"I guess I have to consider where I'll live." I took a breath and didn't voice that it might be in Italy.

CHAPTER TWENTY-EIGHT

Andrew

By midnight, I read on my phone that the governor of New York had declared a state of emergency because of the blizzard and all the roads out to Long Island were closed.

Coming home without Gwen had caused a long, drawn out conversation. I was pretty much told, *You messed up, Son*. If my father, a head-strong, no-nonsense attorney who showed as little emotion as possible said I did wrong by a woman, I wasn't about to argue.

We just had a gross misunderstanding. Once I explained to Gwen what my intentions were, the woman who had revealed herself so intimately to me in Milan would emerge.

I slept at my parents' apartment and in my old bed, too tired to go all the way downtown. That's not the homecoming I wanted. I'd planned to bring Gwen there and make crazy love to her, hopefully with my grandmother's ring on her finger. Going there alone felt empty and hollow.

On Christmas morning, the roads opened back up.

"Are you even going to call her to let her know you're coming?" Ma asked, pouring hot coffee into a to-go cup for me.

"No, I want to surprise her," I said, locating a Martin Mallory in Darling Cove and assumed it was her dad.

Ma stopped mid-pour. "Hasn't that gotten you in enough trouble already?"

I raised a warning look at her.

Rolling her eyes, she said, "A least take the ring

with you."

Shaking my head, I bit out a quick, "No. I'm just driving out there to bring her back to the city."

"This Darling Cove got a lot of snow. Take my car, so at least I won't worry about you two." Ma handed me the keys to her Cadillac.

The roads should have been jammed, but the blizzard must have changed millions of plans for the holiday.

An hour and half later, I rolled down Sound Avenue, taking in the beauty. Even covered in white, the landscape was incredible. The storm dumped inches of heavy wet snow and all the trees looked like its branches were holding little snowballs ready to engage in a winter battle.

The white puffs of smoke from the houses I passed made me fondly imagine families opening presents, laughing, and snacking on cookies. Blankets of powder in front of all the homes were untouched, clean, and smooth.

My navigation app told me I needed to make a right in about a mile. Looking at the screen, swaths of blue on both sides meant I was surrounded by water. The little red upside-down teardrop appeared, and I tensed with excitement. There was my destination.

Gwen. *My Gwen.*

My home. My heart.

Turning down her street brought a rush of anxiety I wasn't expecting. I stopped to catch my breath and noticed a cop car idling in front of the house. My hackles rose, as worry crawled down my neck.

A man bundled in a cop's leather bomber jacket and hidden under a hat came out to the car. He released a quick siren blast and flashed his lightbar only for a moment and drove off. My cheeks ticked up, remembering Gwen's heartfelt story in Milan about how her father used to do that.

Her father! I slapped myself on the forehead.

I threw the car into drive and raced past Gwen's house to follow the cop. As the police cruiser drove through the town, I admired all the lampposts decorated in lights and wreaths. The North Fork and Darling Cove was not what I expected. Every corner dripped with elegant charm...like Gwen.

The car I followed turned and parked in front of a station house with several police cruisers. *Crap!* The cop who'd left Mr. Mallory's house got out of his car and took off his hat. That couldn't have been her father, though. Too young. *Greg.* I recognized him from the pictures. He became a cop...like his father.

I blew out a harsh breath, got out of my mother's Cadillac, and ambled to the steps of the precinct.

Inside, it smelled of fresh paint and metal. A man in a uniform stood behind a wood paneled desk, his hands resting on a polished granite countertop. The man threw a look at another officer and turned back to me.

"If you're looking for the Hamptons, you took a wrong turn about an hour ago," the officer said with a sly smirk.

I accepted I probably looked like the typical Hamptons visitor. "Actually." I wrung my hands to keep them from shaking. "I was wondering if I could speak to one of your officers."

"Who are you looking for?" a voice echoed from a side doorway.

I glanced to my left to see the cop I followed approaching me. "Greg?"

"*Officer* Mallory," the desk captain said in a stern

voice.

"Excuse me, yes. Officer Mallory. I'm actually looking for the *other* Officer Mallory."

"*Martin* Mallory is in the—"

"I got this, Carlin." Greg looked formidable in his long-sleeve dark-blue shirt and matching tie held down by an American flag clip. A gun on his waist, a set of steel handcuffs dangling from his pants, and a long brown stick tucked into another holder stood out the most. Greg's chin lifted defiantly to meet my eyes which were a few inches above his. "Who are you and what do you want with my father?"

If I'd not been surrounded by several guns, one of which Greg's hand rested on, my answer might have been a stout, *That's my business.*

Instead, I said, "My name is Andrew Morgan. I'm a... It's about your sister, Gwen."

Greg's probing words may have been tough, but his mouth curved, and his lips flattened. "Gwen? What do you want with my *sister*?"

Everything. "I'm crazy about her. She's a wonderful woman." I wanted so much for Martin to hear what I had to say first. That was the proper thing to do.

I had to improvise, for no other reason I wanted to get out of that station house in one piece and not end up on the news. *Man dressed in Prada gets pounded by North Fork police officers.*

I cleared my throat and continued. "I'm here to ask your father's permission to marry her."

"You have my permission!" Martin answered from the opposite corner.

I breathed in relief. Ignoring the others, I trekked toward Martin who beamed at the sight of me. "Sir, Andrew Morgan, sir. Thank you. I promise to make her happy, always."

"You better," Greg said, his polished silver badge gleamed with the light coming in from the tall windows.

I strode up to Gwen's brother in an effort to reach out to him. That guy was going to be my family. Hopefully. Martin's affable permission meant Gwen must have at least *mentioned* me.

Greg's curious gaze took me in. All of me. I was glad I shaved and dressed up. In my good cashmere coat, Prada slacks and a dress shirt, I looked presentable, even though I'd gone to bed a wreck. Gwen's brother and dad were cops. They'd want her taken care of. Protected.

Greg's green gaze trailed to my hand waiting for his and after a smile, he gave me an extra firm grip that made me wince.

I nodded and turned back to Martin. "I'd like to see her." I tugged on my coat. "I have a ring for her in the city."

Martin cupped my shoulder. "Let me give you an escort to my house. I think that would make up for a ring. Gregory, get your coat."

♥♥♥♥

Gwen

I yawned while making another pot of decaf coffee. My sister lounged lazily on the living room sofa. A fake log of fire burned on the television while Skye went through her Facebook feed, announcing all the holiday posts. Casey climbed up as well and curled in the crook of her knees. But the dog snapped to attention and began whining, prompting Skye to get up and look out one of the lace-covered windows.

"Hey Gwen, do you know someone who drives a cherry-red Cadillac SUV? I don't."

"No," I answered from the kitchen. "Probably someone who got lost going to the Hamptons."

"Wait a minute, there're two patrol cars behind it."

"Lights and sirens?" I came into the living room and petted Casey's head to calm her down.

"Yeah. I guess someone got pulled over." Skye let the curtain fall back, but took another peek. "It's Dad *and* Greg out there."

I shrugged at the odd coincidence.

"A young guy is getting out of the Caddy. Huh, I thought only geezers drove those things. Good lord, is he *tall*."

I joined my sister at the living room window. "Who is?"

"The guy. Wow. I can see from all the way back here, that man is *gorgeous*." Skye smoothed her hair and opened the front door. "Hey, there *are* crazier ways to meet people. *And* he may need a lawyer."

"Skye I wouldn't—" My eyes sharpened. That walk. Those legs. That jet-back hair. "Oh my God!"

"What?" Skye spun back around.

"That's Andrew." I yanked my coat on and almost got trampled by Casey barking and bolting out the front door.

"Casey, leave it!" Skye ran out wearing only a thin sweater, waving the leash.

"And you don't have insurance to cover a dog mauling, Skye," I mumbled to myself, slushing down the front walkway.

Skye clipped Casey to the leash and stared at Andrew in amazement. He leaned against his car with his hands in his pockets. *That's* his car? His face was even. Greg and Dad's cop cars hovered in front of the driveway, their blue and white lights flashing. They had their doors open, already getting out.

I spun around in confusion. What the heck was happening? A wave of dizziness passed through me and I began to slip in the snow. Andrew rushed to my side first, even though Skye had been closer.

"I've got you," Andrew said, his voice low. "Gwen, it's me. What's wrong?"

I swelled with fear of losing Andrew, so my instincts told me to push him away. "There's nothing wrong. I thought we were just spending the holidays with our families."

"Gwen," he said, moving closer. "I expected to see you last night *and* today. I just never said anything because I thought it was understood. After that incredible week we had and what we did…in Milan."

"I can't believe you drove all the way out here," I said.

"I can't believe you thought I wouldn't."

I squinted at my father. "And you just randomly pulled him over?" Then I turned to my brother. "Both of you?"

They exchanged odd glances. Greg pressed his hat down. "No. We were having coffee at Sadie's and he came in."

"Yeah," Andrew said. "I stopped to make sure I was going the right way and I recognized them."

"How did you recognize them?" Skye asked in her cross-examination voice.

Andrew smiled. "She has pictures of all of you on her desk."

"Oh, right." I looked down, processing that while Andrew kept his arm around me, his hold felt so good, but I was still confused.

Skye smiled and said, "Nice car. You look good for

an eighty-year old guy."

Andrew laughed. "It's my mother's. She wanted me to use it because my Beamer only has front wheel drive."

"She has good taste in cars." Dad folded his arms, smiling. As I struggled for something else to say, Dad ambled toward me. "It's cold," he said, nudging me further into Andrew's arms. "Why don't you two go in the house."

"Um, actually..." I stared at the Caddy again and knew Andrew's parents lived on Fifth Avenue. His downtown apartment was posh and elegant. He wore Prada and was used to the finer things in life. What would he think about my simple childhood home?

And what would Andrew's mother think? She may have handed over a sixty-thousand-dollar car so he could drive all the way out to Darling Cove. Did that gesture mean she approved? A haze of happiness made my cheeks tick up.

But nausea spread through me again and fast. How would his mother feel about a knocked-up girl who, in a way, had no place to live? Would she think I was trying to trap her son? I stepped back, swamped with fear and confusion.

"Gwen, this gentleman made a long drive. Perhaps he wants some coffee?" Dad, nudged me again.

Andrew touched my face. "Gwen, what's wrong? Has something changed since you were in Milan?"

"I—" I sniffed, unable to hold back, his touch felt so warm. But everything was wrong, and everything had changed.

"Are you crying?" Andrew asked full of concern. "Is there something going on with your family?"

Yes. The family inside of me and in front of me were

forming and falling apart at the same time.

I squirmed away. "I think we need to talk."

Andrew released a low chuckle. "I agree. Can I come inside and get out of this wet snow?"

There was no other way to talk to him. "Sure." I walked up the driveway keeping a few steps away from Andrew.

Inside, Skye snagged her wrapped gifts from under the tree. We'd planned to open them later that afternoon during Dad's break. By the looks of things, that just got canceled.

"Good luck." Skye kissed my cheek by the door and held her gifts against her chest. "If the old man got Prada and I didn't, I'll be back. Upset."

I snorted. They all got Prada. Even Greg, a midnight blue tie he could wear for work instead of the stiff polyester department-issued one. And it would look incredible with a gray suit if he joined the FBI.

"We'll leave you two alone," my father said, squeezing Andrew's arm by the front door.

I caught one final look at Skye, who mouthed, *Oh my God*. Greg held Casey's leash for her, his wrapped gift with green shiny paper to match his eyes tucked under his arm.

Andrew closed the door, but watched the crowd marching away through the sidelight. "They're fantastic," he said, turning around. "They obviously adore you. And so do I."

♥ ♥ ♥ ♥
Andrew

I wasn't there to play games. Gwen looked downright terrified. Not making purposeful plans had her thinking I wasn't serious about her. "Now, why are you standing all the way over there?"

She rubbed her eyebrows. "No reason. Do you want some coffee?"

"Sure." My worried eyes followed her as she left the living room.

It gave me a minute to take in the surroundings. The boxy living room had two wing chairs in front of a fireplace. A blue sectional sofa looked damn comfortable and inviting. I grew up in an apartment. I loved the city, but always dreamed of a cozy place in the country to escape to on weekends.

Darling Cove was everything I imagined and wanted for that.

In front of a bay window, stood a Christmas tree that made me smile. Not the fake professionally-decorated ten-foot-high one in my parents' place. No, Gwen's tree was decorated with love. The smell of pine filled my senses. I'd never had a real tree. Gwen's tree was round and squat with colorful lights, some blinking, some not. I fingered a few soft branches and found an ornament. A round silver plate with a year engraved on it. Several years back.

I stepped away to get the full view. Those were the only ornaments on the tree. They were all the same, but different. All from different years. No balls, no tinsel, no garland. Just little milestones that meant something.

My mom passed away right after I graduated high school. And there it was at the top. That year. Nothing before then and just a sea of sparkle for every year since.

There had to be a new proposal plan, my old one had just been blown to shit. I didn't want to go back to the city. I wanted to stay right there. How could I propose if the ring was in Manhattan? *Stupid, stupid, stupid.* Being deprived of Gwen's sweet body had made me unable to think straight.

"Here you go. It's decaf, I'm afraid." She handed me a striped mug.

I took the coffee in my hands and swallowed a sip. Ring or no ring, I was ready to ask her. "Gwen—"

"Andrew, I have something to tell you." She interrupted me with words that pierced me like the sharp tip of an arrow.

Nothing good ever followed that sentence. If she thought she was breaking up with me, she'd have to think again.

I drew a ragged breath into my lungs and put the mug down. "Okay."

"I... Um. I know this is supposed to be some shining glorious moment for a couple."

I hugged her immediately. "Gwen, I messed up. I'm sorry. How could you think I didn't want to see you yesterday?"

"I can't read your mind, Andrew."

"Well, you should have!" I ground out through clenched teeth, angry at myself. "I mean...you should have made that assumption. But I'm sorry I didn't make it clear."

"Me too," she said, but her demeanor remained cold and indifferent.

"Gwen, how do we fix this, what can I do?"

She blew out a breath, puffing out her cheeks like she had no idea how to respond. My mission was going nowhere fast, except south.

I looked back at the bay window. "Your tree is great. I love these ornaments. But..." I held one in my hand from last year. "Where's one for this year?"

She stared at me, probably surprised I noticed. I felt like I was walking blind through a maze, I had to question everything. "Every year one of us buys the ornament. This was my year. But I didn't hang it yet."

"It's Christmas Day. What were you waiting for?"

From under the tree she removed a square box. "I guess I was waiting for the right moment. Here." She handed me the box.

Curiosity rippled through me, wondering why it was important to show *me* before her family. I took the box and opened it. Silver glinted off the lights on the tree. The year was in block letters, all different sizes. Not very elegant compared to the rest. A silver charm hung from the numbers. A baby bottle? What an odd thing to…

I staggered back, my mind racing wildly to compute what was happening. My heart pounded in my chest.

"Andrew?" Gwen called out to me softly.

My eyes shot to her. "What does… What does this mean?"

"I'm pregnant, Andrew."

"*What?* Really?"

"Yes, really." She crossed her arms. "I didn't want to tell you over the phone or email. In fact, I didn't want to tell you at all."

"You didn't want to *tell* me?" I choked out with disbelief.

"I mean, I didn't want to *have* to tell you. This isn't where I wanted us to be now." She turned around.

I sprang toward her and held on from behind. Relief pounded into me, feeling her soften in my arms. I whispered in her ear, "How could you think I wouldn't want to know?"

"I don't want to force your hand, Andrew." She turned to face me.

"*Force my hand?* Like I don't think I have a choice in

the matter?"

She smirked. "I know you. That's not the man you are."

"Let me be the man already." I put the ornament on the tree next to the one sparkling with the year her mother had died.

With Gwen's eyes on me, I gathered her in my arms and took the first *real* kiss from her. One of want and need. The feel of her lips brought my body back to life. I trembled with weak knees as I prepared to kneel down. But I paused. If I proposed now with no ring, I'd feed into her fears and she'd believe I asked purely out of obligation. And she would probably say no.

No. I had to wait until I had my grandmother's ring in hand to show her, to *prove* to her I'd planned to ask her all along.

My proposal *and* my first 'I love you' would have to wait.

The kiss finished in a sweet swirl of her tongue, but Gwen stopped and lowered her head. "Andrew, I need to tell you something else."

Holding her face, I said, "I want you to tell me everything. Always."

Hearing she'd been pregnant once before and miscarried…bothered me. But Gwen and I had lives before we met. The world had turned upside down to bring us together. I'd figured out in Milan Gwen was *it* for me. And so far, nothing had made me even remotely waver from my desire to be with her. A baby only made me want her more fiercely.

I needed to recalibrate my plans to make sure we stayed together. There was so much more at stake.

I gathered her hair in my palms. "It's okay. I'm glad you told me."

"What if…" She stopped and pressed her head into my chest. "What if something like that happens again?"

"*I* got you pregnant, Gwen." I declared my virility, forcing her to look up. "Everything will be fine. And if it's not…"

She took a shaky breath.

"Then we'll try again," I whispered, smoothing her hair.

"Andrew." Her head settled back beneath my jaw. "I missed you so much."

The words filled my body with adrenaline. I kissed her the way I'd wanted to last night. My arms curled around her, tight. Too tight. I let go, worried I would hurt her. I knew what I was capable of doing to her. How would that work now if she were pregnant?

"Gwen, do you feel okay? I *have* to make love to you. Soon."

"I want that, too." She lifted up on her toes and kissed me, more passionately than I expected.

With her arms wrapped tightly around my neck, she began a torturous trail along my jawline with her lips and the edges of her teeth.

"Wait a second." I feared I would get too crazy with her and need a police escort *back* to Manhattan. I clutched her hands and rested them against her thighs. "You know how much I want to put my hands and my mouth all over your body. I'm not so sure I can be gentle. Not after two weeks without you."

"I'm having a baby. I won't break."

The words still shocked me, even though I had no real reason to be surprised. Finding that condom on the bed in Milan hadn't been the shocker I made it out to be. I'd known all along *something* had happened. The sex had turned scorching hot and suddenly very wet, but selfishly, I hadn't wanted to stop.

I ran a hand through the gloriously long hair I also missed. "So, a baby, huh?"

All the sex I wanted to have with her would lead to a baby anyway. My stamina had returned. And then some. We'd had so much sex in Milan, we used up all those condoms in my nightstand.

"According to EPT," Gwen said.

I chuckled. There was no need for shame *or* blame. All I wanted right then was to hold her. My hand brushed against her arm and her skin already felt different. Under my fingers, she felt firmer, and I caught the glow I'd always heard about.

A wild desire to yank her clothes off and be a part of what was inside her fueled my fire like kerosene. "Are you happy about the baby, Gwen?"

"I can think of one thing that might *possibly* make me a little happier right now."

CHAPTER TWENTY-NINE

Gwen

I took Andrew's hand and led him up the stairs.

I brought him to my full-size lumpy childhood bed. "It's not much. But if it makes any difference, I've dreamed of you on that thing."

"Have you now?" He followed me inside the bedroom, keeping a steady scrutiny on me.

I'd lived in that house until I moved to the city so it wasn't filled with juvenile reminders of being a school girl.

"I've even called out your name." My body folded onto the mattress. "I'd love to scream it with you *in* it."

"And you're sure it's okay?" He glanced out the window.

"Dad's working until much later."

Andrew ripped his coat off and climbed in to join me. He was so tall, getting in and out of that thing would be a challenge for him if someone surprised us and came home early.

He wore the same dark-washed jeans he wore our last day in Milan and a simple V-neck sweater — charcoal, the same color of his eyes. "God, I missed your body."

That morning I'd yanked on yoga pants, a tank top, and a boyfriend cardigan from my overnight bag without ever thinking Andrew would be there to peel it all off later on. His fingernails teased my skin, as he skidded the sweater from my shoulders. Removing the thin tank top revealed how aroused he'd gotten me in such a short amount of time. He kissed me with a tongue designed to drive me mad.

He spread his large hands across my torso. His face dipped between the swells of my breasts, tucked inside a pale lavender bra.

Settling sideways onto his lap, I reached back. "Get this bra off me."

He pressed his hands against my back and unfastened the bra while he nipped at my neck and collarbone. His tongue flicked against rock-hard nipples. "I have to have you. All of you. Every part of you."

"I want *this*." I slid my hand down his chest to his belt buckle, but he grabbed my hand.

"No. Wait." He cupped my elbows. "I want to do something else first."

I bit my lip. "And what might that be?"

"Lie down and I'll show you." He slid next to me, cradling my head in the crook of his left arm while his fingers danced down my stomach.

Andrew remained clothed while he pressed down on my damp panties, and his lips brushed against my mouth passionately. How intimate and sensual, kissing me and pleasing me at the same time.

"I was so crazy for you last night," he whispered. "My body literally hurt."

Pulling the thin scrap of lace aside, he slid one long finger into my waiting heat, and I responded with a lusty groan. My grip on his shoulder tightened. I'd been aching for him as well.

With my legs spread wide, giving myself over to him, I rested my free hand on top of his as he pleasured me with his fingers. "You feel so good," he said, pressing his thumb against the swollen knot of nerves.

My hips bucked from the pressure. Steeped in arousal, my desire pulsed through my thundering heart.

A spasm shot through me, making me whimper and arch my back in a deep stretch.

"Oh, Andrew, yes." My tensions stormed up to the surface and hovered, warmth and tightening combining for the coming explosion. I sucked in a breath and tilted my head back. "Yes. Yes. Andrew. Andrew."

Heat soared through me. Andrew kept up the intensity, and the deep thrusts from his finger in a steady rhythm extended my orgasm, intensifying it.

He didn't stop. The sensitivity overwhelmed me, my hands swatted at his to push him away for a quick break of relief. It was too much. What felt like a drenched finger came out of me and now the pads of several fingers were rubbing my aching center.

"Andrew," I panted from the sweet torture.

"That's me. I'm here, Gwen."

"I need you inside me."

"Okay. But… I'm sorry. Not here. I can't concentrate, knowing two men with guns have a key to this place. Please come back to the city with me. Please?"

I glanced around my bedroom feeling like it was time to let go of my safe haven. The teetering I'd felt with Andrew had just been pushed over. We were having a baby. My place was with him. Nodding, I said, "Okay. Let me just text Dad where I'm going."

Back in the living room, I snagged the ornament from the tree smiling. "Greg doesn't know yet."

Andrew's eyes widened and the hand not holding my bag, scrubbed down the back of his neck. "He's gonna kill me, isn't he?"

Laughing, I got in the Caddy, Andrew holding the door open for me. I melted into the buttery leather seat and Andrew held my hand the entire time. The traffic was light considering it was a holiday, and my heart ticked up returning to the city. My city. Our city. I loved the North Fork, but I belonged in Manhattan.

With Andrew.

And our baby.

"My *mother* will kill me before Greg for parking this thing on the street, but I'm not trekking all the way uptown," Andrew said, parallel parking a block from his apartment.

Outside his building, the doorman greeted us with holiday cheer and at his mailbox, Andrew fished for his keys. But I produced my set.

He kissed me in the elevator, our hands clutching around the keys. At the door, fumbling to get the it open, he said, "We'll, um, figure out where to live—"

I stopped him with my lips. I didn't want him stressed about the logistics of our situation. Or to think it was his to worry about, alone. We still didn't know if I was being sent to Milan.

But Andrew didn't know I wasn't going, even if the job was offered to me.

He held me against a wall outside the bedroom and kissed me like I was the source of his oxygen. "I need you. I need to be inside you," he moaned into my mouth.

"I want that."

After shucking the rest of his clothes, he brought me to the bed, undressed me, spread my legs, and entered me with a swift fierce push. "You better find something to hold on to."

No need for a condom now.

Again, and again, he drove into me until stars popped out behind my eyes and he groaned deep and raw from a body-rocking climax.

He roughly kissed my mouth and said, "I told you

I wouldn't be gentle." He rested a palm over my belly button and whispered, "Mine."

"There's no question about that," I groaned, feeling satisfied.

Tangled and kissing, I stayed buried in Andrew's arms. They were wound so tight around me, I couldn't tell which was right or left. It didn't matter, though.

His face skidded down my neck and he took deep breaths. "You smell so good."

"I think part of that scent is you at this point," I said.

He moved some loose hairs out of my eyes. "Are you saying I sweat a lot?"

"That's not what I meant." I took his hand and put it back on my stomach. "Here. It's you."

"You have no idea how this makes me feel. That inside you…" Emotion got the better of him.

His sweet lips found my mouth, and a playful tongue tousled with mine, gearing up for more. "I'll sleep next week. Maybe."

Oh, the next eight months were going to be fun.

The next morning, in front of Prada, I turned to Andrew in the Caddy. "When will you be in the office?"

He dipped a bushy brow over a tired eye. Ha! He thought he was tired now. Wait until a baby kept us awake and not a sexual hunger.

"I have to bring this car back to my mom. Pick up my suitcases…" He began counting on his hand. "Then I have to drop off laundry, dry cleaning. I don't even remember if I paid my rent. I *have* to go to Flagship. My report is still due. And I have…other errands to take care of."

"So, I'll see you tomorrow?" I said with a teasing kiss.

"Nope. I'll be in before the day is over." He took my

hand. "I meant it when I said, we're gonna figure stuff out."

"Andrew, me being pregnant doesn't mean we have to automatically—"

"I know. Just trust me. By the end of the day, you'll see."

"I do trust you." I held his face to kiss him while his hands gripped the leather-bound steering wheel.

His tongue delicately swirled in my mouth, but he stopped. "Now, get out of the car."

I hopped out and the Cadillac drove off leaving me a few feet from the curb. The air smelled sweet and the sun had risen enough to sparkle against the glass of Prada's building. I cradled my stomach. A wave of satisfaction swelled inside me. I had a job I loved, a man I loved, and a baby on the way.

It was *my* turn to have it all.

I skipped to the curb and jumped over a pile of snow, cleanly making it over the mound.

"Good morning," I greeted the guards, sitting at the security desk inside the building.

My cell phone ringing stopped me from getting on the elevator. The number on the screen sent a tiny chill through me—the specialist, a breast surgeon. My hands quivered.

When I'd called to make an appointment, I talked to Sylvie, the nurse and said my films and biopsy results were on their way, only to find out there was a several-month wait for an appointment. If Sylvie was calling me, then everything must have looked all right with my films. Surgeons didn't make their receptionists deliver bad news.

I swiped the call to answer. "Hello?"

"Gwendolyn Foley?"

My shoulders relaxed recognizing Sylvie's voice. Although I had to notify them of my name change. ASAP. "Yep. Hi, Sylvie."

"Dr. Jesse had a cancellation and you're next on the waiting list. Can you come in today?"

"Oh, okay." I brushed my hand down my throat.

Papers rustled. "Eleven o'clock?"

I sighed, now wishing I had Andrew's to-do list instead. "Sure. I'll see you then."

The screen went dark. I brought up Andrew's number, ready to send a text telling him where I'd be, but paused. It wasn't fair to sneak off to a surgeon and not tell him. But, perhaps Dr. Sage at Lenox was just being super cautious. I hoped the surgeon would give me a quick examination and tell me to have a nice year.

Stepping into Dr. Jesse's waiting room later that morning, I felt a chill seeing all the patients waiting.

At the check-in desk, Sylvie, a woman in her late forties with dark comforting eyes, said with a bright smile, "Take a seat, Ms. Foley."

I sat down, grabbed a nearby *People* magazine and scanned a few pages, but closed it unable to concentrate. That miscarriage had been nagging at me since I'd read the pee-stick. I'd not missed one period since, and worried there might be more nefarious things going on in my body than breast calcifications.

"Ms. Foley, we're ready for you."

I tossed the magazine and followed Sylvie to one of the small exam rooms. Inside, she pointed to the paper gown and rambled off well-rehearsed instructions, finishing with, "Dr. Jesse will be in shortly."

After a few minutes, the surgeon breezed in. Beautiful auburn hair sat on slender shoulders and around aquamarine eyes. "Nice to meet you," she said, shaking my hand then dove into my chart.

The surgeon tabbed through Dr. Sage's notes, flipped through the films and began to explain the biopsy revealed the type of tissue that had grown into problematic masses in other patients. I noticed she kept trigger words out of the conversation. "Dr. Sage's recommendation to screen every six months is appropriate. For now."

For now. Ugh.

Now...

I caught my breath and said, "I just found out I'm pregnant." Saying the words out loud brought a rush of warmth tingling across my entire body. Andrew knew and he was...happy about it.

"Congratulations," Dr. Jesse said with the look of a doctor who didn't hear those words too often from a patient sitting on her exam table. "That's wonderful."

"Thanks." I ran a hand through my hair. "It was a surprise."

Dr. Jesse smiled and tapped my knee. "It happens like that more times than you think."

"So, what are my options?" I asked, feeling relieved.

"Let's start with an exam and go from there," Dr. Jesse said. "Lie back."

The surgeon's fingers danced across my right breast—the troublemaker—like she was playing a piano concerto. Up and down the center and sweeping the sides, bearing down on scar tissue from Dr. Sage's biopsy.

"Ouch." It seemed only Andrew touching me there didn't hurt.

"It feels good, Gwen," Dr. Jesse said with her sunshine of a smile as she stepped around to the other side of the table. "I think we can skip more screenings until you give birth."

At least the left breast wasn't filled with the same tender scar tissue. I released the metal bar under the table, expecting to breeze through the rest of the exam.

While I kept my eyes closed, the same dance of Dr. Jesse's fingers tapped across my left breast. Up, down, right, left. *Sigh*. Right, left. Right, left. Left. Left. Press. Squeeze. Crunch.

"Ow!" I cried out from the blast of searing pain.

When Dr. Jesse's warm hands left my body, I opened my eyes. The surgeon had gone back to the counter and swiped through my films.

"What is it?" I asked.

With skilled precision, Dr. Jesse stacked films against a back-lit X-ray illuminator. And then out of her pocket came a brass plated magnifying glass. In Dr. Sage's office, X-ray images on a seventeen-inch monitor showed me the initial set of suspicious cells in the right breast. Here was Dr. Jesse, using a seventeenth century trinket.

She swore and starting sorting films again. At the near end of the pile, Dr. Jesse gripped another film, and held it up to the illuminator. "There's *nothing* here. Damn it!"

"Dr. Jesse, you're really scaring—"

"Get dressed." She put her hand on my thigh. In a commanding tone, she said, "And meet me in my office. I'm calling Dr. Sage myself. You're getting another biopsy, *right now*."

I swung my legs over the table to stand. "Dr. Jesse, what did you feel?"

"A lump."

CHAPTER THIRTY

Gwen

I took the biopsy referral from Sylvie with shaking hands, not remembering if I paid the visit bill. Then I ambled around the corner to the hospital.

Slowing my usual brisk pace to a zombie stagger, I entered the lobby full of anxiety and dread. Even the Starbucks cart with its fresh coffee aroma and tasty looking treats barely registered.

At the Radiology sign-in desk, I gave my name expecting to have a seat. No. I got whisked into a frigid locker room. I robotically removed my dress. The white and heather gray color-block shift dress had slid on my body that morning, Andrew kissing every inch I covered. Stopping at my belly, he smiled so heartily, I wanted to cry. Now taking it off, I wanted to weep for a much different reason. I was going to destroy Andrew, wasn't I? Not only might he lose me, he might lose *his child*.

Dr. Sage appeared in the waiting area moments later to collect me in all my meltdown glory. "Dr. Jesse said there's something in the left breast for us to look at."

I stood, my anger kicking the crap out of my self-pity. "How could something that went undetected in my last mammogram grow into something Dr. Jesse actually felt?"

"Let's go have a look right now and see what we're dealing with." Dr. Sage tried to get me under control.

"Wait!" The words I'd been loving to say now felt like shards of glass in my mouth. "I'm pregnant."

"Dr. Jesse mentioned that." Dr. Sage pointed to the

long cold hallway connecting the waiting lounge and the testing rooms. "We'll do an ultrasound before the biopsy. Both rooms are being prepped for you."

"I need a few minutes." I snatched my phone out of my purse and dialed Andrew's phone. I couldn't go through the biopsy alone. Not when the stakes were so high. My health now affected him, too.

He picked up on the first ring, sounding frazzled. "Hey, can I call you back, I'm talking to the—"

"Andrew, I need you," I choked out.

"Where are you?" he asked in a deep serious tone.

"I'm at the hospital." I'd hoped to find my 'it's no big deal' voice and be strong, but I didn't possess anything but fear at the moment.

"Oh my God, what happened?"

"My breast surgeon had a cancellation. I was on her waiting list. They called me after you left. I didn't know...what being pregnant would mean. So...I went to see her. Figuring it'd be no problem." I exhaled and clenched my stomach to not break down. "She felt something, Andrew. They want me to do a biopsy, right now."

His silence suggested I sent him into a tailspin. After a full minute, he responded, "Wait for me in the lobby, I'll walk up with you."

"I'm already up here." I dug deep to avoid a crack in my voice that would only fire up Andrew's worst fears.

"Okay, honey." There was rustling in the background. "I'm on my way. Gwen, wait!"

"I'm on the third floor."

"No. I... Gwendolyn, I—"

"No. Don't you dare say those words to me *now*." I abruptly ended the call with clammy shaking fingers.

I still wasn't sure if his committing to me was out of obligation. I sure as shit didn't want to hear 'I love you' out of pity.

The sonogram was brief, but painful, and Dr. Sage easily found the mass. I stepped into the biopsy procedure room and answered the usual pre-procedure questions like a lifeless rag doll.

"How is this going to work if I'm pregnant?" I asked, signing the consent form. And stalling.

"It's perfectly safe like this," Dr. Sage did her best to assure me. "We've put down a leaded apron."

My jaw trembled in lieu of a nod.

The door opened. Figuring it was a med-tech, I turned away, but the unmistakable shape of Andrew's body caught my attention. I shot my hands in front of my face to hide the fear pulsing through me.

Dr. Sage did a dramatic double take when Andrew strode into the room. Along with his beautiful face, he brought a surge of emotion with him.

"I'll give you a few minutes," the doctor said, tucking her hair against her neck.

Andrew fell at my feet before I even stood up. I pressed my face into his chest and took deep successive breaths to force the tears away.

"I'm here." Andrew unfolded me and held my chin. "I'm here, honey."

"I'm so sorry."

"What *for?*"

"I feel like I made you some kind of promise this wouldn't happen."

"You did no such thing and even if you had—" Andrew ran his hands up and down my ice-cold skin and felt me shaking. "It's going to be okay."

Our eyes locked. Longing and searching.

I nodded, but still felt afraid and confused.

♥ ♥ ♥ ♥

Andrew

With a weak smile, I exhaled. "I'm here, Gwen."

The entire ride over, fear swept through me. But something else, too. Strength and courage. I'd survived a war once before. I was better prepared now. I'd fight the good fight *with* Gwen. For her.

She was *mine* and I wasn't going to lose her.

The team returned wearing surgical masks signaling the biopsy was ready to happen.

"Maya, can he stay with me please?" Gwen asked the tech.

"Sure, we'll get him an apron as well."

"Apron for what?" I asked.

"The mammogram machine," Gwen answered for the assistant.

"Hang on." I faced the assistant while holding Gwen tight against my side. "She's pregnant."

"I already told Dr. Sage that. I'll be lying on a wooden board." Gwen pointed to an ominous looking table in the back of the room. "The machine is underneath and they put down a leaded apron."

Gwen had put her life into the hands of those people, but that didn't mean I trusted them on day one.

Maya slipped the heavy plastic shield across my arms and I asked, "Gwen, where do you want me?"

"Do you think the table can hold both of us?"

Oh, how I missed her humor. "I'm guessing no. But that's because of me, not you."

She swung her right arm directing me to the space in between the table and the wall. "Can you stand over here, please?"

I stepped around, took her right hand and placed

my other hand across her back. As the table rose, the hydraulic moan stiffened my spine and I filled with fury. The lift stopped at my chest, allowing my arm to engulf her waist.

She parted her lips to say something, but released a howling cry of agony. The sound I expected would come from something that wasn't human. It rocked me to my core. All of Cate's struggles and procedures I'd had to watch her go through rushed to the surface and tried to wallop the piss out of me.

I wouldn't let it.

"What happened?" I asked Gwen gently, sounding strong.

She was strong, she'd get through it. So long as I didn't fall apart.

"The machine tightened. It's so painful."

"I'm sorry, Ms. Foley." Maya's smothered apology from underneath the table provided little comfort.

"It's Mallory!" I barked. *And not for long.*

The procedure crept along. A few moments of being held in the same position allowed the pain on Gwen's face to vanish ever so slightly. She relaxed her jaw and managed a faint smile. Maya continued to ask her to either move up or move down, each time the loosening and then tightening changed Gwen's expression.

I tried to keep her distracted by making encouraging small talk. When tears tracked down her cheeks, I lost it.

"Hurry up!" I demanded through clenched teeth.

Touching my face, her fingers pressed into my eyebrows. She whispered, "Even furious, you're so damn handsome."

"It's not a look I'd like to wear often." I took her

hand again and kissed her knuckles.

Gwen opened her mouth to respond, but instead gasped in relief.

"Okay, we're all done here," said Dr. Sage who'd slipped in unnoticed.

"Um, there's no graceful way for me to do this. Can you wait over there?" Gwen pushed up on her forearms. "I can get down myself."

"I know you can. I'm going to help you anyway," I said and reached for her.

She tugged her gown closed and climbed down with my hands gripping her waist. If she wanted me to carry her through the corridor, I would happily oblige. Instead, she leaned against me as we walked to the dressing room.

It was empty and Gwen dragged me inside. Maya came in and handed over films and icepacks. I placed myself between the assistant and Gwen's dressing stall to accept the package and instructions. The familiar post biopsy routine shocked the breath out of me, but I fought the feeling of dread.

As I stood there shaking, Gwen opened the door. Without speaking, I handed her the icepack.

"Thanks," she said, avoiding my eyes.

We left the hospital, not a word shared between us. In the taxi, I held her so close I felt the frosty package tucked into her bra.

I'd given my apartment's address then leaned in to tell the driver, "But, make a right on 57th. I have a stop I need to make."

"Why are we stopping? What's—" Her eyes widened seeing the creamy white cement building.

The name on the door stood out in tall gothic letters and Gwen dug her nails into my arm.

Tiffany's. A company older than Prada.

Staring at the two large windows and the flags flying overhead, her jaw dropped. "No."

I jerked my head at her. "I really hope that's not your official answer."

"I mean..." She shook her head. "Please don't bring me into Tiffany's. Not *now*."

"Why not now? What better way to turn this day around?"

"Andrew," she squeaked. "Look at me. I don't want to walk in there like this." Her hands rummaged through a tangled mess of hair I couldn't care less about.

"How much different do you think you'd look if I brought you here one morning, the way you and I can go at it every night?"

My bold and provocative statement made her cheeks flush. Okay, maybe bringing her into Tiffany's with sex hair wasn't what she wanted either.

"Talk to me." I tugged at her arms.

"Can we just go to your apartment and talk about this first, please?"

I blew out an exhale and redirected the taxi driver. The deafening silence returned on the ride all the way downtown and in the elevator going up fourteen floors.

In my kitchen, I thumbed through the stack of takeout menus. "Are you hungry at all?" I asked.

"No. I can't eat. I'm still so nauseous."

The baby. Christ, the baby. I hadn't even considered that. I worried about *her*. Now I had two people to...

I had to stop myself.

With a steady breath, Gwen said, "Let me get all this straightened out before we talk about *anything else*. You're assuming I won't have to go off and live in Italy."

I roughly wiped my mouth. "If you think I'm letting

Enrico send you to Italy now, carrying my kid, you're out of your mind. There is no way in *hell* that's happening."

Gwen snickered. "Inferno does mean hell in Italian." She clarified when I stared blankly at her. "*The Divine Comedy.* Maybe Dante was in a long-distance relationship."

Even after an emergency biopsy that might cause a disastrous complication, her humor was sharp and poignant.

"It won't come to that, Gwen. I'm prepared to quit if it does. You'll be more valuable to Enrico in New York, if I'm not there."

"Do you see what a mess I've caused?" She threw her hands up. "Wait, when did you make *that* decision?"

"When you left Milan." A look passed between us. "I made a lot of decisions that week. And I didn't even know about..."

"I'm so sorry." She looked down and tangled up her fingers.

"Please stop apologizing."

"I can't eat anything now. I just need some tea." She pulled out a mug from the exact right cabinet. Plopped in a tea bag from a box I didn't even know I had and then stuck it in the microwave. Her fingers swept over the keys without any hesitation.

I released a slow whirl of laughter. "You sure know your way around here."

"It hasn't been fun sleeping here by myself," she said, leaning against the counter with her back turned.

That burned me. I couldn't be with her because of Marcello.

"I need to lie down." Without looking at me, she took the mug of steaming tea and disappeared into the hallway leading to my bedroom.

I stepped into the bathroom a moment later to find her brushing her teeth with a toothbrush that wasn't mine. A visual sweep of the counter revealed all the things she'd purchased and kept there. All good signs, but something was going on in her head. Something darker.

"Gwen, I need to do some work. I lost a lot of time today."

With cold eyes, she said, "Sorry about that."

"Stop apologizing already." *Good going. Yell at the mother of your child because she's upset about her health.* "I'm... I'm sorry. I didn't mean to yell."

Gwen pushed past me and slammed the bedroom door. With me on the wrong side. Frustrated, I stomped to my desk and fired up my laptop to work on my year-end report.

Hours dragged by and my eyes grew tired. I woke up in the middle of the night with my head on the desk. A startling fear pulsed through me. I rushed to the bedroom and opened the door. Gwen's body under the covers settled my heartbeat. While it would have driven the sanity right out me, I wouldn't have been surprised if she'd crept away while I was passed out.

How had so much gone so wrong in such a short amount of time?

I brushed my teeth and undressed using the bathroom light creeping out of the door. Wearing only my boxers, I slipped into the bed. And waited. I sensed she was awake and hoped she would roll into me. Let me apologize properly.

Nothing. Not a stir. Empty sheets between us.

So different from last night, when she was panting and writhing beneath me. Now she was shattered and broken, clinging to the other side so she didn't fall off.

The rough and traumatic events of the day should have made me toss and turn, except I passed out and woke when the sun peeked through the bedroom curtains.

Gwen wasn't next to me.

I opened what felt like one blood-shot eye and found her frantically getting dressed.

CHAPTER THIRTY-ONE

Andrew

"Where do you think you're going?" I asked Gwen as she rolled on a pair of day-old stockings.

"Home," she answered emotionless.

"You are home." I pushed the covers away and got out of the bed.

"To the North Fork, I need my family."

"*I'm* your family now. We're having a baby. You're *mine* to take care of."

She stopped and laid empty eyes on me.

I bent down in front of her. "Gwen, please just stay here."

"I have some serious thinking to do."

That jolted me. "Thinking about what?"

"Everything." She stood and grabbed her wrinkled dress. "Do you *want* to be a widower again?"

The question sent blood boiling through my veins. "This is different. Okay. You're going to be fine. We don't even know…" I couldn't finish when the breath in my lungs vanished. What if she were right?

"Exactly. We don't know. And until we do, *this*…" She pointed to me. "Is on hold."

"On hold?" I got to my feet and grabbed her arm. "You're having my baby and I love you. I'm not putting *anything* on hold."

She blinked and said nothing. It took a moment for me to realize why she couldn't speak. I just told her I loved her. *Damn it!* I wanted to do it with the ring in my hand. The ring I planned to pick up later that morning. Her not returning the sentiment made my stomach flip.

"Please…" I had trouble breathing. "Just…give me

a few hours to get all of this straightened out. Please, Cate?"

Through heavy breathing bordering on what looked like sobs, Gwen said, "You just called me Cate."

"I... I did?" *Uh-oh.*

"Yes." She yanked one boot on and grabbed the other.

I caught her wrist so she wouldn't fall. "I didn't mean for that to happen."

"I won't wreck your life." She began throwing everything she brought with her into a pile.

"Whoa? Where did *that* come from?" I blocked her body from leaving the bedroom. "Stop. Let's talk about this. You have not wrecked my life. I'm right where I want to be, *Gwen*. With you."

"Oh yeah?" She spun on her heels and walked to my closet. From inside, she grabbed a golf club and jabbed at the hat box I'd tucked away. After two pokes it popped off the shelf, tumbled over, and all its contents poured down.

"I don't want to be another woman you have to tuck away in a box," she said half angry, half sad.

My eyes blinked looking at the pieces of my life she just let spill on the floor. The room began to spin. My ankles gave out and I sank to the parquet tiles.

I caught Gwen staring at me. She'd turned white.

"Oh my God. Andrew, I'm so sorry. Please, let me clean this up." She grabbed my wrists, but I wrenched away from her.

I didn't recognize what was going through me. All I felt was her trying to hurt me. To push me away, so I'd leave. I wouldn't give in so easily, but it didn't mean I wasn't destroyed in that moment.

I crumpled papers and photos in my shaking hands

until I threw them all down again. That was my past. That's why it was in a box. I stood and tried to collect my frazzled thoughts, but she caught me before I could turn away.

"I'm so sorry. I don't know what I'm doing. I'm just confused. I saw pictures of the perfect life you had with Cate, and all I could think was..." She looked down. "I just don't understand."

"Don't understand what?" I asked through gnashed teeth.

"Why you want to be with me." She sniffed. "It's why I didn't tell you about the baby right away. I knew you'd do the right thing. How will I ever know if you really want me? *For me?*"

"I'm trying to show you, but you're fighting me at every turn." I bit my lip, and said, "Perfect, huh?"

"What?" she squeaked through tears.

"You thought my life with Cate was perfect?"

Her breath escaped her. "I meant before. Before she got sick."

"And then she did. And the *perfect* life disappeared fast, Gwen."

"So why do you want to be with me?" she asked quietly.

"*Why?*" I looked around like she'd just accused me of something terrible.

"Yeah, why? Why would you want a life with me when that terrible history could repeat itself?"

"Because I *love* you!" It was hard not to scream curses at her, anything to emphasize how I felt.

"Stop..." She slid to the bedroom floor and held her head. "Just stop saying that."

I scrubbed a hand down my neck. "I have to go to work. I have to make sure *neither* of us has to move to

Italy." I walked toward her, still frozen and silent, slumped against the wall.

I bent to press a soft kiss on her forehead and squeezed her hand. "I'll clean all that up when I get home. I *really* want you to be here when I get back."

Gwen stood and smoothed her dress. "I'm sorry. I have to leave." She didn't wait for an answer and fled out the door, taking my heart with her.

After a ridiculously short shower, I dressed and left my apartment heartbroken and alone. The cold damp air outside made my lungs tighten in my chest. More snow, maybe. I'd love it if another blizzard stormed through and grounded all trains and planes so no one could leave.

As I made my way down the dank stairwell to the subway, my phone buzzed. I looked at it, hoping it was Gwen.

But it wasn't a call. It was an email I'd been cc'd on. From Marcello. *To* Enrico. His year-end report. He sent it several days early. Without me having one last look.

Jesus, no!

I climbed out of the stairwell and ran down the street for a taxi. I fumbled with my phone searching for a way to retract the message on behalf of Marcello. Even trying to sign in as him, using an old password I'd known about. It'd been changed, though.

Damn it!

My hands shook. I had to get to the office right away and repair whatever damage that email may have already caused. But Gwen's ring was ready to be picked up. I'd dropped off my grandmother's ring at Tiffany's the day before while running errands. I'd picked out a setting to complement the stone, and as a favor to my mother, they'd set it right away. Gwen's meltdown after the biopsy yesterday had prevented me from getting it. I didn't want to force it on her.

Now, given all that'd happened, I *had* to get that ring. Tell her everything. That I'd been planning to propose all along. I wasn't asking her out of obligation. I'd made those decisions weeks ago.

The baby was *proof* I'd made the right call.

Standing in the street, I stood frozen. Go get the ring, find Gwen and propose. Or…go to the office and work some kind of miracle where Gwen doesn't have to move to Italy…then propose. My body darted back and forth, deciding which was more important. If only I were two people.

Wait, I already had another version of myself.

I activated a call on my phone and frantically murmured, "Pick up. Pick up."

"For Pete's sake, it's been two days! *Am I planning a wedding or what?*" my mother answered, sounding anxious to hear the news of an engagement that may never happen.

"Ma, I need your help," I said and gave her a severely abridged version of what had happened. Leaving out the hospital scene, I let her assume Gwen and I had been too busy having sex and I'd not gotten around to picking up the ring.

I got to my office and sat at my desk. Staring at my monitor, I waited to meet with Enrico. Every ding from incoming emails churned my gut. I'd been waiting for an explosive email from my boss before I could repair the damage. The *'no news is good news'* proverb meant shit to me at the moment. Besides, I wouldn't be surprised if Enrico had put Gwen's transfer to Milan in motion regardless. The way she'd looked at me that morning, I bet she'd go willingly. With my child!

What she'd said about me and Cate being perfect and me not really wanting her tore through me, leaving me hollow and breathless.

I wrote out a resignation letter to keep Gwen in New York. *There is no goddamn way I'm letting her go.* I just didn't think I'd have to quit *today*. Before I had a chance to propose. My mother better be on her way with the ring to save me.

Saved by Mommy, great!

The body in my doorway broke me out of a trance.

"What do you want, Salvatore, I'm busy," I asked, refusing to hide my annoyance.

The designer lunged over the desk and grabbed me by the throat.

♥♥♥♥
Gwen

On the southwest corner of 34th Street and Seventh Avenue, I stared at the entrance to the Long Island Railroad. Worried that if I got on a train to go home, it would really be over between Andrew and me. If I continued to push him away, he'd eventually give in and leave.

That's not what I wanted.

Dizziness had been coming and going, and the damn nausea that made the few bites I'd eaten rage in my stomach.

I stood frozen and let the bright winter sunshine blind me while I collected my thoughts. Opening my eyes, I couldn't find my footing and down I went.

For all the homeless people laying all over the streets of Manhattan, a cute girl wearing Prada made people stop. Questions flew at me and all I did was clutch my purse watching out for hands grabbing for my cell phone or my wallet.

"Hey, let me through. I know her," said that voice. *That* voice.

When I opened my eyes, a halo of long fire-engine red hair swayed over me. "Gwen?"

"Faith," I breathed.

"Are you all right?" Faith asked, tugging me to a seating position."

"Okay, nothing to see here," another voice said, sharp and sassy.

"Lily, this is Greg's sister. Help me."

"I got ya, girl."

Next, I was lifted to my feet.

"Lil, get to the studio and tell Carter..." What she said to someone named Lily, I missed. But a brunette scurried off talking on her phone.

"Do you need water?" Faith reached into a tote bag. "Here, I have a bottle."

"I'm fine."

"Passed out on the sidewalk is not fine. Come on."

She steered me into a café further down 34th Street. All the food buffet style was too much for my sense of smell to handle. "Have a seat. Do you want coffee?"

"Tea would be good, decaf?" I lowered into a metal chair and planted my elbows on the table so I wouldn't fall down again.

"Coming right up," she said, putting her work bag down in the chair across from me. But my sense of pride kicked in.

Standing, I said, "Wait, no. I'm fine. I'm sure you have to get to..."

"Your brother will never speak to me again if he found out I let you just wander through the city looking ready to pass out."

"So you do want Greg to speak to you?" came

flying out of my mouth and I slapped it.

Faith exhaled. "Let me get us some tea and we'll...talk."

I sat back down and pushed my issues aside. Greg and Faith never seemed closer to...talking. I knew they belonged together. The way they loved each other. I'd never seen anyone love someone like Greg loved Faith.

Except my Dad and the way he loved my mom.

And...

You're having my baby and I love you. Andrew's words came rushing back to me. I barely processed them earlier. He doesn't realize I'm trying to protect him. I saw what losing my mom had done to my Dad. I couldn't...

Faith returned with two white slender cups and tea tags hanging from the sides. "Plain with sugar, right?" She let packets drop from her hands and I noticed she wasn't wearing a ring.

She'd left the ring my brother gave her—my mother's engagement ring—in Darling Cove before she left town. Before she'd died, my mom had told Greg to give it to Faith.

"Just plain is fine." I held the cup, the warmth felt good in my hands.

Faith took a sip and her eyes, blue like mine, stared. "Go ahead. Ask me."

I swallowed my tea. "Do you still love him?"

She choked and held her chest through a few coughs. "I wasn't expecting you to ask me that."

"I think that's all that matters." I shrugged.

"Do you think he still loves me?" Faith asked, terror in her eyes that I might say no which answered *my* question.

"He won't talk about it. But I think so. He's not had

anyone steady in his life since…"

"Me too," Faith said and looked away. "I'm sorry. For everything. I know how Greg adored you and how you loved him back. It must have hurt to see him so…"

"Devastated. Damn right." I felt some sassy coming on.

Faith took a breath. "I deserve that. For what it's worth, I was devastated, too. I didn't want to…" Faith blinked tired eyes.

"I get it. Tell me, how's work going?" I asked to keep her sitting, and drinking, and most importantly…talking.

"I'm producing now. Lily and I work one of the overnight news shows." Faith Copeland rose the broadcast news ladder from photojournalist to executive producer. She was beautiful enough to be in front of the camera, but her razor-sharp mind must have convinced the news gods she did more justice producing news stories than reading cue cards.

A stare stretched between us.

Blowing on her tea, Faith said, "You're gonna tell Greg everything I say, aren't you?"

I exhaled. "We were best friends up until the day you left. I knew you liked Greg since you were ten years old. Did I say a word to him in all those years?" I'd been grossed out back then by *anyone* wanting my fifteen-year-old smelly brother, but that was irrelevant.

Faith's jaw dropped and after a few moments, the love of Greg's life exhaled. "I'm sorry." A few more seconds passed before she spoke again.

"What *did* happen, Faith?" That feeling of sharing with my childhood best friend thrilled me.

"It's bad enough Greg doesn't know why I really left. I can't tell you and leave you hanging with that information on your conscience."

So close...

"I understand. Greg has access to interrogation rooms and bright lights."

Faith released a soft laugh. "God, I've missed your sense of humor."

"I'm here all week." I appreciated the break in tension as well.

"Are you still with that lingerie designer?" Faith asked, a career girl like her knew what buttons to push.

"No. I just started a new job a couple of months ago."

"Oh yeah? Where?"

"Prada." Damn, I liked saying that.

"That's amazing, Gwen. Good for you. Get your money's worth from that FIT education." Faith had understandably changed the subject from Greg.

I wanted Greg to take small steps with Faith. I needed to go slow with her as well if I were to rebuild a friendship that once meant the world to me.

"Thanks," I said. "It is kind of wonderful. I was just in Milan." I squeezed my shoulders together and slurped more tea.

The memory of wonderful Milan dissolved when I realized if I didn't take Marcello's job, Enrico would have to send Andrew. What if he refused?

I put everyone's future in jeopardy.

"Gwen, *are* you okay?" Faith asked when I'd gone quiet and probably pale, based on how my stomach turned again and again.

"I don't know." I gave an honest response and lost my breath from the impending decisions I faced.

Faith narrowed her eyes. "Man trouble? I heard you and Dan are getting a divorce."

"Yeah. But I'm...seeing someone else."

"Been with him long?"

"No. That's part of the problem. Things sometimes just move so fast. First it's all great sex and then..."

Faith's head fell forward, red hair spilling all around her. "God. What I wouldn't give for some great sex."

And what would Greg give to know *that* little confession?

Sympathetic eyes wandered again to Faith. Now that I had a taste of fantastic sex, I never wanted to *wonder* when I'd be rocked with another orgasm.

Whatever had made Faith run out on her wedding must have made sense to her at the time. Or she felt she had no other options.

Faith shook those red waves and said, "Don't make the same mistake I made, Gwen. Strong, deep emotions can cloud your judgment."

And *hormones*. That had to stop right now. My fears made no sense, yet they were driving my behavior. My breath came in short bursts, realizing I was about to make the biggest mistake of my life.

I shot to my feet. "You're right. I feel much better. I have to go. Happy New Year, Faith." Bending down, I kissed the girl I *knew* my brother still loved deeply and completely. "Please think about talking to Greg. I promise you, you won't regret it."

"I promise to think about it, Gwen." Faith smiled, her back a little straighter like I'd give her a nugget of hope she never expected.

On the street, I jumped into the taxi lane to hail a cab. I had to put my money where my mouth was. I had a man I loved and it was time to tell him so.

CHAPTER THIRTY-TWO

Andrew

"You!" Salvatore's garlic-laced spit flew in my face. "You had a hand in this, didn't you?"

"Hand in what?" I loosened myself from Salvatore's grip, sending the man stumbling back a few feet. "What the hell is wrong with you?"

"Don't play *stupido* with me, Morgan."

"I'm not playing stupid. I have no idea what you're talking about."

The designer smoothed his dark-blond hair in place using the reflective surface of one of my awards hanging on the wall. "I'm being transferred to Milan because of you."

"What?" I shot to my feet.

Salvatore sent a derisive scowl up and down my height. "I will not let some *ex-model* dictate my career." He said *'ex-model'* as if I'd been a prostitute.

I held my tongue. So, Salvatore had known all along. *How* was the least important thing to me at the moment.

I rounded my desk. "I assure you, *I* had no idea you were being moved to Milan."

As much as I despised the man at times, I wouldn't have let the top New York designer go willingly. Salvatore Corella was the key to Prada-New York's *brand* success.

Salvatore puffed out his chest. "Enrico calls it a *favore*, of course. He needs a seasoned designer there to make Prada-Milan more productive. I have to clean up the mess *you* made with Marcello."

How had I lost control of my own department?

Enrico chose to send Salvatore to Milan to help *Gwen*.

My body seared hot with anger. "Salvatore, you'll just have to live with Enrico's decision. I've *been* in Milan. I had no idea about any of this. I would love to stay and fight some more with you, but I need to speak to Enrico about something else." I geared up to quit. Right there and then.

My shoulder slammed into Salvatore as he stormed out of my office. The look that passed between us dripped with pure rage and hate. I needed to stop all that mess from happening.

I'd only made it a few doors down from Enrico's office, though.

"*Yo, stronzo!*" Salvatore yelled. "I have one more thing to say to you."

I spun around. Every head in the office looked up and most of them knew *stronzo* meant 'asshole.' The way Salvatore charged in my direction made Thalia turn ghostly pale.

"*What?*" I met Salvatore several feet away. "Don't do this in the office, Salvatore. This shit ends up online."

"Have it your way." Salvatore pulled me by the shirt collar into the copy room and slammed the door.

Oh, great!

Salvatore stepped right up to me, his chin raising to meet my eyes. In a low maniacal tone, he said, "I hope you and that little *cock tease* will be very happy together."

The comment sent a shock wave through me. I curled my fingers into a fist, and without thinking, executed a perfect jab into Salvatore's pudgy jaw. The designer flopped against the copier and hit the floor like a bag of rocks. Blood and spit flew from his mouth.

I shook my aching wrist, feeling nothing but panic.

"Oh, shit."

♥ ♥ ♥ ♥

Gwen

I feared Andrew really would quit to prevent me from going to Milan. He may have said he wasn't looking for a princess, but I wanted to be the ultimate warrior princess—Wonder Woman—and save my man.

I prepared to march into Enrico's office and turn the tables on them both by quitting first. Without me to use as a pawn to move to Milan, Enrico would be forced to tough it out with Marcello and let Andrew keep his job. His New York job. The job I knew he loved.

He'd been through so much. Andrew deserved to get his life back. I just hoped he still wanted me to be a part of that life.

In Prada's lobby, I rushed to the turnstiles with my access card in hand. At the guards' desk, I spotted a beautiful older woman bundled in an ivory wrap trimmed in brown leather looking quite annoyed while the guard made a call. My feet moved toward the woman as if I were being pulled by a magnet.

The woman turned in my direction and her carbon colored eyes lit up. "Gwendolyn?"

A bubbly feeling spread through my stomach. I absorbed the woman's features, particularly the nose and faint lines around the mouth. "Yes?"

The woman held out her hand. "I'm Sarah Morgan, Andrew's mother."

I just met my baby's grandmother. The *only* grandmother my baby would have. I choked up and thrust my hand out. "It's so nice to meet you."

"Oh, dear." Sarah's inky black bob, the same color as Andrew's hair, swayed against her high cheekbones. "You look like you've seen a ghost."

"It's because you look... I mean Andrew looks so much like you." Except the height. His father must be tall.

"Gwen dear, this is my husband William, Andrew's dad."

The man stepped around a pillar dropping a phone into his pocket and my jaw dropped. Crippling good looks must be a dominant gene in the Morgan family.

I tucked my hair behind my ear with trembling hands. "Hello, Mr. Morgan."

"Call me Will." His handshake felt firm and warm. "It's good to meet you."

Andrew's parents gawked at me for several seconds. How much did they know? They looked too chipper to know about my health scare and not ecstatic enough to know about the baby.

Sarah glanced at her watch and asked, "Working today, dear?"

I answered with a nod. "Does Andrew know you're here?"

"This new guard has been trying to reach him." Sarah folded her hands. "Don't let us keep you."

I opened my mouth to ask if they wanted to come up with me, except my cell phone rang. "Excuse me."

I looked at the screen and my heart fluttered. *Dr. Jesse*. The flashing name knew my fate. So soon. That can't be good. I couldn't bear to have bad news go to my voicemail, sitting there to listen to again and again.

I tapped the green phone icon. "Hello?"

"Ms. Foley? This is Sylvie from Dr. Jesse's office."

I clutched the edge of the guards' desk. It was Sylvie! "Yes?" My heart pounded in my ears. I missed most of the message, other than the lump came back benign. I was fine. There was something about another surgery to clear out margins of the same tissue, but that could wait. "Thank you. Um, yes, okay. I'll make an appointment in the New Year to discuss next steps."

"Happy New Year, Ms. Foley," Sylvie said and hung up.

Happy indeed!

"Dear, is everything all right?" Sarah stood behind me and softly rested a hand on my shoulder.

"Yes. As a matter of fact." I dropped the phone back in my purse, relieved enough to do a happy dance. "I'm great. And I want you to know… I am so in love with your son."

Sarah smiled tugging at her heart, and Will cupped his wife's elbows.

I approached him. "Mr. Morgan, you and Mrs. Morgan have raised such a wonderful man. I just hope that I…" I broke down and couldn't continue.

"Oh dear!" Sarah moved in and held me.

A *mother's* arms around me shot through me, the sensation I'd not felt since high school. Not just warmth or love or safety. There'd been plenty of affection from my father and even Greg. A mother's hold felt different. A mother/daughter bond was *sacred*.

I squirmed out of the embrace, but only because I was shaking. "Thank you."

"Excuse us for a minute, dear." Sarah squeezed my arm once more then nudged Will away a few feet.

I grew too anxious to wait anymore. I needed to be with Andrew, but didn't want to rudely ditch them.

"Mr. and Mrs. Morgan?" I called out to them. "I *do* need to get upstairs to see Andrew. We have a lot of things to talk about it."

Sarah whispered into Will's ear one final time. He pursed his lips looking at his wife, but nodded.

"You should take this with you then." From her Prada purse, Sarah removed a perfect square of a box.

Teal blue and tied with a creamy white satin ribbon. *Tiffany's.*

I stumbled back. "Wha—what's that?"

"Isn't it obvious?" Will said with what looked like tears in his eyes.

"But how…when?" I asked.

"We're already ruining the surprise Andrew's had for you since Christmas Eve," Sarah said. "And he'll probably kill us for this."

"Kill *you*." Will nudged his wife. "This was your idea."

"Christmas Eve?" I took the box in my hand. "He wanted to give this to me on Christmas Eve?"

"It was still in its original setting then," Sarah said, nodding, and she brushed my cheek. "The stone was my mother's. It'd been in a Wall Street safe deposit box for *years*." Her emphasis on the time frame made me step back. That ring would be mine and only mine. "My son didn't have to ask me twice if he could give it you. He went to Tiffany's yesterday morning and picked out a beautiful new setting. This ring is now yours, Gwendolyn."

All the dates lined up perfectly. Andrew had intended to give me his grandmother's ring on Christmas Eve. Before he knew about the baby. I wasn't forcing his hand. At all! "So…how do you have it?"

"The jeweler set it yesterday as a favor to me, so Andrew could pick it up the same day. He never made it there for some reason and this morning he had some kind of work emergency. He called me and asked me to pick it up and bring it here."

"This was at Tiffany's yesterday. Ready to be

picked up?" I asked in a flat voice, unbelieving almost.

That's why he wanted to stop there after the biopsy. When he'd dropped me off at the office yesterday morning, he'd asked me to trust him and I would know everything. I *never* expected something like that.

Nodding, Sarah stepped closer and closed my hand around the box. *This is now yours.* "Now go find my son already, and let him give this to you properly, for Pete's sake."

I hurled myself between Andrew's parents and hugged them both. "Thank you. Thank you."

Andrew had intended to propose all along. Before the baby. Before the biopsy. He wanted me.

Just for *me*.

♥ ♥ ♥ ♥

Andrew

"Andrew, Enrico wants to see you," Thalia said, standing by my office door.

"Okay, thanks." With a heavy groan, I stood. "Does he know about Salvatore?"

"*Sì.* I'm jealous. I've wanted to hit that *stronzo* for years. You beat me to it."

I needed a touch of humor at the moment, considering in the next few minutes my entire world would be blown apart. Marcello was going to be fired. Gwen was being transferred. And I just laid out New York's head designer. I wondered if Enrico had ordered in lunch. Flogging me would probably take all day.

It took a lot of willpower to not cast one more warning look in Salvatore's direction. He sat in a chair with what looked like a harem of women tending to him.

I gently knocked on my boss's open door.

"Ah, *Rocky*," Enrico joked, flipping over papers.

"Come in."

I walked right up to the desk with a hand on my heart and apologized in Italian out of respect. *"I'm very sorry I hit Salvatore. I will sign whatever apology is necessary to make this right."*

"For a scuffle?" Enrico waved his hand. "Salvatore is very passionate, and he gets under *my* skin. No need to apologize to him or file any report. And if *he* does, I will take care of it."

I caught my breath. "Why didn't you tell me he was being moved to Milan?"

"I had planned to discuss it with you today." Enrico removed his glasses. "He found out on his own. He has little spies all over the world. I'm sorry *you* had to find out this way."

My heart pounded in my chest. *"Va bene."*

"Siedeti, siedeti." Enrico pointed to his guest chair. "And how was Christmas with your family?"

I'm your family now, I'd told Gwen that morning.

My *famiglia* was Gwen and the baby. Was everything all right with *them*? I had no idea, but I nodded to answer anyway.

"Quello è buono. And have you seen this?" Enrico pointed to Marcello's annual report printed out on his desk.

"Sì." I just couldn't stomach to read it.

"Andrew, I need you to be honest with me." The way Enrico put his glasses down made his reaction hard to read.

"Of course."

"Did you write this for Marcello?"

My eyes widened. "No. Not at all. I gave him the report I handed in last year to use as a guide."

My boss nodded and flipped over a few more

sheets.

Before Enrico spoke again, I leaned forward. "I think I've gotten through to him. I've been monitoring his performance almost daily and he's coming along. That report is hard to write." I pinched the cover. "I can send it back to him to—"

"There is no need." Enrico closed the report and tapped the top sheet with the stem of his glasses. "Andrew, I am disappointed in you."

I hung my head low. I failed. Licking dry lips, I said, "Enrico, I think it's best if I—"

"I am troubled that you do not take enough credit for yourself."

"What's that?"

"Andrew, this report is *stellar*." Enrico opened it again.

"Huh?"

"He organized it with a table of contents. And look at this." Enrico slid his glasses back on and pointed to his monitor. "The sections jump right to the page. He even embedded moving graphics."

Okay, so he prettied it up. "But what do you think of his projections?"

Enrico took off his glasses again and put them on his desk. "Don't worry about that. Marcello will be fine. And with Salvatore making beautiful clothes, the brand will market itself."

I felt the world spin beneath me. It was done. it.

"Gwen…" I grumbled under my breath.

"Oh yes, Gwendolyn." Enrico pursed his lips. "Do you think she will be disappointed not to move to Milan?"

I stood and closed the office door. "Enrico, I have a lot to tell you."

CHAPTER THIRTY-THREE

Andrew

I tapped the toe of my left shoe...discreetly, since I wore Mezlans and not Prada. Their shoes never fit my size-thirteen feet very well.

Enrico Petrillo blinked his dark Italian eyes as I explained the events of the past two months.

Hearing the happy baby news, Enrico came to life. "You are going to be a father. That is the best news a man can get. And with such a beautiful woman. *Amore* is a wonderful thing to have in this life." He took a deep breath and said, "We specialize in love here at Prada, you know. Why else would we design such things of beauty? We want people to fall in love. *Vai*. Go. Go find your love, your *amore,* and make things right."

"I don't know. She's pretty upset with me right now," I said breathless from Enrico's words of love and Prada.

"It is just the hormones." My boss waved a lazy hand. "I could swear my wife wanted to poison me every time she was pregnant."

"That's amusing," I said with a soft laugh.

"Kiss Gwendolyn and make up." Enrico handed me a manila folder. "These are the details of a last-minute showcase I need you *and* your *amore* to work on."

"Where will it be?" I asked, taking the folder and smiled reading: *Mui Mui Handbag Collection*.

Enrico smirked back. "Where do you think? Marcello will never be as good as you and Gwendolyn *together*."

"I can't agree with you more, Enrico." I propelled out of the guest chair and flew down the corridor.

I barreled through the office with little regard for the bodies in my path. There was so much to do, including telling the neighbor in Milan who'd been taking care of Casper, that I'd be back in a few weeks. The cat was coming back to New York.

Getting inside my office, lost in my excited thoughts, I tripped over my feet. "*Gwen!*"

She spun around and…smiled.

Next to her, a woman with warm dark eyes, exactly like mine stared at me. "Ma?"

♥ ♥ ♥ ♥

Gwen

I stood shoulder to shoulder with Andrew's mother. I was gonna have some fun. I loved how Andrew looked so adorably confused. He raised his hand to scratch his head, exposing a pair of bruised knuckles, softening my stance.

"What happened to your hand?" I rushed to look at his fingers.

"I'll tell you later." He closed his hand around mine. "You've met my mother?"

"Hello, dear." Sarah moved in his direction and kissed him on the cheek. She glanced at his hand as well, but with it sitting in my comforting grasp, she nodded, seeming pleased.

"When did you get here?" Andrew asked his mother.

"Your father and I have been downstairs for thirty minutes. No one has been able to get ahold of you. He had to get back to the firm."

"I had an emergency meeting." Andrew raised his eyes to me.

Sarah clasped her hands together. "It was a good thing we ran into Gwen in the lobby."

Still looking at me, Andrew asked, "And what are you doing here?"

"I work here…don't I?"

Andrew nodded and glided his fingers across my cheek, his touch so warm and silky. Perhaps the hormones intensified all the feels. "How do you feel?"

Sarah closed in. "Is something wrong, dear?"

"No." I bore into Andrew's eyes, hoping my answer cast a wide net to let him know everything was almost *perfect*.

He squeezed my hand, looking completely befuddled. Andrew leaned forward to discreetly whisper something to his mother, probably trying to signal for the ring.

I coughed. "I could use some water, though."

"Right." Andrew dropped my hand. "I'll get it for you. Ma, why don't you come with me?"

Sarah gave me a sly look. "You need my help to get water?" his mother argued.

Andrew grunted.

Sarah waved her hands. "Tell you what…I'll get the water for her."

Andrew reached out to snag his mother's wrap, hoping to stop her. But the woman moved quickly. "Let me make sure she doesn't get lost," he said.

"Andrew, wait." I rushed into his arms lightning-fast.

It took a second before he responded to me, suggesting my need for him after what had happened a few hours earlier surprised the heck out of him.

He leaned his forehead against mine. "I'm so sorry about this morning."

"No, I'm sorry. For everything. I was out of line. But listen, it was a false alarm," I whispered. "I'm fine. The lump is benign."

Andrew's grip on me grew to bruising strength. "I knew it. I knew it would be okay."

"You were right. But it made me realize a lot of things. Life is short." I straightened my back. "I'm resigning today. I refuse to leave you and go work in Italy."

Andrew didn't say anything and stared at me, stunned at the sacrifice. He folded me back into his arms. The cottony scent of his shirt was the smell I'd missed the most.

"Turns out Marcello isn't getting fired," he said. "I'm keeping my job here in New York. And you're not quitting. I need you. *Here* in New York with me." Without even checking to see if anyone was watching, he kissed me passionately with a warm and sensual mouth.

A crushing weight dissolved away with his surprising news. We would no longer be two people resting our heads on pillows many miles and an ocean apart. Now I could have a life where I worked with Andrew all day and made passionate love to him all night. Every night.

The last twenty-four hours had been a crazy whirlwind. I didn't even know what time it was. With Andrew's lips on mine, days could slip by as well.

We were in the office, so he stopped kissing me, but kept a firm grip on my hands. "Oh, before I screw this up any further, what are you doing for New Year's Eve?"

I snuck a look at his groin and smiled. "It's not like I can have any champagne."

"Oh, right." His eyes skimmed across my body, protectively searching every inch.

I stroked his face, touching his eyelids. "After seeing your mother, I bet the baby will have those dark, rich eyes."

"*Baby?*" Sarah cried out from the doorway with a cup of water. It almost spilled out of her hands as she pulled me and Andrew into a killer bear hug.

I sank into the embrace, trying to figure out who was hugging whom harder. I considered it a three-way tie. Sarah dabbed under her eyes when she stepped back, letting me and Andrew stay connected.

"Ma, can I take Gwen home now?"

"Mmm," she answered, smiling.

He cleared his throat. "Do you have that...*thing* for me?"

"What thing, dear?" She secured the strap of her purse against her shoulder.

"Huh? Ma, wait!"

"Call your father later, dear. I don't know how long I can keep this exciting news to myself." Sarah gave me one final hug and a kiss on the cheek. After a wink, she left the office.

Without her there, it turned whisper quiet.

Andrew grunted as we stood in front of his desk, his hand in mine, much like my first moment with him in that office.

He nodded, seeming to realize it, too. "I really want you to go back to the apartment. You need to rest. I'll meet you there in a little while. There's something I need to take care of."

Figuring out where the heck the ring was, I bet. "You know, let's just leave and go for a nice walk."

"Anything you want, Gwen. But I have to stop someplace first."

"For what?" I whispered, "It's not like we need

condoms anymore."

He choked and turned red. "True. I, uh, need to pick up my suits from the dry cleaners."

"I'm the only one who can walk around the office with the same clothes and messed-up hair?" I ran my hand across his forehead, smoothing the stress lines away.

He cinched his thick eyebrows together. "Now that you're the mother of my child, I'll have to rethink all of that. But seriously, I have to get my car to the mechanic, it's been sitting for a while."

"I don't know." I tapped my chin. "This is a slow week. Lots of people take off."

"Gwen!" He gripped my shoulders and gave me a dose of close-talking, as if he were spelling something out for an unwilling child. "I. Have. To. Pick. Something. Up. For. *You*."

"Do you mean this?" From my pocket, I removed the blue box.

His head fell into the curve of my shoulder. "Ma!"

"Don't be mad at her," I said.

"Did you open it?"

"Not yet."

"Were you surprised?" he asked.

"Everything about you surprised me." My chest grew tight thinking of the journey we took to get to that moment.

He sucked in a breath. "Please let me do this right. Gwendolyn Mallory, I—"

"Wait!" I placed my hands against the lush surface of his lips. "Andrew Morgan, I love you. You've changed my life and made it so much better. The moment you looked at me, even last year, I felt this pull. I didn't realize it then. But I know now it was my soul connecting to yours. It's not just your child inside me. *You* are inside me. Coursing through my veins. It draws me to you. I belong with you. I belong *to* you. And I want to spend the rest of my life with you."

Andrew turned pale, a slight tremor taking over his body, like he'd not been expecting such a heartfelt declaration. "I...I can't say exactly when I realized I loved you. It didn't hit me like a thunderbolt. It felt more like of slow-moving wave. The kind that starts far out from the shore, and builds slowly, and steadily."

I smiled. "The kind that when it hits the beach, it knocks you over?"

"You've definitely knocked me over, Gwen." He took me in his arms and kissed me against the back of our office door. "Gwendolyn Mallory, I'm *crazy* in love with you. You've turned my world upside down from the moment I saw you." He lowered to one knee. It made sense to ask me right there, the place where we grew to love and respect each other, the place where we turned from work enemies to passionate lovers.

"Every breath I've taken since then has either been filled with your scent in my lungs or my longing for it to be there." He pulled my hands to his lips. "Let me into your life and let me light it up the way you've brightened mine. You've led me out of the darkness, and I promise to be here for you. Forever."

"Oh, Andrew." Warm tears rolled down my cheeks by the time he got to the question.

"Gwendolyn Mallory, will you marry me?"

I straddled his bent knee, so our lips were even. "Yes. Yes. Yes!"

"Why three yeses?" He took a bundle of hair into his grasp for a hearty breath of my scent.

"Just putting some answers in the bank for other

questions you may have for me...later," I whispered in his ear.

"Okay, then." Andrew lifted me up so he could stand. "Can I have your ring please?"

I smiled and handed him the blue box.

With it nestled in his hands, he said, "This stone has been in my family a long time and...what?"

"Your mother kind of told me where it came from."

"Of course, she did." But he smiled. "What's most important is that now it's yours, Gwen. And you are mine." He placed the teal blue box in my hand.

With shaking fingers, I began unraveling everything. Past each layer, the ribbon then the box, I found another box, a dark blue velvet cube.

"Open it," Andrew whispered, leaning against me.

A gentle popping sound from the top flipping open surprised me. For a moment, I wasn't sure what I was looking at. "It's a sapphire?"

"No. It's a diamond. A blue diamond. They're very rare. But the color, it matches your eyes." Andrew slid the ring out from the indentation.

His grandmother's classic round stone had been set into a circle of accent diamonds creating a halo effect. "Andrew, this is overwhelming."

Sliding it on my finger, he said, "Appropriate, since you've completely overwhelmed me, Gwen."

With our fingers in a tangle, I noticed the bruises again. "What did happen to your hand?"

"I kind of punched Salvatore in the mouth."

Slapping his chest, I cried out, "And I missed that?"

He chuckled. "Trust me. It was intense. I'm glad you weren't here. I wouldn't have wanted you to see me act like that."

"I'm in love with every version of you. Even the

manly and protective guy."

"I've got a lot to lose now. I'll be keeping my hands to myself." He brushed my stomach. "Not from you, of course."

I breathed deeply, his scent filling me while I rested my head on his chest. "So, the riddle is supposed to go: Gwen and Andrew sitting in a tree. K-I-S-S-I-N-G. First comes love, then comes marriage, then comes—"

Andrew lifted my chin and placed a gentle kiss on my mouth. Breathing me in, he whispered, "Yeah, we got this *way* out of order."

CHAPTER THIRTY-FOUR

Lenox Hill Hospital
New York City
January

Gwen

I opened my eyes and needed a minute to process where I was. Cottonmouth and the searing pain under the flimsy gown reminded me I was in the hospital's ambulatory recovery room.

"Oh, hello," a nurse said, while taking my vitals. "How do you feel?"

"Thirsty," I answered, knowing they wouldn't give me anything to drink.

The nurse lowered her chin. "We'll get you breakfast and something to drink in a little while, okay honey?"

I nodded and closed my eyes. I didn't want food. In fact, I knew I'd eventually be sick.

"Oh, and your husband is here," the nurse said, typing into a mobile records cart. "I'll send him in. You're a lucky girl."

"What?" I said, still foggy. "Um…no. My sister is picking me up."

"I think she's here, too."

"No…wait," I protested, but the nurse left. *Skye!* Why would she call Dan of all people? "And why am I lucky?"

"You're lucky because the surgery went great." Skye sauntered in with Dad and Greg following closely behind. "Dr. Jesse came out and said the lump was definitely benign and she removed it cleanly. You'll have a smaller scar than she thought."

Lucky me.

"Hello, pumpkin." Dad pressed a kiss on my forehead and looked at Skye. "She's a little warm."

"I'm surprised. It's cold in here," Greg said, looking uncomfortable.

The Mallorys hated hospitals.

"She's recovering," Skye answered, stroking my cheek and winked. "That burns calories."

"Where..." I pushed through the post-anesthesia haze. I braced my arms to sit up, but a shooting pain made me think otherwise. "Who..."

"Why is she so confused?" Dad asked.

Greg stroked my cheek. "Gwen, what's wrong?"

"The nurse said my husband is here," I said.

"He is," Skye answered with a shrug. "He's getting your prescriptions all settled with the doctor on duty."

"Why would *Dan* be doing that?" I snapped at my sister.

Dad snuck a look at Greg, but Skye informed me, "Gwen, you're not married to Dan anymore."

"Then who the hell *am* I married to?"

"I know we had a simple wedding, Gwen." The man I had a one-night-stand with eighteen months ago strolled into the room. "But I hoped you would at least remember *I* was there."

Wedding? I'm married to *this* guy?

"Simple for now." A bold woman with short sable hair waltzed in behind him. "We'll do something bigger soon."

It all flooded back to me in a rush that formed heavy sobs in my chest. Andrew... I married my one-night stand! And I'm having his baby.

"Why is she crying?" Greg asked. "Andrew, why is

my sister always crying around you?"

"Greg, stop it already." Skye pulled him away.

"Honey, what's wrong?" Andrew's body blocked everything from my view.

"I just got confused," I said. "I forgot where I was. And...well the date, the year, really. Waking up here, in this hospital, I thought..."

"It's just the anesthesia wearing off." Andrew secured the paper hat on my head. "Do you really not remember our wedding? It was three weeks ago."

The drugs made everything fuzzy. Thinking hard, it had been simple, but oh, so elegant. A Milan designer surprised me with a white organza empire dress when we were there for the showcase.

Andrew and I brought the dress *and* Casper home. He turned out to be the most expensive free cat in history, considering what it cost to bring him to New York City. He was still getting used to his new home. Trying to escape out the window of our Manhattan apartment like he had in Milan. When he wasn't sitting on the windowsill pining over all the birds he'd love to 'play' with, although I'm not sure how he'd fair against a city pigeon, the cat curled between me and Andrew, purring against my stomach. He always looked all handsome and formidable like one of the lions at the New York City Public Library.

Skye used her legal connections to convince a judge to not only move my divorce papers to the top of the list for his signature, but he also performed our quick impromptu marriage ceremony.

I became Gwendolyn Morgan as I exchanged vows with Andrew in Central Park with both our families watching. Next to my beautiful engagement ring, Andrew slid a simple platinum band. His grandmother's diamond was more important to me.

Staring at my bare fingers now, I asked, "Where are my wedding rings?"

"You don't trust me that we were really married?" He flashed his new wedding band, two-tone platinum and copper. He kissed me on the nose. "Your rings are at home. Safe."

Home was his downtown apartment, but we were looking for a bigger place on the Upper West Side which felt more kid friendly. Well, Sarah was looking, and emailing me pics of granite countertops and stainless steel appliances all day long.

I reached up to touch Andrew's face, but whimpered from the pain. A stormy tension grew in his eyes. His anger engines fired up whenever I felt any kind of discomfort. His hand closed around mine and he glanced at our families. Together, again.

His dad and mine talked quietly in the corner. Will Morgan had agreed to help with Dad's case. Sarah and Skye chatted politely. Those two were in a death battle to see who could spoil the baby more.

Greg turned and looked out the window. With all the love around him, I hoped he'd find happiness. My brother was a wonderful man with a lot of love to give. Beyond it all, I prayed he chose a path to bring Faith back into his life.

Dr. Jesse appeared, and the room fell into a hush, forcing me from her reverie about Greg.

Dad began moving people out. "Come on, let's give them some privacy."

Yeah, get Greg out of here before Dr. Jesse tries to take him home. My handsome brother belonged with Faith, the only woman he ever really loved.

One by one, everyone slipped out of the hospital

room. But Sarah stood next to the bed, opposite her son. Sarah would not be an ordinary mother-in-law, the kind to take a backseat, or be the first to leave the room.

"Can I get you anything, dear?" she asked me.

"No, Mom. I'm fine for now."

Sarah's face lit up whenever I called her that. After our quick ceremony, the original Mrs. Morgan had taken me aside and said, *You're my daughter now. It would be an honor if you called me Mom.*

The invitation had come as a surprise, leaving me weepy. *Okay. I'll give it a try, Mom,* I'd said with a baritone melody of the song: *You're a mean one, Mr. Grinch.*

Sarah had released a howl of laughter. *You'll have to practice. And I cannot wait to hear you call me Grandma, little one,* she'd said to my belly.

Andrew had squeezed my hand with a face full of emotion. He'd given me something he couldn't have realized would be so important...a mother. *His* mother.

Sarah, however, did leave, winking at her son, and the surgeon moved to take her place opposite Andrew.

"How do you feel?" the surgeon asked, pressing a stethoscope on my chest.

"Thirsty."

"Can we get her something, please?" Andrew asked.

"I'll have the nurse send in some ice chips." The surgeon hung the device around her neck, and said, "I need to check for any bleeding." She gently pulled the sides of my hospital gown open.

I caught the surgeon's hand and said to Andrew, "You don't have to watch this."

"Of course, I do," he answered, even though he seemed tense.

"No, you really don't," I argued. "Trust me, when this baby gets ripped out of me, that will be traumatic enough."

He brushed my cheek and moved to the other side of the bed to stare out the window with his arms crossed.

My skin cooled from being exposed. My stitched-up breast felt so tender under Dr. Jesse's touch. "Looks good. Just what I'd hoped."

"That's a relief." I tugged the gown closed.

"I'll have your discharge papers ready in about an hour." She tapped my shoulder and moved toward the door.

"Thank you, doctor," Andrew said and turned back around, his face even.

"I didn't mean to imply you couldn't handle that, Andrew. It's bad enough I have to sit here with no makeup on, wearing this stupid hat." I pulled it down further. "Meanwhile, you look all GQ as always."

"Honey, stop. You have to keep the hat on. If I write Prada on it with a Sharpie, will that make you want to keep it on?"

"Ha ha." I kept the collar of my gown closed, but Andrew's fingers were sliding inside.

"Please let me look." Andrew's hands gently pried mine apart. "I want to see it."

I exhaled and released the gown wondering how he'd handle blood stained stitches, swollen tissue, and the beginnings of yellow and purple blotches.

"Does it hurt?" he asked with a catch in his throat.

"A little," I answered softly.

At the mention of pain, Andrew's body stiffened and his face hardened. Not from fear, from protective-based anger. His hand hovered over my sensitive skin.

Andrew smiled and tied my gown closed again. "I know this will heal up fine. We *got* this, honey."

The 'we' still made my heart flutter. We were both healed and I really did have it all. "You know I plan to work even after the baby is born," I reminded him.

"I have no intention of keeping you barefoot and pregnant, Gwen."

"Barefoot no. But pregnant..." My cheeks flamed with heat. "The way you and I *go at it*, I'm guessing this won't be our only kid."

And the way I'd been enjoying sex while pregnant, I didn't see a downside to getting knocked-up again soon after this baby was born.

"Tell me the truth, Andrew. Are you upset we're not having a boy?" We'd learned we were having a girl at my last doctor's appointment.

"I know I said I'd been picturing a boy before we found out." He'd made a heartfelt confession, saying he'd heard having a son was like getting to live his life over again. I'd give him a boy if I could. Give him anything he wanted. "Now, I can't wait to watch our little girl blossom into someone smart and beautiful like you. How can I possibly ever thank you for that gift?"

"I can show you when we get out of here." I responded with a kiss way too heated for our situation.

I'd already been ravenous for sex, thinking my surging hormones were to blame. More likely, my attraction to a man so masculine he had the power to alter my body had me in a sizzle quite often.

Yep, there will be another kid.

♥ ♥ ♥ ♥

Thank you for reading Wait for Me.

Will Greg Mallory and his runaway bride can get out of their own way when she comes back to town and needs his help?

Grab *All For Me* today!

How long does it take to get over being left at the altar? Greg Mallory hasn't figured that out yet.
But his runaway bride, Faith Copeland, is back in town, so he's going to find out soon enough!

Greg wants one thing: **Answers**.

Faith needs one thing: **Redemption.**

Small town love *always* wants a second chance.

ABOUT THE AUTHOR

Deborah Garland is an Award-Winning author of emotional and funny, steamy romances!

She lives on the beautiful North Shore of Long Island with her very patient husband and their mischievous pug. She had to learn how to make her own Cosmopolitans and right now there's a bartender who will NEVER see her again. She eats cheap mac and cheese with expensive red wine, her heroes are ALWAYS over six feet tall, and they fall, hard, HARD for the girl.

STAY IN TOUCH WITH ME...

My newsletter followers get not only a good laugh each month, but also updates on new releases, sales and giveaways. Sign up at my website:

www.deborahgarlandauthor.com

Don't forget to follow me on any of these great platforms:

Amazon, TikTok, Goodreads, BookBub, Facebook, & Instagram

Printed in Great Britain
by Amazon